ARNOLD WESKER is
three books of short stories, two collections of essays and
THE BIRTH OF SHYLOCK AND THE DEATH OF ZERO MOSTEL
published to great acclaim by Quartet Books in 1997. Best
known for **THE WESKER TRILOGY** his work is continually
performed worldwide and has been published in eighteen
languages. His early prize-winning plays **ROOTS** and **CHIPS
WITH EVERYTHING** were revived last year for a national
tour and at The Royal National Theatre respectively —
reviews claimed them as 20th century classics.

ARNOLD WESKER

The King's Daughters

TWELVE EROTIC STORIES

QUARTET BOOKS

First published in Great Britain by Quartet Books Limited in 1998
A member of the Namara Group
27 Goodge Street
London W1P 2LD

A catalogue record for this book is available from the British Library

ISBN 0 7043 8089 7

Phototypset by F.S.H. Ltd
Printed and bound in Great Britain by C.P.D. Wales Ltd

CONTENTS

The King's Daughters

THERE WAS A KING

𝔗here was a king. Old, sad, disappointed, his face creviced from endeavour.

He had been a good king, attentive and just, who felt deeply a solemn duty to protect his people. He had fought wars to gain more land that his people might thrive, then more wars to defend the thriving land his people had cultivated and others now coveted. Rebellions by ambitious knights had needed to be quashed; internecine quarrels between avaricious lords had cost the precious blood of his subjects. His nerves strained, his wisdom was taxed. He was an embattled king.

The king's name was Melania; his kingdom, Melandia. King Melania lived a long life full of appetites, not only for ruling and justice but for knowledge, beauty and women. He had twelve wives. Each brought him a grace and skill. His first wife converted to Christianity and, before retiring to a nunnery, taught him about the one God; his second, skilled in diplomacy, entertained his ambassadors and inspired the trust of near and distant states; his third was a

1

spinner of tales picked up and recited throughout the land by itinerant story-tellers; his fourth built alms houses for the aged and poor, and, together with the wife founded hospices, for which travel widely to engage the most learned of doctors; while studied law and helped her husband legislate. A seventh sang, accompanied by the playing of an eighth; another landscaped his gardens; another wove tapestries; his eleventh copied manuscripts wonderfully illuminated. Only the last wife was without a skill. She he took when he was sixty, a seventeen-year-old who brought with her a strange silence and melancholy which permeated the court, a child poised between two worlds, two eras, a waiting child, a child with knowing eyes, knowing she knew not what, waiting for what never came. She died with foreboding – I or was it promise – lingering between her lids.

All died. As the land flourished by their works so the king was blighted by the calamity of their deaths. The lines in his face spread, deepened by the confusion of good and ill which plagued his years. But each wife left a daughter, twelve daughters who were the king's joyuntil, in his seventy-fifth year, after the death of the last wife, a disturbing event began to occur each night. His daughters would disappear from the castle grounds without trace, and return next morning tired, to sleep until midday.

He had them watched. The guards saw them enter their rooms but never emerge. Nor would they be seen again till they gathered in a certain part of the vast garden in the early hours of the morning and made their way through the hall and passageways of the palace to their rooms. How they left unseen, where they went unseen, how they returned and assembled unseen in the garden remained a mystery.

The king became anxious, remembering the foreboding of his last young wife. He questioned them one by one. Each had inherited the grace and skill of her mother, and replied to him with her mother's intelligence. As they came to give answers, it seemed his life was paraded before him. In each child the mother resided, the years echoed.

Thus do I, Coaxandria, the king's chronicler, begin my story which I here order, interpret and summarize for the king, and for those who will read after him.

FIRST CAME LENOTA

𝔉irst came Lenota. The oldest and, of all his daughters, the strangest. Short-limbed, black-haired, with orphan's eyes asking to be forgiven any mistake she might make. Though her eyes were vivid with intelligence, they were uncertain. They understood but doubted, were capable but begged, knew what should be done but could command nothing. Among her sisters, she was the most devoutly religious, and contemplated taking up the veil. Doubts plagued her. Was she strong enough for sacrifice? A restless mind drove her into the fevered arms of the mystics, one of whom she suspected herself to be, so fiercely did her body burn with love for all things.

To the king's questions she replied, 'Do not ask me, father. These are disturbing times. My mind is not my own. I disappear at night into my doubts. Sometimes I cannot find myself, know not who I am. There is no ill done. Have no fear. Just pray I will emerge. Forgive me.'

Next came Meliora, the diplomat. Tall, proud, auburn-haired

and green-eyed, she spoke slowly, calmly, the skilled assessor of character, estimator of worthiness, evaluator of virtue. Members of court were intimidated by her judgements, feared her contempt. As she assessed, fortunes changed. The king listened to her advice, for even though her certitudes were haughtily delivered, she was fair — according to her criteria. She said, 'We are dutiful, we grow, soon we shall be married and your blood will be spread to nourish many lands. All problems can be solved, though perhaps not all should be. For consider — resolution often brings pain. Do not worry, father. Our nights are not spent in harm. Leave us our privacy.'

Which made the king fret more, till came Dionis, third oldest of his daughters, the spinner of tales. Like Meliora, she too was tall. Brown hair, brown eyes, features alert with caution and disbelief. She walked with an anxious stoop, her chin sometimes raised, poised to observe and gently mock; at other times with her head sunk into her shoulders, resigned to the world's folly. But of all the sisters she was the one most concerned for their well-being. She listened endlessly to their fears, complaints, problems, shaking her head from side to side in mute sympathy. So long-enduring was she that her head-shaking became involuntary, whether the problem called for it or not. None of her clothes seemed to fit and, poor child, her hair was prematurely streaked with grey, about which she was wry.

To the king, she said, 'Of course you are right to be anxious. Would we love you so much were you not? But trust me when I tell you that my sisters are well. They confide in me. I know their problems. They need cause you no concern. Eat regularly, take your strolls, visit your people, and leave your daughters to become women.'

★

The fourth to come before the king was Liticia, whose intense grey-blue eyes and thin lips implied a stern nature. She stood elegant and straight, determined to be her own mistress. Only a trembling square jaw betrayed vulnerability. When she laughed, her eyes filled with tears and her intelligent features became gay. From being intimidated by her one minute, the king relaxed the next, aware that she could be teased.

'Father,' she said, 'you know my public passion is for the poor and the aged, and that I will continue my mother's work of building alms-houses throughout the land. I will be dutiful in all things but those which affect my life. I do not want to die regretting how I lived. The hours of light are for you, the dark hours are my own.'

Before such determination the king lowered his eyes, blessed his daughter and awaited with relief if not hope for his fifth oldest, Beatrix, who had a cure for everything except what ailed him most – his confusion.

Voluptuous Beatrix. In her all temperaments met. Coy and sharp, sensual and intelligent, submissive and strong-willed. Her obsession was time. No moment must be lost. Each hour had to be filled with an experience, even if only listening to her sister, Amissia, sing. She was where she promised to be when she promised to be, and those who were not were whipped with her fury. Her obsession with time led her to an obsession with health, for illness was time lost. She studied medicine in herbs, urged the building of hospitals, trained other young women of the realm who had the gift of healing. Between them they discovered relief for depression in mustard, a remedy for exhaustion in the hornbeam, control of temper in the cherry plum.

She told the king, 'Dearest father, you are like an over-protective mother harassed by unwanted thoughts for which the remedy is three drops from the red chestnut and six from the white.'

'I am not a harassed mother,' he complained, 'I am a lonely old man weighed down by the past.'

'For which you need the juices of heather and honeysuckle. I will provide them and you will fret no more.'

From his sixth oldest daughter he expected truth: Margeria, his help and pride, whose passion for and knowledge of the law made justice in his kingdom the envy of the world. If there was an *éminence gris* behind his throne it was her, though Meliora the diplomat might think it was she. But poor Margeria, she had not beauty. The king regarded her and knew the promise in her features was unfulfilled. He could see what she was meant to be, but her handsomeness had been arrested in mid-bloom. Only in her smile did he understand – her intelligence had accepted the lack.

She told him, 'At night, dear father, we disappear into our dreams.'

'That is playing at words with me,' he rebuked. 'It is not worthy of you.'

'Be patient,' Margeria reassured him.

But he was not, especially after his sixth youngest daughter, Amissia, left him.

Amissia. All aflame. Almost black-skinned. It was she who sang, whose mother came from the Islands, and who, he suspected, led the others through their nights. Her spirit was restless. She travelled more than her sisters in search of songs to sing. 'For you, father, only for you.' Quick-tempered, she imagined insults behind each phrase, hostility behind each glance. But when she entered a room, it was sunlit and vibrant. Her anecdotes created laughter, her swift conversation left others breathless. She urged, persuaded, encouraged, made things happen.

'Now then, father. Each in her time. No king has daughters more adoring, faithful and intelligent. You may regret I only sing and have no skill to help you rule, but do not silence the one who sings. As long as I sing, your realm is happy.'

Which told him nothing, of course. Nor was his fifth youngest more illuminating. Mabylye.

A large and carefree girl who refused to treat the king her father seriously. He would remonstrate and she would gaze with bovine eyes, playing her lute, attempting to quieten his anxieties. She was – how can she be described? Luscious? Loose-limbed? Careless? Sensual? All those things. Playing her lute, she sat with her legs spread. Stepping over streams, she raised her skirts higher than needed. Her dresses were cut low, she was forever leaning forward. Once she was discovered asleep by a garden wall with her legs propped high on a boulder, her thighs bare to the gaze. She had no relationship with her body; rather she followed it around, acquiescing to its movements, as incurious about its demands as she was about her father's need of explanations for that which she herself could barely understand.

'I follow where my body takes me,' she said, playing exquisitely meanwhile. 'I ask no questions, for I would understand no replies. The music, father, the music! Listen to the music.'

Which he did, soothed by sounds from a world he knew he would never inhabit. He offered no resistance.

By the time his fourth youngest daughter appeared, Etheldra, he realized he would hear nothing from them about their nocturnal disappearances. She was the keeper of his gardens, which her mother had created, and, like her, was fair, rotund, red-faced and radiant from the elements to which she exposed herself. Rough skin, hands scratched from the roses' thorns, her fingernails clogged with earth, she smelt of honeysuckle, sweet shit and mown grass. Long hair fell in knots to her buttocks. She talked to the animals and the wind but rarely to people, though many were drawn to her, for, like Mother Earth, she was dependable, even-tempered and had no corners in her mind behind which she hid.

She explained simply, 'You are an oak, father, you must expect some of your branches to reach out of sight.'

Amy, third youngest, had always been an enigma to him. He could describe her parts but not add them up. Brown curls burst from her head. Her eyes waited wide-open for mysteries. She competed with no one, effaced herself, glided quietly through life. Though she was not without gaiety, she uttered nothing that was frivolous. A stillness in her gave the impression that she was shy, but her laughter was deep and passionate. She was content with her weaver's skill, which, like her passion, was sought throughout her father's lands and beyond. Patiently, as one who knew all pictures finally took shape, she explained to the king, 'Just as your daughters cast shadows, so shadows are cast in them.'

'Riddles! Riddles!' he exploded. 'You all talk to me in riddles!' But riddles they were not, as he was to discover.

Now entered the oddest of his daughters, Enota. Short trunk, long legs, oversized bosom, a body out of proportion. The intensity of her fierce brown eyes defied their awkward slant to convey beauty. Rich auburn hair fought with protruding teeth in a mouth that was too small and with a nose whose line was one with her forehead. Yet all flowed. Where each part failed, the whole assembled in harmony driven by a passionate nature. The king wondered at this offspring. She resembled neither himself nor her mother, rather she belonged to a seed impregnated long ago, dormant, waiting for its day. But the monasteries fought for her skills, which shone from the exquisite copies of manuscripts they begged her to re-create for them.

She stood before her father, hands clasped low, head flung back, eyes staring straight at him. She was the penultimate child but looked the oldest. She said, 'You have forged a kingdom, you have nurtured a family, your citizens flourish in freedom and justice. Do you wish less for your daughters? We honour you and ask nothing but that you stay on the pedestal which is yours.'

The king said little. He marvelled at his unreined daughters, considered their sagacity, retreated before their singularity, and remained confused.

Delight, as often, came with his youngest, Amabilia – sweet-natured and giving, still plump with adolescence, driven as yet by no skill, eyes full of questions, a heart burning with expectations, features animated by surprise at all things. She attempted to emulate her sisters but played the lute heavily, painted clumsily, sang raucously, and could neither retain a fact nor pursue an argument with logic. Her imagination was a butterfly's, her mind a grasshopper's; she had no tact. But tantrums distressed her, so she patched up quarrels and laughed with each turn of the wind. Her sisters spoilt her. The king adored her.

'Look how you frown,' she scolded him. 'Is your court in

arms against you? Does someone poison you with rumours? Silly old goose. We sleep elsewhere. What of that? It seems strange to me, but my sisters want it that way and I have promised secrecy, though what there is to be secret about I cannot understand. Do not ask me, father. We are close and sworn, and you would not have it otherwise. Now, laugh! Laugh! Go on, laugh!' And she began to prod and tickle him.

From what she said it seemed that nothing untoward was taking place. And for the moment nothing was — to Amabilia! He was almost reassured, but not quite. He resolved to send out a call for help, the king to his subjects.

He was loved, many came forward, none could help. The kings' daughters slipped away each night, and he felt, unreasonably, they took with them their love for him. Knowing they were not somewhere in the palace, his nights were lonely. The rewards of a lifetime of caring were denied him. Homage and the gentle respect due to old age were withdrawn. It seemed nothing would be done, until...

THERE IS AN OLD
DRUID LEGEND

There is an old Druid legend that once every seven years the four winds blow from all corners of the earth upon the same place; and if at that place a living person stands, sits, sleeps or is at some task, then upon that person is bestowed the power to become invisible. Man, woman, child, wise, foolish, rich or poor – the winds meet and where they meet the power is gifted.

During the days when the old king sent out through the land his pleas for help, the winds met and hurled their breath through one of his subjects, a sweet young man of twenty-four whose name was Jonas. Jonas was keeper of the king's first stables. He became an Unseen. It happened just as he was feeding a fine grey mare. He and the mare were amazed. She neighed, backed away, then bolted. The young man, seeing he had no legs, fell to the ground, where he lay for a long time, unable to know how to move a body which it appeared he no longer possessed. His amazement turned to fear, then confusion, then delight, then fear again. If I am not seen, how will I be believed?

When an hour had passed and his thoughts had settled, a most extraordinary process occurred. His fear became panic. I want my body, he cried urgently to himself. I must have my body back. Panic focused concentration. Slowly he became a shadow of his former self. He concentrated harder. The harder he concentrated, the more he solidified, until, straining, he willed his body visible again.

With joy he stood, jumped, skipped, walked round in circles, and somersaulted. Then, in the midst of rejoicing that his body had returned, a vague longing for his body once more to fade, become invisible, came upon him. It had been so pleasant. He concentrated hard, trying to recall the nature of unseenness. So hard that he became shadowy. The harder he concentrated, the more shadowy he became, until, straining as before, he willed himself invisible again. This time he did not fall. He jumped. He skipped. He somersaulted. Then he stood still and willed himself seen again. It worked. Unseen. It worked. Back and forth – seen, unseen, seen. He had learned to control the gift of the four winds.

You must know a little about Jonas's nature. Sweetness was only a part of it. He was innocent and trusting as well, a soul to whom good had to be very good and evil very evil before he could distinguish between them; he knew his trust had been misplaced only when it was betrayed. Such sweet and trusting innocence irritates others, it measures their bile. He was an uncomfortable companion.

Add clumsiness to his simplicity and it will be understood why his company was avoided. With horses he worked efficiently, among people he lost co-ordination. Especially among women! Though handsome, he held no lasting tryst. He rushed an entrance, clamped an embrace, sandpapered a cheek, tripped to a kiss, banged with his lips. Girls ran from him bruised, bewildered and in tears.

Instead, Jonas watched horses mate, and took his pleasure helping them. The winds could have blown upon no lonelier soul.

Thus do I, Coaxandria, continue my story, which an excited and confused stableboy related to me and which I order, interpret and summarize for the king, and for those who will read after him.

MANY WEEKS PASSED

Many weeks passed before Jonas comprehended the power of his gift. When he did, he perceived how it could be applied in the service of the king. Twelve daughters disappearerd no one knew where – who better to follow them?

The young man came before the old king, who looked at him and thought: Here is a strange one; every part of him appears to have a life of its own. His hair falls this and every way, his left leg moves forward when his right has inclined sideways. And what are his arms doing? Fighting one another, it seems. Never have I confronted such awkwardness, thought the king. But he saw a luminous glow in the boy's eyes, a light leaping and begging to be listened to and trusted.

'What makes you think,' asked King Melania, 'that you, a keeper of horses, can succeed where so many wise men have failed?'

Jonas, his taut nerves alert with fright, knew he must withhold knowledge of his power. He replied cautiously,

'Nothing makes me think I could be wiser than the wise, Majesty. But think this, can I be more stupid than the stupidest?'

Majesty thought: My land is plagued with riddles! But Majesty smiled, gave the young man freedom of the palace and its grounds, and placed no limit upon time.

For payment Jonas received one silver crown a day, with the promise that, if he succeeded in solving the mystery, each silver crown would be made into a gold one, each gold one multiplied by ten, and the total increased a hundredfold.

He was astounded. What had the old king seen in him to offer such wealth? Perhaps I seem more than I am, he thought, or am I more than I seem? One thing was certain, there must be no haste. Success depended upon time enough to gather his wits.

He found a place beyond the estate, high on a hill, willed himself unseen and sat thinking. After three days he was blessed with an insight: the secret was to work backwards and discover from where they *came* rather than where they *went*. An inspired insight.

From that part of the garden where the princesses were always first seen, he surveyed the landscape. The palace was set high on a hill, nothing surrounded it. Flat. Except for a river. Did they rise from that? Misty majesties from a liquid dream? In days when a stableboy could become unseen, everything was possible. Unseen, he waited, straining to discover something unusual. At first, nothing. The landscape appeared sharper in form and colour, that was all, until he looked at the grass around him. He was standing in the midst of rare small creamy flowers called ceratium. He had seen them before, spaced out, but never in such profusion. What struck him as odd was their presence here where he stood and in no other part of the landscape. But was it *so* odd?

Soon all changed. A chill struck the back of his neck. He shivered, looked about. A cage of thick air was enveloping him. It happened swiftly. The breeze hummed like a swarm of approaching bees. Swallows dipped in and under the wind as though on alert. Trout leapt like scouts out of the river; leapt, looked north, leapt, looked south, leapt leapt, looked east and west. The ceratium yawned open their creamy bells, and into the cage of thick air corporealized the forms of the king's twelve daughters.

Jonas drew in breath.

One of the daughters froze, Lenota, the mystic. 'We are not alone, sisters,' she said.

But they could see no one and told her not to be foolish.

She insisted. 'I know it. I sense it. We are not alone.'

Jonas's instinct against haste was helped by his patience. Every morning for forty-eight mornings he came to the same spot among the ceratium to watch where the daughters filtered from miasma into form, hoping a glance, a stray word would reveal a clue as to where they were filtering *from*; *how*, he would discover later.

He began to enjoy the caged world of thick air, thrill to the crazed humming of the breeze and the heady atmosphere it spun. He felt no fear, though every morning the same daughter would say, 'We are not alone, sisters. I know it, I sense it. We are not alone.'

But he discovered little. Except this: a pattern of fatigue and recovery. At the beginning of each twelve-day cycle they would grow tired, till by the end they were exhausted. Then, during the next twelve days, they regained energy and sparkle again. Everyone, that is, except Amabilia the youngest. She remained unchanged. What could it mean? He understood nothing. But once the pattern was established, it did no more than repeat itself. After two cycles, he decided upon the next stage: Where had they been? How did they get there?

Lenota, plagued by both religious guilt and a sense of the boy's presence, was unable to sleep, troubled that their nights would be revealed to an unseen being. She turned to her books. There she read in the writings of St Claryssia, the anchoress of Mastabillion:

> I stood still and the hills moved. I moved and the hills were transfixed. I closed my eyes and the landscape was before me. I sealed my ears and the seas roared within me. I was silent a whole year, yet my head filled with a voice I recognized as my own. Nothing was as I had once known it, nor seemed to be itself. But I was not afraid.

Which did not help Lenota, for *she* was afraid.

TO FOLLOW THEM, JONAS THOUGHT, WOULD BE SIMPLE

To follow them, Jonas thought, would be simple. Each daughter had a maid who opened the bedroom door for her mistress, time enough for three people to enter.

Jonas abruptly swept into the bedroom of the youngest daughter, Amabilia.

The maid cried out.

Her mistress exclaimed, 'What was that?'

'Your gown made a sudden rush of air, perhaps?' suggested the maid.

'But my gown is tight about me.'

'Then spirits are abroad.' And they both laughed.

The maid prepared water for her mistress's ablutions, laid out her nightgown, placed a warm earthenware bottle between the sheets, then helped her mistress undress, folding away each garment before unbraiding the princess's luxuriant hair. As the last garment was removed, Jonas, despite that he could not be seen, turned his head, delicate and embarrassed. Such was his nature – for the moment.

Behind him he could hear the swish of cloth, the splash

of water, the gasps and sighs of a body pleasured clean. When Amabilia told her servant she could go, Jonas judged it time to turn. How radiant she looked, her eyes sparkling for a ball rather than bed. The servant left. Now he would discover their secret. A door in the wall? A trap in the floor? An iron staircase from a panel in the fluted ceiling? None of that. The princess blew out all the candles but one, entered between her sheets, curled up and prepared herself for sleep.

Jonas watched and waited, watched and watched and waited. Till he dozed, only for minutes, he was certain. The curled shape was still there and remained there all night. As dawn came he wondered: Is there a night when they do not go where they go? Or a night when one stays home? That could not be. He had observed them through forty-eight mornings, all had been present. His tired brain demanded sleep and was given it.

An hour later he awoke in fright, jolted by the loudness of his snoring. She has heard me, he thought. I will be found out. Worse! He was visible! He had forgotten that will-power slips away in sleep. He heard footsteps outside the door. The servant girl was coming to help her mistress prepare for the day. Panic! He must will himself unseen. But the first moments of morning are not the best in which to gather powers of concentration, especially after a night of broken sleep. The young man closed his eyes to command his will. Youth was on his side. He faded away. Just in time. For the door opened. He was amazed.

Through it stepped the princess, Amabilia, covered in a cloak. He looked to the bed. The shape was gone. Bewilderment engulfed him and he could not contain a groan. The princess froze. Was someone in her room? Lenota's warning echoed in her ears: 'We are not alone, sisters, we are not alone.'

Luck blew for the young unseen. A wind had arisen, making the boughs groan. Amabilia's fears were assuaged. She moved quickly. Her cloak was off, revealing the nightgown in which he had seen her enter her bed. She pulled back the sheets, fell between them and was soon asleep.

Jonas crept from her chamber and thoughtfully ambled to his thinking hill to consider his first problem. How could he go with the young princess where she went? Enter her bed he could not – the unseen are not the unfelt! What had he missed? Little could have happened in the few minutes he had dozed, surely? He would have to observe with greater care. After a sleep on his hill and a bath in his cottage, he returned that night to Amabilia's room. Again he watched her undress, again he turned his head before the last garments fell, again he listened to her splashes and sighs, then closely watched the young body into its bed, and waited.

Half the night passed. She did not move. He *had* to investigate. Holding his breath, he tiptoed to the bed and pulled back the sheets. It was a wide bed, for two, and on it the princess lay very still, too still for sleep, more in a trance. He touched her, pushed her, pinched her. She did not awake. It was as though she were not there. He stood in the middle of the room, scrutinizing each object, each part of the wall. He moved slowly around the bed, searching for something that would leap out at him and reveal a secret. A clue, a clue! If only he could chance upon a clue!

Chance was unreliable. Inspiration was needed. Which at that moment came. From nowhere. As inspiration does. Follow her movements, he reasoned to himself, travel her route.

He entered her bed. Fit for a princess indeed, he

21

thought, at the touch of fine linen. He stretched by her side. Nothing happened. In different positions, nothing happened. He pulled at panels. Nothing happened. He sat up, stood up, knelt down, leaned over, looked on shelves, tried turning gnarled embossments, attempted to move wooden posts. Nothing happened. Exasperated, he flopped back into the bed and embraced one of the silk-covered pillows for comfort and contemplation.

And there it was. Beneath the pillow. A small purple glass phial filled with liquid. Without hesitation, he opened the bottle and moistened his tongue with drops from it. What happened next he would remember for ever.

From the centre of his head arose a familiar sound: the humming breeze. It grew in pitch. A sensation on the surface of his skin, beginning from his toes, moved up and over each curve and bump of his body like a knife shaping him out of the air, as though his body were being sculpted and defined for the first time into a shape he had not known before. Everything met high in his head – the last contour, the last vein, the last shrill note, all drawn together by the humming breeze which was now not of this world. And to his astonishment, his body rose sharp and singing. He could see himself. Not only was he no longer invisible, but he no longer belonged to himself!

Then began a journey of sweet terror. Through dusky mists heavy with dank, odious smells one moment, the next luscious and sweet-scented. Through sensations beautiful then fearsome, through sounds soothing then distressing, through howls of pain, smells of decay, scents of spring, glimmerings of promise, harmony, dissonance. He travelled, it seemed, through tunnels designed by perverse spirits to confuse him, suspend him in uncertainty.

And yet despite its threatening vacillations, as he

travelled this giddy journey, a calm descended. He knew he would be safe, that mother and friends, childhood and thick soup, hands bathing him, warm old hay, all were with him. He could suffer with grace and silence, for there was a lovely light at the end.

LIGHT INDEED

Light indeed. A forest light. Jonas found himself in a forest of high, mad trees. They should have been oaks, elms, birches or pines. They were none and all of these. The oaks had branches of elms, the elms had leaves of pine. He felt as he had felt when he first became unseen and his legs had crumbled beneath him seeing nobody there. Nothing in the forest was what it should have been.

Fearing that fear would diminish his power to will himself unseen, he focused hard to ensure the gift of the four winds was still with him. He faded into shadow. But where was he? How could he return? Alone in the forest, he was frightened as never before.

Youth conquers fear, however, or persuades itself that it has done so. He climbed an oak – or elm? – to identify his whereabouts. From where he towered in the tree he could see a hut; behind it another and to the left another still. He counted twelve huts. Was the answer to be found in them? What he was to discover would intrigue him but reveal no clues. As we will see.

He clambered down from his perch and approached the first hut. Through the window he saw the green-eyed diplomat, Meliora, alongside the lump-with-no-waist legislator, Margeria, posing before Enota, whose body tensed with concentration. She was painting a most curious miniature portrait of her two sisters. Though dressed simply, each revealed a naked breast.

Jonas thought them odd sitting thus. For whom could such a portrait be intended? Not the king. Not for their own rooms. Certainly not for the churches or monasteries whose manuscripts Enota illuminated. They were in conversation but Jonas could barely hear their words. How could he enter? He could not knock. It was a moment for bold and simple action. He threw open the door and strode through. Meliora and Enota screamed, imagining intruders, but seeing no one concluded it was the wind, the wind. Only Margeria said, 'I heard no wind.'

Once inside, the boy could hear their conversation. Would it explain their portrait? Would it reveal an explanation for their disappearance each night?

Margeria picked up where their exchange had paused. 'And so the time for change is approaching.' Her voice was sad, lugubrious. 'I have guided our father towards just laws which are a force in the land. Now he must face the question: which is more important – the demands of law or the demands of majesty?'

'Strengthen law, strengthen trade – majesty will be strengthened,' exclaimed Meliora.

'The barons are not interested in trade,' lamented Margeria, 'only in draining power from the king, imagining this will increase their own power.'

'The barons are fools,' cried the haughty Meliora. 'I want us rich and trusted rather than powerful and feared. They have had their day. The merchants must now take over from the warlords.'

'And father will have to relinquish his power.' Margeria sighed, as though she did not care to be intelligent and would exchange her power of thought for any one of the attractive physical attributes of her sisters. 'Such are the times. I hear them.'

Jonas was amazed to hear such conversation from the lips of women, even though he understood nothing of what they discussed. They exuded a strength which made him feel – he was reluctant to confess – insignificant. Was it for this each had endured the terrifying journey, for no other reason than the chance to engage in such exchanges in private? The palace and its grounds were full of private places, he reasoned; there must be other explanations.

He surveyed the interior of the hut. The walls were covered with furs and rugs, the floor with an abundance of cushions multicoloured of weave. For furniture there was a wooden stool, a carved armchair, a washstand and a table laden with fruits, poultry, meats and wine. For whom, and why? The confused stableboy could piece together none of it.

What of the other sisters? How was he to escape from this hut to investigate their activities? Nature came to his assistance. All God's creatures must piss – Kings, poets, beautiful women. Princesses too. Meliora was called upon to relieve herself. Jonas followed her through the door, though not without a glance from the alert and suspicious Margeria, and moved towards the other shacks.

He discovered that the sisters passed their time in similar ways. Lenota the mystic, Dionis the story-teller, Amabilia the youngest had gathered in the hut of Amy, who was sitting before a vast, awesome tapestry, patiently weaving a world which, like the forest, was at once both recognizable and unrecognizable. Animals familiar at first glance were, on closer scrutiny, unfamiliar; buildings thought of as dwellings were like no dwellings known to the inhabitants of this world; marvellous machines of pulleys and pivots for construction unlike any we who have travelled afar have encountered; strange foliage from God knows which fantastic soil. What had nurtured the imagination of this tenth daughter? Whence came her imagery? Her colours – bold, primary, startling? It was a mystery. The tapestry dominated the hut, the travail of two years.

The other sisters seemed indifferent to the glorious blaze of weave. Instead they were entranced by Dionis's story. In her lap lay the youngest, Amabilia, with eyes clear, bright, alert, enraptured. She lived every moment of her sister's tales, their characters' pain and joy reflecting themselves in her mobile features. The strangest was Lenota, aeons away, tucked into a corner of the hut, which like the first, but in different colours, was shrouded in skins and carpets.

In the third hut Jonas found the remaining sisters. Even-tempered Etheldra, flushed and roughened by the elements; intense and elegant Liticia, on whom the poor and misfortuned depended for their houses and alms; voluptuous Beatrix, dark-haired, dark-eyed, dependable in crisis and ill-health; all listening to the lute-playing of loose-limbed Mabylye, and the tremulous singing of brown-skinned, restless Amissia.

Here were no secrets to reveal to the king. His daughters passed their nights relaxing from their duties of the day. The king had been over-anxious, as ageing fathers often are for grown daughters. And so Jonas's first impulse was to report at once and give his sovereign peace of mind. His second impulse was caution. Nothing, he had heard tell, was ever simple. What of the twelve-day cycle? Should he not wait and watch during more nights?

Now, in this last hut cosy with music and song, he must wait for the king's daughters to return to their palace. How would they achieve this? Jonas waited in a state of pleasure the quality of which he had never before experienced. The atmosphere was warm from the smells of food, wine, perfumes and the heavy, alluring odours of young womanhood. And though he relaxed like a sister among loving sisters, yet the stableboy's confusions did not entirely ebb. He felt stirred by he knew not what.

His attention was drawn by Mabylye. The lute player had been sitting with her back to a wall, her legs outstretched, her instrument hugged to her bosom. Now she shifted her position, drawing her right foot under her left thigh making a bowl of her lap into which the lute's head rested more comfortably. In the process, the careless player revealed a huge expanse of woman's flesh. And more. Jonas was embarrassed but gazed and gazed. And gazed.

Amissia said, 'I see your nest, sister. I see your nest and it is moist.'

'So soon?' asked Beatrix enigmatically. 'Mabylye, how impatient you are.'

'Not I, but "it",' replied Mabylye as she began to finger a fast and complicated melody on the long instrument.

Jonas understood nothing of this brief exchange, nor, with his feelings in turmoil at the sight of Mabylye's heavy thigh, was the poor, excited lad inclined to fathom it. Instead came a longing from nowhere. He was anxious to return, to wake out of his dream into the familiar.

Half-way through the night the sisters, tired from music-making, chattering, food and wine, fell asleep. Jonas, fearful of following them, and remembering how he became visible once he was asleep, fought his drowsiness. To no avail. Within minutes the close and heavy atmosphere numbed his waking senses. He slept and slowly appeared. A boy among five women. It was not possible they could avoid seeing who was among them now. However, good fortune stayed with him. Good fortune certainly for me, the chronicler Coaxandria, who, had Jonas been discovered, would have had no twelve tales to chronicle.

Dawn hauled itself out from the earth. The cry of the wide-winged sky-madden pierced awake those whom the king missed. Jonas shot upright and — horror — he saw himself! The unseen was seen. The daughters stirred. He concentrated hard to fade away, but mornings, as we have observed, do not lend themselves to instant action. He thought he would never fade in time, but the princesses were heavy with sleep. He faded out before life faded in for them. Etheldra, being the healthiest, opened her eyes first and saw the last faint image of Jonas flicker out. She was not alarmed, however, explaining it as the end of a dream.

Jonas watched with curiosity to see how they would return. He should have known. Each daughter reached for a phial, moistened her lips and waited. The humming breeze welled up from the earth. It was the daughters' turn to fade away. As they had come, so they must go. He should have known.

He reached for a phial, moistened his lips, heard the sound of the humming breeze, experienced once more the sensations painful and tender, the scents sweet and putrid, the sounds of balm and disquiet, and was returned home to sleep and think and sleep again.

JONAS SLEPT,
BUT THOUGHT LITTLE

*J*onas slept but thought little. How could he, a young, inexperienced stableboy, think through twelve complex female lives? All he could do was observe and hope that events would explain themselves.

They did. Events of such privacy and power they changed his life, even though he was unable to piece them together coherently and could only describe them to me, Coaxandria, who now relates, shapes and sets them in their time.

Jonas returned the next night and the next and again for nine nights. Usually he found them engaged in the same activities. Margeria and Meliora posing, discussing the affairs of state, the problems of law; Enota painting them. Amissia singing, and Mabylye playing to Beatrix, Liticia and Etheldra. Amy weaving and, together with Amabilia and Lenota, listening to the tales of Dionis. But the pattern was not always the same. For two nights Beatrix was not present. She had travelled to meet and persuade Arab and Jewish physicians to work in her hospitals. For three nights

Dionis sat at the feet of a teller of tales named Malory, who had many adventures to relate about a king named Arthur. Only on the tenth night did they all come together, assembled in one hut as though summoned to a royal conference.

At first they seemed preoccupied with nothing in particular, engaged merely in the common pursuits of eating and drinking, humming and strumming, whispering in corners. Yet there vibrated between them a presentient atmosphere. Jonas could feel it on his skin. And it was so.

Meliora broke the mood. Her words were abrupt and unexpected. 'I am tired,' she said, 'of my loving.'

Although the sisters would have sworn that not one could disturb or surprise the other, yet each felt a quickening of the senses.

'You cannot mean that,' Enota stated.

'I mean,' Meliora corrected herself, 'that I am tired of the *way* I love.'

Ten princesses held their breath. What Pandora's box was about to be opened? Only one princess was distressed, Lenota.

'We agreed never to talk of this,' she said. 'We agreed!'

'Why so frightened?' her sister asked.

'There are shadows in our lives which must not be put into words,' Lenota warned. 'Besides, we are not alone, sisters, heed me, we are not alone.'

'And did we not,' Beatrix spoke next, 'agree not to talk of these things in the presence of Amabilia?'

'Because I am the youngest?' protested Amabilia.

'No, because you are the virgin.'

'Which is a state,' said the firm Meliora, 'that should cease to be.'

Pandora's box was unlocked, the lid inched open.

All eyes turned on the youngest sister, who stood up, her eyes dark and confused, between eagerness and trepidation. She looked from one to the other of her sisters, searching for their response to Meliora's pronouncement. One by one they smiled. Amissia burst into a wild song and Mabylye struck vibrant chords on her guitar. Soon the room was brimming with chatter. Only Lenota was unsmiling and silent.

Amy's voice rose above the unleashed spate of gab and song, defiantly raising Pandora's lid.

'Two nights from now he will come to my door. He will knock. I will tell him "enter". He will enter grinning, and say, as he always says, "Twelve days have I been waiting for this night." And he will throw off his clothes, in great haste, as he always does, and I will ease off my gown, slowly, as I always do, lie on my back, pull open my skein of cream, into which he will slip and slide with his furious finger, oohing and aahing and uttering meaningless words such as, "Oh, my honeysuckle, my sweetness." Such as, "Oh, my midnight oil, how you burn me burn me burn me!" And it is true. I burn him burn him burn him till he splutters out before I have begun even to smoulder. Then he will eat what has been prepared, drink a little, look at my tapestry and tell me "it grows it grows". And he too will grow, and stoop once more to nibble my nipples, tongue my tummy, and slither about in search of my cream again. Thus will the tedious night pass.'

'He will come to my door,' said Liticia, pulling Pandora's lid higher, 'burst in upon me with the authority of a spoilt lord. He will stumble towards me, fumble about me, lop out a breast, hoist a skirt, place my hand on his long john which will be short and I must stroke into full vanity. He will ask have I been pining for him, and I will say "yes", which is

32

always true until with dismay my eyes actually behold him. And as I stroke he will growl and scratch and go thumping around my flesh till he can stand no more and must plunge between my legs, sinking to the bottom of my sea. Then he will sleep before eating, and having slept must begin again his dismal floundering foraging floundering. And there are such other things I would do and have done.'

'We should not be talking of these things,' insisted Lenota. 'Loving is a private, sacred act. It betrays the men to talk of them this way.'

'Nothing is betrayed,' declared Meliora. 'Certainly not love, for love this is not.'

'Besides,' said Enota, 'they talk of us I am sure, and more cruelly.'

'He will knock on my door.' Etheldra took hold firmly of Pandora's lid. 'Wait till I say, "enter", and enter. With flowers. He will stretch beside me, close his eyes, tell me his dreams, and wait. I will kiss his eyes, kiss his ears, kiss his neck, his throat, his lips and slowly unbutton, untie, unfold and reveal his nakedness until – my turn! I stretch beside him and off he goes – unbuttons, unties, unfolds, revealing my nakedness and making ready his hoe for my damp seed-bed. Oh, he is sweet and his dreams are about me, and I will not deny our pitch and toss is pleasant sometimes but – nothing *grows* in me. I do not mean child, I mean – my breath is even, no storm heaves, I am as bored as an unweeded patch.' Thus spoke the princess of the gardens.

'He will come,' said Beatrix, who cared for the sick, 'dressed elegantly and, each night, variously. He will recite new verses in a low, passionate voice. He will declare his love, which I will be unable to return, because soft words embarrass me. We will talk for hours and hours, eating and drinking until I am almost too tired for passion. He will never fail to be thoughtful and gentle, which is why once I wanted him, once, once, ah, once!'

'Mine will burst in upon me,' laughed Amissia, 'full of swagger and pride, and boasting his bugle was blowing its song long before he reached me, and will I please, please, pleeeeease sing along with it! Which I do while I disrobe and he disrobes, both of us singing as though to inflame our passion, which – may God forgive this confession – grows in him more than in me. But I sing and I sigh and I blow his bugle now and then – '

'You *blow* it?' cried Lenota, horrified.

'You *dare*?' asked Amy, thrilled.

'He *asks* you to?' enquired Dionis, surprised.

'Not too much,' replied Amissia, delighted to have shocked her sisters, 'just sufficient to draw from him a few strange sounds. I would like to blow harder but it seems to worry him. So instead I let him blow his own bugle under my arch, which I make on all fours and pleases him better.'

'You see,' said Meliora, 'there *is* imagination among us. Amissia blows and makes arches.'

'My falconer bounces in,' revealed Enota, 'and says each time, "Here is my cucumber, where is my pie?" And I can laugh no more.'

'I lie with my one,' said Dionis, 'always beneath and him above, and as he parts my lips and heaves, I beg him tell me a story. "What kind of story?" he asks. Any story, I say, any that will make pictures in my head. So he plunges and puffs and thinks and pauses and always always always in the end cries out breathlessly, "I cannot, I cannot, I have no breath left." Heavens! I am so drained by his windy silence.'

'You will hear nothing from me,' said Lenota, whose mind was drifting to horizons she could barely perceive.

'And from me there is nothing to hear,' laughed

Margeria, 'for the truth must be faced, I am too unlovely to be loved.'

'While from me,' said the loose-limbed Mabylye, 'well – I – I would be too ashamed. My desires frighten me. He thrusts me like a happy hound but I think, I think...' She hesitated, unable to finish her thought.

All waited.

'Be bold,' urged Meliora, 'these are new times. Lift the lid higher.'

'You lift it,' said Mabylye. 'It was you who spoke first.'

'I have,' said the daughter of tact and diplomacy, 'imaginings untried.' She paused. 'I have advised our father in foreign affairs and trained his emissaries for foreign lands. I have watched time pass, and thought – I need to explore that which is foreign in myself; foreign, dark, intoxicating, rainbow-coloured. Senses to be released or imprisoned. But first – ' she turned to the youngest, Amabilia – 'new beginnings must be newly begun.'

Pandora's box was opened. What would rise from it, take wing and fly?

All this Jonas heard and saw about the king's daughters and related to me, Coaxandria, who have here ordered and interpreted and summarized for the king, and for those who will read after.

AMABILIA
- THE YOUNGEST

When she was seventeen, Amabilia had been told by her eldest sister that in one year from then she must know a man, but one of *her* choice.

'A princess can never be chosen.'

'And what of love?' the youngest had asked.

'Love is a sweet, pure stream which will find its way through any mire,' her sister had replied. 'First comes experience. With experience comes memory, from memory comes pleasure. With the memory of experienced pleasure the turbulence of love may be the better savoured and protected.'

The princesses had gone where men gathered, worked and bartered in this topsy-turvy land at the end of the tunnel. Bargains had been struck. Each of her sisters, one a month, had spoken with Amabilia about their own plans and expectations. Each in their way told her that the metamorphosic emotion called love was set aside for another time, another place.

During her twelve months she had met and considered

many men and in the end hovered between two of them. One young, handsome, bursting with energy but of uninteresting skills and shallow curiosity. The other, old, or so his fifty years seemed to her, old and weather-beaten, possessed an orchard from which was made cider. During the years he had nurtured his orchard and had taught himself to read and write. People purchased his skill for writing contracts and composing love letters. He and his sons delivered them. Sometimes to faraway places.

Important for Amabilia, who laughed a great deal, were his eyes, which smiled; and in his gentle features she could see the young man he once had been. She thought: In the one I have both – he that was and he that is. Her choice had about it a sense of inevitability.

The day arrived. Amabilia sat in her hut trembling. Of carnal pleasures she knew and did not know. In her mind were pictures but, as her eldest sister had pointed out, no memory of sensations. An array of foods selected by herself stretched the table's length between lit candles. She had decided there were to be no perfumes or wines, no artificial stimulants. The occasion promised turbulence enough, she wanted him alert and herself awake. This first experience of physical pleasure must be pure, she told her sisters.

Her hut, warmed by a fire whose burning wood produced an incense of its own, was cosy and comforting, with culinary smells and the subdued hues of red, brown and sienna woven rugs. No skins on her floors, they seemed too pagan to her, but plates of brass and copper flashed from her walls, and tiny sheep bells maintained a continuous trembling. Trembling with them, she waited.

He came with a bracelet of plaited gold engraved with birds in flight, which pleased and relieved her. She had expected nothing.

'Must come with something,' he said. 'It would be brutal to arrive with nothing but my battle orders.'

He smiled his young man's smile through his old man's wrinkles. She did not know how to respond to the soft irony of his banter. He recognized her confusion.

'I have five sons,' he began, taking meat from the table and offering it to her mouth.

Her eyes held on to him like an apprentice awaiting each new instruction.

'Five! And each is different. Is that not strange? So different you would think each had a different father.'

She listened to him carefully, looking for other meanings in his words. Was this all he had come to do, talk of his sons?

He continued, his voice deep and mellow like a bassoon, reassuring. 'But I am their father right enough. I just marvel at their difference. In fact I marvel how different every face is. Each one surprises me. Do you not find that?'

She thought about it. 'No, it does not surprise me. I marvel at it but it is so in the nature of things that I *expect* people's faces to be different.'

'Ah!' he responded. 'We miss much because of what we expect, take for granted. Next time you see two faces in the same room, you just look at them closely and ask yourself – is the difference in features only a difference of shape or does the fall of a mouth, the slant of an eye, reveal a difference in character?'

As he spoke she stared at him.

'I see you looking more closely at me,' he said. 'Are you wondering what the difference is between my face and yours? That is not difficult to describe.' He took her hand and ran it down the side of his face. 'Mine feels like leather. You can run your nails in the lines on my face. But yours – ' his finger, slow as a solitary tear, slid from her temple down her cheek and curved under her chin – 'your skin is soft like an early summer's evening.'

'You live in your orchard,' she laughed, 'I still live in my head.'

He reached for a mirror and placed his face alongside hers. 'Look. Look and describe the differences you see.'

'My eyes,' she began, 'are large, round, black and – ' She paused.

'Go on,' he encouraged her.

'I do not like what I see,' she said sadly.

'Young girls often distort the truth of what they are,' he countered with a smile. 'What is it you see that you do not like?' he asked. 'For I see beauty and dawn dancing in your eyes.'

'"Dawn in my eyes",' she mocked. 'Look again. They protrude. Spots on my skin, fat cheeks, thick arms, the mind of a grasshopper my sisters tell me, and heaviness all over. The only beauty you see is the devil's beauty called "youth".'

Her mentor ignored her self-deprecations. 'You have lips that curl,' he said, running his finger over them.

She shuddered.

'Feel mine.' He pulled her finger over his lips. 'Cracked and drawn. Now, put your finger in your mouth, suck it in and out, feel its shape.'

She did so.

He told her, 'Smooth. Long. No bumps. Now mine.' He put his finger in her mouth. 'Leather again, and bumps. All gnarled.'

She slowly sucked his finger, feeling its shape, gazing all the while into his eyes. Yes, it was gnarled. But she felt tenderness for it, held it in her mouth and lapped her tongue around it. How strange, she thought, my tongue knew what to do. His finger moved and stroked the roof of her mouth. She closed her eyes to concentrate on his touch. He made her aware of her mouth's cupola, of her gums, her strong teeth. She bit his finger gently, laughed, then withdrew it from her face.

'Look at me,' she said gaily. 'I am on my knees, my arm is outstretched holding a mirror, a man has a finger in my mouth and my eyes are closed. Surely all this is for laughter?'

'Laugh,' he told her, 'but your shyness is gone.'

'True, true!'

She jumped up, threw her arms around his neck, kissed his cheek, treating him like a father from whom she had just received a present. The embrace would have been innocent but he held her in it and turned his lips to hers. She remembered why he was with her and at once behaved as she imagined was expected, pressing her lips hard into his and squeezing his neck.

He pulled away, spluttering. 'No! No! No! Not like that, child!' He paused. 'You *are* a child, aren't you'. He paused. As he said 'child' his mood changed. 'I am thinking, is this an honourable arrangement?'

'I am eighteen years old,' she assured him, 'have no fears. Take me on this journey with you.'

'Then like this.' He showed her.

They were both still on their knees, facing each other. He cupped her face in his rough hands and brushed her lips with his.

'And this, and this.' He lightly kissed her lips. 'Feel them first,' he said. 'If you press too hard, you press away feeling.' He gently sucked her lips, bit them, slid his tongue along them. 'When feeling is stirred, *then* you may press.'

Which he did, firmly, darting his tongue each time deeper, until her mouth was wide and his tongue circling and creating such unfamiliar sensations she could not contain a moan. Nor stem strange juices between her thighs, or control her knees, which buckled beneath her. She swooned to a heap.

'Oh,' she gasped, 'what power in a kiss. How helpless it made me feel. Wait. We must wait a little.'

She lay on her back, wanting to wrench her body open to become one huge mouth for his tongue. She reached up her arms to pull him down. His tongue seemed longer. She had learned how to open her mouth wide for its tip to flick her throat, till she became breathless again and pushed him away.

'I want to swallow you,' she gasped. 'Is that not madness? I feel I want to take every part of you in my mouth.'

At which she drew him down again, her energy in full flight now. This time she thrust her tongue into his mouth and with it heaved him over. Now she was above him, thrusting and searching and uttering joyful sounds, as one who has learned to ride a horse and could not be reined to a halt.

'Whoa! Whoa!' he was forced to cry out, winded. 'There is more to loving than mouths and tongues. Do not tire yourself out in one mad gallop. Nor me for that matter,' he added.

'Have respect for my elders?' she asked with affectionate cheekiness.

'No. Pity!' he puffed, sharing her humour.

'What more?' She flung herself on her back, her arms outstretched, her legs wide, her look bold and not without a touch of sweet wickedness.

'Aye, thou's lost thy shyness then,' he said, feeling the need to retreat into his dialect.

She turned her face away and coyly shifted her eyes back, taunting, waiting. He looked down on her.

'I can see the shape of your body as your dress falls over it,' he told her.

'And what does it make you feel?'

'An uncontrollable pulling between my groin.'

'Why? Can you say why?' She was still outstretched.

'Why? I am not sure. Perhaps because I look at those shapes and remember what it feels like to touch them, to lie on them. I remember the sensations, the warmth, the smells, the juices. I remember.'

'So you feel what you feel not because of me but because of a memory?'

Questioning him made her feel it was she who was now controlling events.

He thought about it. 'A memory, yes, but stirred by the sight of *you*.'

'Is memory so important? My sisters keep telling me it is.'

'Some say memory is all, both for what we love *and* what we fear.'

She seemed not to have understood.

'Thoughtfulness adds beauty to your face,' he told her.

'Thank you,' she responded, 'but beauty is no help to stupidity.'

'Inexperience is not to be confused with stupidity,' he reassured her. 'You will come to understand the power of memory. Tell me, have you seen a man naked before?'

She shook her head; his question took both her breath and speech away.

'You have not seen the long arrow men use to pierce passion from a woman's body?'

She shook her head again, her eyes widening with anticipation.

He stood up. 'Then I will show thee.'

He began, with slow confidence, to unpeel his clothes till he stood over her, heavy with muscles and used flesh.

'There,' he said, looking down, 'he's at rest now, though

had I been a younger man you would have cast eyes upon a bolt-upright attentive thing. But *I* am not young, *he* attends not, and we are both hard-worked. Look, he merely throbs and waits.'

'For whom? For what?'

'For thee.'

'For me?'

'For thee to control him. Do you want to discover your power over him?'

She nodded vigorously, unable to tear her gaze from the dark cascade of flesh before her.

'Then do as I tell thee. As you lie there, slowly pull up your dress. Slowly, slowly. Over your calves, your knees, slowly, slowly... and watch him. Watch.'

Amabilia did as he bade her. She raised her dress slowly, slowly, mesmerized and marvelling at the change taking place before her. Where at first had appeared soft flesh now rose thick bone saluting as her dress retreated above her knees, her thighs and finally the nested mound and belly which she was exposing for the first time to a man. She was bewitched. It had been as he had said. She had made it happen. The power was hers; she thrilled to it.

Oh, now she was agitated with curiosity. How would that grown stem feel to her touch? Childlike, forgetting how she had made it rise, she eagerly sprang to her knees, her clothes covering her again.

'May I touch it?' she asked.

He nodded.

'He has risen to be touched.'

'"He"? You talk as though 'he" is someone else.'

'He is. With a life of his own I have never been able to control. As you see, you control him better than I.'

She curled her fingers round it, warm and hard. 'He

moves.' She laughed with the delight of discovery. 'He jumps in my hand.'

Her other hand was cradling the sac beneath. 'And these, these round things which hang, they too move and swim around.'

She squeezed too hard. He leapt away with a howl.

'That – you must never do,' he admonished.

She was distraught. He pacified her.

'The slightest knock there gives great pain.'

She moved in once more, gentler. 'Now does my touch please you?'

'You know my real pleasure?' he replied as he stood over her, legs astride, his fingers caressing the skin at the roots of her hair.

'Tell me. Tell me everything. Talk to me all the time. Explain.'

'My real pleasure,' he said, 'is your surprise. Everything is new for you.'

It was true. The tumescent form transfixed her. She stroked back the hem to reveal a red dome and felt she did not ever want to let go; there was a warmth, a comfort in it. The aged and wrinkled flesh, the dark hues and thick veins, all conveyed strength to her, while in the smooth red dome, faintly moist now, she saw an oval hole revealing a tiny tunnel into which she felt an urge to thrust her tongue. She wanted to cover the dome with her lips, gently sink her teeth into the length. She did none of these things, fearing she would give pain again, or that he would think her foolish. Instead she stared and stared.

'What does it make *you* feel?' he asked her.

'I feel very wet between my legs for a reason I do not understand.'

'I will explain later,' he promised. 'What else do you feel?'

'Protected,' she replied.

'Nothing more?'

'Well, I – ' She hesitated. 'See! I have not lost all my shyness.'

'Try.'

'You will not laugh at me or become angry?'

'Of course not, child.'

Again that epithet, but this time her youth excited him and the old man's stern 'old man' jumped once more in her hand.

'I love it when he does that,' she said, stroking the strident stalagmite, imagining she calmed it, unaware she agitated it further. Then she dared: 'It makes me feel I want to put my tongue in this hole.'

'Do that and it will never stop jumping.' He laughed.

She did. Tentatively. Her tongue toyed its tip. Not only the long thing but the man too jumped, so that what she held jerked from her hand.

'No, no!' she cried. 'Come back. I want him back.'

What had she done? She reached to curl her hands round him again and looked closely where her tongue had flicked. Had she given him pain?

'You have found the centre of unbearable pleasure,' he explained. 'Move carefully.'

She had satisfied one urge and wished for another to be indulged. She placed her lips around the red dome. Again her tongue moved to the small opening. Once more he recoiled, gasping, but this time she held on and followed, so that suddenly the whole bone was in her mouth. The sensation was such as she had never experienced – pleasure and power in one. She wanted it in her mouth for ever.

'Gently, gently,' he cautioned, withdrawing despite her protestations. 'Do you want me to lose passion so soon?'

She did not understand. He explained.

'There comes an ending to all this,' he said. 'For a man it ends when a thick white stream bursts out from this tunnel. They call it 'stream of life'', for it contains the seeds of our beginnings. And with its coming ends passion.'

'For ever?' she asked, wide-eyed.

'No, child.' He laughed. 'Just until the body is rested, has regained its ardour, then you can begin once more. A continuous cycle, like the seasons.'

'And where does it go, this 'stream of life''?'

'Where between your legs it is moist. I will show you soon.'

The prospect of endless pleasure made her mouth open with incredulity. It could not be possible. Of course it was not, as he explained.

'As you grow older you need longer rests. You, being so young, could continue all night without stopping, as could I when I was eighteen. But at fifty, well, because you are young and fresh you could stimulate my ardour for a whole night, perhaps two, but then I would need days to recover. Nor,' he added, 'is it possible to find pleasure with everybody. Some have looks, manners, smells, rhythms which you will not like. And it is a distressing experience in this life to discover you do not desire the person you love and often desire a person you do not love.'

'And with us?'

The kind, hired lover had difficulty in responding. She understood.

'Desire but no love?'

The question saddened him. Her instinct was to reassure him.

'But affection,' she declared eagerly, and reached once more for her comforter. She gasped, distressed. 'Look at him! What have you done to him? He is dead!'

'He is not dead. I talked too much. Loving demands concentration. My tongue wandered. No matter,' he continued, 'the moment has come to teach your young body about itself.'

Her first thought was that he wanted her to repeat the first action. She flung herself on her back and began slowly to hoist her dress. He stopped her with a laugh, fell to her side and kissed her with great affection for the innocence of her ways.

She asked, 'Do I too have a centre of pleasure?'

'And why should you not?'

'Where? Where?'

'Soon! Soon!' He echoed her with smiles and reassurance. 'I will show you. But first – '

Unhurriedly, button by button, he opened her dress to the waist. Beneath was a bodice of fine cotton, which he pulled up slowly, caressing her with fabric, till her full round belly lay exposed before him. His rough fingers circled the small saucer. She closed her eyes, sighed, and quivered with anticipation at his touch. He bent to circle his tongue there. Her sighs heaved faster as instinctively she raised her body to him, offering. But he did not stay there. Instead his tongue slid down the sides of her flesh, pausing sometimes to suck gently, sometimes gently to bite. Her young body writhed in small movements, instinctively knowing what to do with itself. When he stopped, her eyes sprang open at once.

'Why? Why? Is that all? Are there no other parts to discover?' She was so eager and anxious he had to laugh again.

'Oh, many parts,' he assured her, 'many, many parts. First, remember where I have just touched.'

His fingers retraced their path, this time with his nails. Her body moved again. It did not seem possible that the same areas could offer a greater sensation, but with his fingernails skimming her flesh they did. And she comprehended the power of memory – the second journey across her flesh doubled her pleasure: the pleasure of knowing the touch that was to come, the pleasure of the touch itself. Anticipation followed by fulfilment.

He raised her bodice higher, the first man to see her breasts. She gazed at him gazing. Here was a new pleasure – to be looked at and feel the emotion her body aroused in the eyes of the beholder. He blew gently on her skin. She closed her eyes to enjoy the caress of breath. She quivered. His nails moved up her sides, circling under her arms, from whose thuriferous pits she smelt her own musky sweat, down the soft side of a breast, round and round in ever decreasing circles until – aah! Here must surely be the unbearable centre of all pleasure. Her nipples hardened. She experienced a reversal of feelings. Whereas with his flesh in her hands she had felt power and domination, now on her back with rough fingers stroking and sharp nails pinching the brown studs on her breasts she felt total surrender. Restraint drained from her. She knew she would do anything, desired to do everything, ached for everything to be done.

This feeling intensified, for now lips replaced fingers and the tiny dark mounds of hardened flesh were sucked and bitten, his mouth moving back and forth from one teased nipple to the other. He knelt behind her, above her head, both hands played her buds as he bent his head to mouth and tongue the taught skin of her offered throat. He plunged into the cavity where neck meets shoulder and she moaned for the threefold sensations making her writhe and plead.

'Your lips,' she cried, 'give me your lips.'

Holding still to the pinnacles of her breasts, he shifted to kiss her lips, from which her tongue lashed about in his mouth.

The young princess thought no pleasure could surpass this. But something felt incomplete. She was on her back, his body was behind, her breasts and face were receiving his warmth and caress – but her legs! Writhing had caused her dress to rise and now the lower part of her body was exposed. Who would touch her there? Why had he only two hands? Without knowing what she did, she pressed the ground with her feet and pushed up belly and mound like an altar pleading for offerings.

He recognized the movement and recognized too that he must cool the blood of this virgin, his charge. He kissed her cheeks to calm her.

'Why? Why?' she again asked, this time petulantly, not wanting to be calmed.

He made no reply but instead drew her clothes from off her. Both were naked.

He rolled her over to lay on her stomach. She understood. New parts. She was to be shown new parts. She felt his hands part her black hair, his warm breath upon the nape of her neck. No flesh had been touched, yet she shuddered. His tongue circled the back of her neck. Who would have thought a nerve end lived there? She wriggled her shoulders and laughed. He was astride her. She could feel his flesh resting on her rump, limp it seemed. Why did it keep retreating in this way? She reached behind and felt it leap at her touch. That satisfied her and she sank into the cushions to await his further explorations.

They came: fingernails marked her back and sides, finger-tips toyed and pressed. No part of her flesh failed to respond to his touch. Down his hands circled, down, down till he had to remove her hand from his thickened old faithful – it impeded his tracing. Where was he now? Aaaah! One finger had reached the top of the crevice where back ended and plump buttocks began. She cried out, arching upwards. Amabilia was a fleshy young woman, the smooth cheeks rose high from her back. She felt him part the cheeks. Oh – what next? Between them pressed his warm hard rod while hands continued to knead and stroke and gently pinch.

Till this moment, waiting for him to reveal pleasure in new parts of her body, each touch had been a discovery. Now, her rear end exposed to air, she became conscious of that most private part, the clenched hole. Inexplicably he had not touched there. She clenched and unclenched expectantly, feeling ashamed of her desire. No one would want to touch there, surely? Abandon overwhelmed her. Uncaring she raised her rump, reached for her comforter and placed it between her young buttocks. The action mortified her. She dropped flat to her stomach and burst into tears.

'For what?' cried the old man, dropping to her side in surprise. 'For what?'

Like an anxious father, he kissed her calm. Then. Change again. Her sobbing eased into moans. His tongue was elsewhere – her ears. No emotion remained still in one place. She shuddered from unhappiness into pleasure into elation. But where was he now? He seemed to have left her altogether. She could not believe it. What was he doing? He had parted her buttocks and his tongue was there, just where she had ached to be touched, in that most private of parts. Was this the centre of all pleasure? She thrust herself high and wove her thick cheeks in circles rhythmically with his thrusting. She had never known such ecstasy.

Unaccountably her hand reached between her labia.

'I am so wet,' she moaned, 'so wet from I do not know where or why.'

He stopped his movements and drew a hand between her legs as though to wipe away her juices. What was he doing? She turned and flopped on her back. He was sucking her moisture from off his fingers.

'That is the right juice,' he said, 'the juice a young woman should be flowing with now.'

'Has it a taste you enjoy?' she asked, surprised.

'No juice is like it,' he replied.

At which she leapt to her knees and playfully pushed him over to his back.

'Lie there,' she ordered.

She thrust her fingers between those thick lips to scoop out the juice the old man had said he loved, and wiped them on his lips. He sucked at her fingers. She scooped more. He sucked again. Here was something she could give him. Suddenly, she jumped up and sat astride his mouth.

'Here!' she cried. 'Take all.'

She did not comprehend what she was embarking upon, desirous only to offer. But in this offering was return a hundredfold, a sensation surpassing all others taking her breath away. His tongue thrust in and out. His lips sucked the plump slices hung between her legs. His fingers parted the succulent flesh, revealing a small, spiralling bud from which he drew pleasure like pain, pausing only to say, 'Prepare, child, for here is the centre of all ecstasy.'

He bit, he licked, he circled his tongue. She did not know what to do with her body or voice. Another person shrieked within her. The shriek became a cry, the cry a sob. So unbearable was it that she fell back in a swoon with her legs apart. She writhed, bent double, stretched and then arched up, calling for she knew not what. He was there between her legs, his fingers prising her open, his teeth biting, his tongue circling, his lips sucking. She grabbed his hair, squirmed and sobbed. No thought was in her, no sense of place, person or time. She was enveloped in pleasure that was not of this earth. How could such ecstasy grow from second to second when each second seemed a pinnacle to pinnacle until her blood burst within. She dug her nails deep into his flesh, drew blood, and moaned piteously, 'No! No!' as though to a heartless marauder. She was a confusion of protest and submission. Life drained from her in a flood and she cried the haunting cry of lost innocence till she could bear his touch no more and pushed him away. But this old man knew not to stay away. Comfort was called for. He lowered his body, covered her face with kisses and cradled her in his orchard arms.

It was what she craved, his comforting. She had pushed him away but oh, how he knew her needs. She clasped him and returned his kisses with joy and energy, each kiss saying thank you, thank you, till a most wonderful tiredness overwhelmed her. Her arms relinquished their grip, her body its eagerness. She looked up at his face, which was watching her every movement. A guardian smile was in his eyes. Returning his smile, her eyes felt heavy. Now it was sleep demanding submission. The old man knew it, and knew as with everything what next to do. He lay at her side, eased her into his arms and drew a cover over them both. She snuggled into the crook of his neck, enveloped by the smell of apples which rose from his weathered body, and slept. Her last thoughts before drifting were a conflict of wonder and wonderment at the strange ecstasy which had driven from her memory of the world.

When she awoke her shyness returned. He was leaning against a wall by the fire which he had rekindled, gazing at her. He seemed sad. Her breasts were uncovered. She pulled the cover over their nakedness. He had long been awake and had peeled her an orange, offering slices to her mouth. She bit into them and sucked, her eyes on him all the time waiting for meaning – of what had happened, of his sadness. The taste was sharp and refreshing. It brought her sweetly awake, and with it came the raven's hunger for food. Her body tingled full of memories. She could not keep still.

She leapt up, shy no longer, and fell on the table, grabbing greedy mouthfuls. The amused old man watched. She filled her hands, ran to him, threw her arms about him, heaped upon him kisses, and into his mouth thrust food from her fingers. She ran back and forth, feeding him this, feeding him that, kissing him constantly. On every part of him was food. From every part of him she lapped it up, not knowing what to do first or next or thereafter, and ended in wild spluttering and coughing.

'Oh, I am shameless!' she cried. 'What is happening to me? What have you done? I feel like an animal with no power of thought. Food and phallacking! What else is there in life? Nothing! And that is a dreadful thought. I feel so ashamed.'

'You must not feel ashamed, little lady,' he told her. 'At such an age it will seem there is no more to life. But all things settle and take their place.' His sadness deepened.

'Why, why, why are you so sad?' she asked.

'I love your youth,' he answered her. 'I love it dearly, believe me, but it reminds me mine is gone. So I am sad.'

'I will not hear it!' she cried imperiously. 'No sad or angry thoughts. I command you to think no thought that might dilute my passion.'

'Nothing will dilute that, my young princess, but a tiny twist of lemon deepens the sweetness of honeyed apples. It is good you should discover the mysteries of such pleasures with an old, pealing bell like me. Now, eat your fill; there is a veil to be pierced before you know all that lies beyond youth.'

They continued eating. She kept glancing at him to drink reassurance from his eyes. A question had to be asked.

'I was too far from this world to understand what was happening,' said Amabilia, 'yet I am certain nothing comparable happened to you. I was up and away shrieking and swooning, but you remained very earth-bound.'

'True,' he agreed, 'but you will not up and away alone next time. Next time I will come with you.'

She sensed that what he meant was more than what he said.

She rose hurriedly and left the hut. He heard the confident gush of her young stream part the night-time grass. Soon she was beside him again, on her knees, breathless, running from the night's chill, the smell of her body sending out messages of need.

'Are there,' she asked, 'parts of your body that burn to the touch as mine do?'

He laughed.

She pushed him on to his back. 'You think I cannot pleasure you?' She parted the hairs of his chest to reveal his nipples. 'These, do they feel as mine feel?'

'Try,' he invited her, 'and watch.'

She knelt behind him as he had knelt behind her, lifting his head to rest in her lap. With fingers and thumbs she rubbed and twisted his dark buds and watched. The limp lord flickered, squirmed and rose from the lake of hair like the fabled sword. She was spellbound and again experienced a sense of power. But it seemed to rise, and with difficulty she flashed her fingers between her legs to gather the thick juice the old man had said he loved, and spread it upon his lips and buds.

'Your imagination is at work I see.'

She was happy to be encouraged. Was this how food evolved? People made connections? Juice sweet for one thing could be sweet for another!

The effect was instantaneous. The long arm of his law stood firmly aloft. She lifted his head carefully from her lap and shuffled to grasp it. Hard, veined, warm, palpitating. There was its red dome. Her mouth covered it and moved down. Up down, up down, bright excited eyes watching him, seeking praise.

'Oh, how you know to take wing,' he whispered, 'as a young bird from its nest.' His eyes were closed, his head moved from side to side. He moaned as her tongue found the tip of his tip. 'Not yet, not yet,' he cautioned.

He changed positions, pinioned her arms and returned his mouth to that centre between her legs where pleasure was wild. Memory worked. Ecstasy was twofold: knowing what was to come and the excitement anticipating it. She could not reason why, but excitement was intensified by the power of his hands locking her arms to the ground.

Then, before she could burst from herself again, he withdrew his mouth and whispered urgently, 'Now! Prepare! There will come some pain, but bear it. Bear it and trust me. Close your eyes, and feel. Feel and remember where my lips have been.'

He relinquished grip of her arms and placed a cushion under her back. His fingers parted her moist petals. He lowered the loved hard thing into her. Here was an utterly different sensation as the tip slipped in and out, eased by her juice. Then the pain! A jab of pain. Where was he going? Skin was there, a wall. There was no way into her from this end. The lance seemed to have swollen and become a weapon of threat rather than pleasure. The thrusting went on, the pain increased, the memory he had asked her to retain was fading. But then his fingers were at work on her tiny mole. Pleasure and pain! Confusion! She cried, protested, pushed at his chest with the palms of her hands. Nothing stopped him. Here was ordeal not joy. He plunged and plunged, and though she understood he was trying to be gentle yet the pain seared, till – ayeeeee! She screamed. The wall was pierced and he sank with his lance to its hilt in blood. Youth and innocence were truly fled. She wept.

The pain was ebbing but so too was all memory of pleasure. Only one thing remained, the warmth and home-liness of what lay inside her. It belonged there. For ever. No ecstasy, just comfort and homecoming.

Thus they lay for many minutes as mood and feeling changed and a restlessness like a spring breeze urged her to move. Small movements at first, like tentative pleas. Her lower parts thrust up and down. She felt his log throb and jump inside her. Excitement was returning. The cushion arching her back helped her to new sensations. She wanted everything. Her body moved urgently, thrusting up, asking for more. He responded. He too began moving up and down, and that other creature in her came awake, moaning. She felt new parts come alive where the piston rubbed and cloyed in her bloodied honey. It must not stop, she thought. What will I do when it stops? He will go. I shall be emptied and alone. Life will end.

Her nails dug into his flesh. There it was again, a draining of her body's juices, streaming out with sobs and gasps. But what was that? Another voice cried out. Was someone else in the hut with them? It was a cry of anguish long and sad that told of pain and loss. At the same moment she felt a warm pouring inside her. She uttered words that she had never before uttered.

'Come! Come! Flow in me! Come! Oh, never stop. Cuuuuuuuum!'

She realized there was no other in the hut, it was his voice with which hers mingled. Only the two of them. Old man, young princess.

'Do not ever move from there,' she commanded.

'*I* will not,' he laughed, 'but *he* will.'

Soon he rolled off her, took her into his arms and covered them comfortably together.

'Before you sleep you must bathe,' he taught her. 'Wash deep inside you.'

'I will,' she promised.

'For it is not my child you must carry.'

'I know,' she reassured him. They were silent for a long while. Then she asked, 'Tell me about your sons.'

He began. 'The eldest has a good head for inventing machines. He is in Holland now with a man who studies the stars. The next is at sea. He brings home strange-smelling spices. The middle one and the next are at home with me tending the orchards. And upon the youngest I have spent all my savings that he be sent to study for the church. I have loved each one differently for the difference I found in them and for the freedom they have which I never had. Once I was a bondman, you know. I knew what servility was.'

All this Jonas heard and saw about the princess Amabilia and related to me, Coaxandria, who have here ordered and interpreted and summarized for the king, and for those who will read after.

ENOTA
~ THE SECOND YOUNGEST

She was pleased with her painted map. Attention to minute detail gave her profound satisfaction.

Though Enota's commission was to paint dogs, unicorns, mermaids, firedrakes, centaurs, doves and other sweet, pacific creatures to inhabit the foliage surrounding the map, she had added falcons perching among sinewy vines and curled leaves. Why, she wondered, had she done it? Merely because her lover chanced to be a falconer? Well, that too is art, she concluded. Life intrudes. Her lover was a falconer, therefore this tenth painted page must have falcons.

What a boring book it was, compiled by a travelling monk who claimed to have reached the end of the world, looked over its edge and seen hell. With what absurd luridness on the fifth page had he described hell. She had scrupulously re-created his bleak, puerile imaginings – winged beasts, quadruped serpents, insect-headed canines, gargoylean fish life, rainbow-fired amphibians – all saddling or devouring ugly, pain-ridden humans damned for eternity. But she had delighted more in the painting of this latest page, woven with living nature, rather than the fifth, sinuous with death.

This oddest-shaped of the king's daughters was exhausted. Her fingers ached from the tense gripping care of tiny strokes. Her sharp eyes were losing the intelligence of concentration. Henricus, her falconer, was asleep. The young village-helps sat in a corner, the boy complaining about the late hour, waiting to be dismissed; the girl sourly agreeing with him.

Enota put down her brush, ordered the adolescents to clear away, leaned back against the wall hugging her knees and watched them move, sluggishly bored, as they stacked clay pots, packed easel, chalks, multicoloured powders and sheets.

Her eyes became heavy. She closed them. The colours of her illustrations danced in spots before her. She longed for them to fade, for her mind to become blank. With effort she emptied her head of pictures and dwelt instead upon the sensations of the night air blowing through the loose sleeves of her garment, and the smell from her armpits where she had sweated with exertion. A pleasing smell, thick and familiar. Henricus claimed to enjoy it and nuzzled into the damp hair, breathing deeply as though he were on a high mountain. Enota, however, did not enjoy *him*. As she had told her sisters, she could laugh no more neither at his cucumber nor his cucumber mind. Like Meliora, the second eldest, she was tired of the way she loved and was loved.

At the sound of a thud her eyes opened. The boy had knocked over the silver falcon which she had been using as a model and he was now regarding her anxiously. At first she did not look at him but at her array of objects – gifts brought by those who knew of her need for models. Joyful Buddhas from China, profusely breasted goddesses from Turkey, scheming bronzed eagles in flight from Albania, coiled copper snakes poised for vengeance from Egypt, startled monkeys in mahogany from a new land so far away across oceans that its name till now had not been discerned. All were standing. No damage had been done to the silver falcon from Germany. The boy was waiting for reprimand, his eyes brimming with appeal. How vulnerable is the face of youth, she thought. Or was it the vulnerability of a servant's face that she saw? She nodded reassuringly, all was well. He continued with his work.

Enota was now wide awake, her fierce brown eyes following the gawky, eager actions of the village young ones. They threw to the forest peel and rind, core and bone; covered the almond soup and the pâté of game; filled two pitchers, one with water, the other with wine; stacked away platers, knives; replenished candles and oils; laid out mats and rugs for the night's bed; swept, then came to stand by their mistress for payment.

What age could they be? The girl fifteen, perhaps less, perhaps more? The boy? Difficult to tell. He was delicately featured, small-framed, with hard-worked hands and knowing eyes – fifteen years? Sixteen? Both stood before the squatting princess, whose eyes fixed upon the boy's face. Suddenly, to her surprise – though she did not show it – without shifting her eyes from his face, she placed her hand upon the bulge between his groin and slowly rubbed, watching him, waiting for his reaction. The girl gave a tiny laugh. The boy blushed, backed away and held out his hand. It was only money he desired. Why had the princess been surprised? It had seemed a natural action, like stroking a cat or clucking a child's chin.

She reached for her pouch and emptied the coins in her lap; their weight sank her garment between her legs and raised it over her knees. The blushing boy could not help gazing into the dark corners of flesh and hair. The princess felt his gaze and took more seconds than were needed to sort out his wage. She found the coins, closed her legs, offered the boy his day's pay and smiled a smile intended to melt him. The boy fled.

The princess turned her attention to the girl. At once the relationship was different. Instant sisterhood, the division of station gone. They smiled together, sharing a perception of the silliness of young men.

Enota said, 'Turn your face sideways.'

The girl did as she was requested. Enota reached for paper and chalk. Within minutes a scurry of swift movements shaped the girl's likeness, giving the lines of her eyes a hint of the smile which came from the thrill of being model for a princess, a smile which grew into a squeal of delight when she was shown the finished cartoon.

'Sssh!' hushed the princess. 'You will wake the falconer. I do not want him hovering around me for yet a while. Pour me some wine, please.'

The young servant obeyed. Enota offered her cup. It was declined.

'You want to be going home, I know.'

The young girl held out her hand for payment.

'Would you like me to do another drawing of you?'

She dropped her hand and smiled her pleasure.

'Slip off your gown,' requested the artist.

'Why?' asked the surprised girl.

'Your body is more interesting than your dress,' replied Enota.

The girl hesitated.

'Come,' encouraged the princess, 'see if your breasts are bigger than mine.' At which she tucked a hand into her blouse and lifted out her left breast. 'Let us compare.'

The girl complied. Truth was she had often played 'compare' with the other girls in the village. She pulled the cord to the top half of her dress and drew aside the rough flaps. Two soft mounds were there.

'Oh, mine are much, much bigger,' said the princess. 'But I can see that when you are grown your nipples will be larger. Look how small mine are. Silly little pimples. Hardly there at all.'

She began to sketch. Soon another drawing was completed. When shown it, the girl's eyes widened.

'How I wish I could do that,' she said.

'Perhaps I will teach you.' Enota's voice was gentle. 'Now slip out of your dress, don't be embarrassed.'

The girl obliged and revealed a slim form with a bush like spring at the base of her belly. The princess made her change places, arranged her lengthways upon her cushions. She drew. Sheet after sheet, shifting the girl from pose to pose, showing her each one after it was done. Her servant quickly learned how to move and arrange herself. With each new position she relaxed more. The princess drank meanwhile. After the seventh sketch the girl relented and drank with her. Soon both were tired. The girl stretched out on the rugs as though ready for sleep. The princess sat beside her, cup of wine in her hand. They were silent for a long time.

Idly the princess drew out both her breasts and rubbed her nipples with the wine, watching them grow.

'Do you ever touch yours?' she asked her maid.

The maid nodded, seeming ashamed to have confessed. 'They say it's a sin,' she whispered, then smiled, dipped a finger in her mistress's wine, and circled it round and round her buds till they too grew.

'Has anyone else ever touched you?' the princess asked.

The girl nodded. 'We do it to each other down in the village.'

'Like this?' The princess dipped her finger into the wine and circled the girl's young teats. 'And this?'

She leaned forward, took a nipple between her teeth, bit and licked it with her tongue. The girl sighed and offered up her breasts. The princess slid down to the damp hole in her belly, where her circling tongue drew even longer sighs. But she knew not to hasten and leaned back against the wall, contemplating new thoughts.

'Do you touch other places?' she asked.

'Other places? What other places? There's only lips, and girls do not kiss.'

'Some girls do if the urge comes upon them.' Enota's fingers played over her servant's skin.

'Kissing is for boys,' the maid insisted, 'but kissing between girls, now that *would* be a sin.'

Enota ignored her declaration. Again silence. The girl feared she had gone too far, contradicting her mistress.

'Would you like to discover new parts to touch?'

'What new parts, ma'am?'

'New parts. You trust me, don't you?'

'Always have done, ma'am.'

'You *can* go home if you like...'

The girl jumped. 'Oh no, no, no, ma'am. I would stay here for ever if I could.' She clapped her hand to her mouth. There! A secret revealed. Was it, though, a secret? Who could be surprised that a girl from the village would want always to be near abundance, soft finery, ease of manner? 'Show me new parts, ma'am. Please.'

'Lay back again, then,' coaxed the mistress. 'Stretch out.'

The village girl did as the royal girl told, staring up, wide-eyed and expectant. The mistress knelt before her servant's feet, the toes of which wriggled tense with anticipation.

'Close your eyes,' said the princess to her midnight maid.

The midnight maid closed her eyes. The princess caressed the maid's ankles and the maid's toes.

'Tickles, ma'am,' said the maid, opening her eyes.

'*Close* your eyes,' admonished the mistress. 'The tickling will pass.'

But the maid could not forbear from opening them with each touch.

'They must be covered, then,' said her mistress, reaching for a length of cloth to blindfold her young companion. 'Now you will *feel*. When it is dark, you *feel* more.'

Thus blindfolded, the maid felt fingers press here, press there and move in firm sweeps around her feet and ankles up, up along to her calves. There was a pause. What was the princess preparing? Hands parted her legs. The princess knelt between them. Fingers crept to her knees, around her knees, behind them, a hand to each thigh, a hand to each hip. She trembled as the caressing nails dipped into her sides and rose with her belly. She raised her haunches from the ground, permitting fingers to travel where they wished. There was another pause. There had been many pauses. Each pause excited her. Where next? What next?

She felt hot breath like summer air waft over her. She trembled. Why breath? Where were fingers? She longed for fingers. They came, this time creeping into the oddest of places, the soft crease inside her arms. No, she had not been touched there before. And what strange place now? Up and down inside her thighs. That too was new. She trembled again. And now where? Surely not to her most private of parts? What could be there? Only a slippery clamp of flesh, a soft part which she and her friends called the spitting lips. She became embarrassed. A wetness spread, a small flooding. Sensations shuddered through her which she had never before experienced.

The princess spoke. 'Was I right?'

'Yes, ma'am. Oh, yes. I never knew. None of us did.'

'And you never knew this part either, did you?'

She prised the peeing part apart and gently rubbed the moist flesh between thumb and forefinger until the maid felt no other part of her body existed. She writhed and pushed the fingers away. But fingers fought back to conquer again that spot which felt like – felt like – what? There was no describing the sensation. It was like no other thing. It was itself.

'Where *are* you? What have you found? Oh, ma'am, ma'am. I never knew it, oh, ma'am, do not, I feel so hot, I can't breathe, please do not.' She felt tongue and lips go down to that centre-fire and suck what seemed all being from her body. 'No, no! I come wet and wet and wet, no, no, no! Aaaaaaah!'

The maid wrenched the blind from her eyes and dug her nails into the shoulders of her patroness. A sound unlike anything in her known earth came as the waters of her flesh came. Both from she knew not where.

The cry brought Henricus awake. He sat upright and was about to protest. The princess put her finger to her lips. He watched, wide-eyed and not without some hint of annoyance. She ordered him to feign sleep. The girl relaxed. Twisting and turning ceased. Warmth. Peace. As never before. The two women lay side by side. Comforter and comforted.

There was movement. The princess peered into the shadows.

'Look who has returned.'

The girl raised herself on an arm and smiled. Standing by the door, sheepishly, was the village boy.

'Have you been there long? Did you see it all happen?' the princess asked.

The boy was silent, his head bent, eyes riveted to the floor.

The two women leaned back against the wall, the princess in her favourite position, knees tucked up into her bosom, the girl with her legs stretched out, now modestly covered.

'Pour us some wine,' the princess commanded the boy. He obeyed. She patted the ground, indicating he should kneel between them. He obeyed. They sipped their wine. Her eyes pierced him. The sensation of her touch had lingered, she knew. He had returned to be touched again. But she did not oblige. Instead she drank on and rocked her legs open and closed, open and closed, until the boy was drawn to raise his eyes, at which moment she held her legs apart. His eyes widened. The princess placed her hand on her knee and began slowly caressing down the inside of her leg to where hair glistened with her dew. Damp fingers found damp cut and slid provocatively in and out. The boy was hypnotized. The princess watched him. The girl watched them both.

She stopped. The boy lowered his eyes. Though she knew the answer, she asked, 'Why have you returned?' Her foot reached as though to rest on his lap. Something moved. 'Ah. He is with us,' she said to her companion. 'Let us see it,' she commanded the boy.

No reassuring tones for him. He had resisted her first advance, now he must suffer. He blushed, thinking to regret his second thoughts but secretly thrilling to the princess's stern orders. 'Do it!' she ordered again. He unflapped the thick cloth and prised out his shy stem, which she suspected from the way he handled it had only ever been shown to the wind. The long thin flesh hung limp and forlorn. No one moved. The women sipped and stared. The boy raised his head to the ceiling, humiliated but held. His humiliation grew as the princess picked his private limb in her two fingers and flopped it around.

'What a funny, lifeless thing,' she said. But she took pity on him as his humiliation deepened to distress. 'It looks lonely. Shall we give him company?' She placed her wine by her side. 'I have nothing as big as that,' she told him, 'but look!' She stretched out her legs, drew up her dress and revealed her furry mound. 'Here is this small thing.' She opened her legs and parted her 'spitting lips' to allow the tiny bead to appear. She caressed it. 'There. See? You are not alone now.'

The young maid too found her bead, the newly discovered place from which her centre's fire had come, and, following her mistress's example, caressed it. The boy stared from one to the other. Fascinated. Fingers touching parts he had never seen before. Still nothing happened. He was not in the grip of pleasure but of curiosity, which is no stimulant.

'Ah,' said the princess, 'I see your body must learn to know itself.'

With one hand still caressing her bead, she reached out the other to hold the lad's limp thing. Gently she squeezed it, again and again. It stiffened. The girl stopped her own movement and watched. It was her turn to stare wide-eyed. The flesh grew and rose. As it did, the princess plunged fingers into her cut to gather her cream, which she rubbed up and down the boy's high bone till it shone.

'There!' sighed the princess. 'Now it is a handsome thing, a proud and raging thing indeed.'

'But why did it grow?' asked the amazed girl.

'For the same reasons these grow.' Plunging fingers once more into her slit, she gathered creams to rub into her maid's dark nipples.

Suddenly there came a roar. It was the boy. He had risen and was tearing off his clothes. He seemed possessed. Animal noises came from the stirred lad. He leapt threateningly towards them, small body, adult eyes, hard-working hands and tool erect like a standard raised to honour a new-born state. The women crept close to each other, waiting, watching to see what came next. He stood for he knew not what and, not knowing what, his standard lowered. The boy was perplexed and sank into himself as though betrayed.

'What happened? Where did it go?' The girl from the village was full of questions. 'Can we make it happen again?'

'Yes,' replied the princess. 'Just do to it what I did.'

The girl obeyed. She took her friend's warm flesh into her small palm and squeezed. It began to swell. She was entranced. She thrust two fingers between her legs to gather the cream with which more easily to push back the hanging skin and reveal the red bulb. The movement pleased her. Strange things were happening to the boy. His eyes glazed over and seemed to roll out of control. He gripped her hair as she had gripped the hair of the princess. She felt a power over him. She did not understand exactly what was happening, only that it was *she* who was making it happen. She drove on, excitedly rubbing and pulling until the boy roared and a huge jet of warm jellied milk exploded from his flesh over her face, running down her cheeks to her lips. It was a moment so strong that she too screamed, pushing and pushing, calling forth more jets of this strange-smelling, salty liquid, till the boy could bear no more and swooned over on to his back.

The princess crawled towards her bewildered maid, wiped the sticky tears from her cheeks with two fingers, sucked the juice from one and offered her the other. The rest she rubbed first into the girl's nipples, then into her own.

'Now rest,' she told her. 'Lie back. Passion explodes and must cool. We will explore more later.'

Soon the young ones were asleep.

Her falconer lover sat up. His squinting eyes had witnessed all. She whispered to him not to talk loudly. He crept to her side.

'That was a wicked thing to do,' he whispered.

'I know,' she whispered back. 'Why did it please me, then?'

'That is the nature of wickedness,' he replied, not without some pomposity, 'it pleases.'

'Then I must be a wicked person.'

'Be troubled.'

'I am.'

'I must go away and not return,' he suggested unconvincingly.

'It will never happen again,' she promised unconvincingly, and stretched out to sleep her guilty sleep.

The falconer looked from one sleeping shape to the next. He was not tired. The pattern of his night had changed. His role had been usurped. Either falcons needed to be trained or cucumber pies to be made. What more, after all, *was* there to life? And if his cucumber was no longer needed to make cucumber pies, what here was left for him to do? He was not an adaptable man.

An hour passed. He rose to revive the fire. The noise disturbed the young bodies, which moved their positions. Two moments of reassuring truth dawned on him. His odd princess with slanting eyes, a nose with no beginning, protruding teeth, mouth too small, her body all awry, stirred – a clumsy being, no doubt of that. Not that *he* was a young god! She opened her eyes briefly to smile at him before returning to sleep and with that smile came the first truth: beauty comes from eyes, character resides there.

Both youngsters, however, had rolled on to their sides with*out* opening their eyes. He watched the girl's body edge in sleep towards the boy and fit itself into his 'S' shape. Her arm cuddled him close and safe to her young bosom. The second truth: conscious thought invites wickedness, unconscious instinct offers comfort.

Henricus looked around at the sleeping flotsam, smiled, covered the two young people with rugs, then picked up his oddly shaped mistress in his arms, laid her on their bed, and settled beside her. He slept. Half the night passed.

When they awoke, princess and lover sat with their backs to the wall, cups of wine in their hands, watching and waiting for their young servants to creep from sleep, which they soon did.

'Nice times, my lasses and lads,' said Henricus, who spoke like a different being. 'Growing-up times. Growing-up and standing-up times!' He laughed at his humour, thus diminishing it, though they joined him politely. One laugh sounded louder than the rest.

'There are five people laughing,' cried the princess anxiously.

'Nonsense!' said her man. 'I count four. Now, to passion. Passion is dead and needs reviving.'

'Dead?' she cried, and flung back their rugs. 'Dead?'

True! His singer of songs lay slumped and silent. She threw her wine at it and swooped to lick the sorry sight. It responded eagerly and was soon erect, dashing and quite pleased with itself.

'Oh, sir,' cried the village girl, 'it is bigger than *his*.'

'Like my breast is bigger than yours,' said the princess, protecting the boy's pride. 'We are older. But one day this – ' She tried to pull the rug from off the serving-boy, who, intimidated now, clung to his cover for fear his hard-done-by thing would appear puny beside his master's. 'Let go,' demanded the princess. 'Let go I say!' Her command was fierce. The frightened boy released the rug and offered up his naked body to their sight. 'A lovely body,' declared the strong and regal ma'am. 'Never be ashamed of it. It has youth and dew and the sweet smell of young sweat. Many women would say their preference was for your smoothness rather than this – ' she pointed to her part-time lover – 'with hair in every hollow and crease, and muscles round every corner for a soft lady to bruise herself upon. So be proud.' She turned to her maid. 'Size, as you will learn, is not all.'

The maid sat back, prepared to learn. 'It gushes,' she said, 'like the fountain in our square, but what more can be done with it?'

'Watch,' said the princess. She knelt between her lover's legs, and where before she had merely licked she now took the tall cock in her mouth and sucked.

Everyone was amazed. Especially Henricus, upon whom such a bold, bawd act had never been lavished. He whooped like a crazed man, which made the youngsters laugh. Enota too. She had to pause. 'Fool!' she admonished. 'Behave!' He ceased his whooping, but not his heavy

71

breathing, as she rocked back and forth plunging deeper each time till the huge thick thing was lost from view and his breathing, poor man, rose to alarmingly high registers. The princess stopped before top C was reached and turned to instruct the young ones. Before so doing, she slipped on her dress and bade her maid do the same. 'Now, boy, kneel upright behind me. Girl, do to him as I have done to my amazed falconer. When his cock crows high, stop and I will instruct you further. One thing more. Hoist your dress so that your small rump can be seen. I will do likewise.'

Both women bent forward to their tasks. To Henricus was revealed the small cheeks of his maid's behind with the pink and sparsely haired oval slit between. To the boy came in view a sight even more succulent – cheeks, red hair, oval slit, but bigger, juicier. He was transfixed by the visual, agitated by the felt. Over his lank member came the girl's lips, fast and clumsy from inexperience but rousing nevertheless; her tongue had stumbled upon a strange spot at his tip which made him jerk each time it was touched, while there, before him, were the round thighs, the flanks, the moist centre all in motion and belonging untouchably to his untouchable royal mistress. Then it happened.

Impelled by nothing he understood nor could control, he wrenched himself from the girl's lips and lunged into the lips of his royal mistress's royal rear.

'Ah!' she cried, raising her mouth from its task. 'That was not meant to be.' But her fevered falconer pulled her face down again. She was forced to suck on and accept the driving spear from behind.

Now that it was happening before her eyes, the girl recognized what else could be done with it. Of course! The proud stallion's act! How foolish of her not to have understood. The sight had thrilled her in the field and thrilled her now. She wanted it done to her. She tried to pull the boy away. To no avail. He gripped tight his mistress's hips. Nothing could stop his thrusting. Frightening noises rose like summer storms from everywhere. Princess, lover, village lad were all uttering loud moans and cries which harmonized like a trio of instruments. To her amazement the girl saw the same burst of jellied milk come from lover to royal mouth. She tasted the sticky cream. Salt, bitter, sulphurous like the body's lava, like the burnt-earth taste of wine. Men were the same. All could give pleasure. The thing must be thrust into her, she knew, and demanded it.

'But his! The big one! I want his!'

'Child,' said an exhausted princess with what remnants of her imperiousness she could muster, 'you forget yourself.'

'We all do,' said her deflated but delighted lover. The grown ones exchanged smiles. Not so the young ones. Life had become too serious for them.

All this Jonas heard and saw about the princess Enota, and related to me, Coaxandria, who have here ordered and interpreted and summarized for the king, and for those who will read after.

AMY
- THE THIRD YOUNGEST

While waiting for him to arrive, the princess Amy worked on her tapestry – a glory of stars and planets between which floated, as in all her tapestries, the fabulous mythological being, the five-headed Mabillon from Syreus, upon whom nations called in times of conflict and crisis.

One head was pure intellect; one, unimpeded intuition; a third was driven by emotion; a fourth shook with unbridled laughter; last, the most terrifying, was chillingly, penetratingly devoid of any feeling or thought whatsoever. In her tapestries, though the shape of the other four varied depending upon which history they were illustrating, the features of this fifth face never changed. No matter how different the quality of thought through which the thinking head travelled, nor how variously riven from pale smile to convulsed mirth was the laughing head, yet the head with no emotion was repeatedly portrayed by Amy again and again with the same compelling severity. Let the eye move over her canvas, it would find change, variety, animation. Not so in the visage stern. That one intimidatingly peered out upon the onlooker, full of portent, a strange stability among the changeful others. Her tapestries were instantly recognized by this singular study of unmotivated response. They were powerful works.

He arrived, Boldiman, a sandy-haired, freckled young fellow, boyish and plump, his fingers inked from his trade of cloth dyer, grinning as he came through the doors of the spacious if temporary abode.

'I have been waiting twelve days for this night,' he said, shuffling to view what spread had been prepared for him. He drank a little wine, turned to her and said, 'A good table,' and proceeded with smiling haste to undress.

Amy moved not, but sat weaving her heavens and contemplating her hells. When he was without a stitch, he realized she was still clothed.

'What is this? Must I wait in the cold till you have patched up a planet? Have I rushed from my mother's cooking, my lance at the tilt, ready and polished for battle, only to watch you stitch up stars? Are you to prick away at your canvas while my prick pricks air? Am I...'

He would have continued in this vein, for he was a keen mummer whose thespian pleasure spilled over from Christmas mysteries into his bland life, had not Amy turned her head of massive brown curls and enigmatic eyes upon him and quietly said, 'You bore me, Boldiman. You bore me very much. It does not make me happy to tell you this, for I am fond of you and have passed many sweet hours in your company. But there is more than sweetness to life, especially to the night hours of life. There are shadows and sharp edges, thorns and bitter herbs, there are cruel winds, dreams of terror, fears of madness and berries sour to the bite. You bring your workshop humour to our midnight pleasures. You bring your daylight rhythms to our midnight frenzies.

You play with me as though I were your naughty school-mate. Why bother to wait twelve days merely to splash your lance about my pot of cream and call me honeysuckle and your midnight oil? Have you never considered that the night is for our dark sides? Can you even conceive our dark sides? These times will not last for ever. They have an ending, as all things have.'

He was astonished. He looked down to where but a moment ago his lance loomed large with eager threats of vague pleasure. It had melted as though before an inferno. The princess described it less flatteringly.

'Oh dear,' she observed with some hint of remorse, for she was not naturally unkind, 'look how he has recoiled, slunk off. Like a whipped dog. Too trusting, perhaps? Poor thing!'

Sandy-haired Boldiman sheepishly reached for his vest to cover his lapsed sinner. He was stunned. 'Would the princess like me to go?' he asked.

'No,' she replied, feeling all men must be given a second chance, 'the princess would like you to tell her stories. Sit, look at the flames, stir your imagination, find inspiration in fire.'

The bold young Boldiman sat in his nakedness before fire and flame, desperately stirring his imagination. The more he struggled to trap it, the more it clouded over with murkiness. 'I think I will return home,' he said. 'You have become strange and beyond my handling. I have nothing you want.'

The princess regarded him with silence and indifference. He left. She felt its inevitability and knew exactly what next to do.

She walked through the forest to its edges and followed the path to a place where people gather. Like her sisters, she was known, and soon a group invited her to share their final drink of the long, sweaty evening. These rough villagers felt at ease with the princesses, each confident in their place, neither side assuming airs. They were in the midst of clapping their hands to a young man dancing an unfamiliar dance on a table. He had peat-black eyes with hardly a centre to them, and a mass of black curls on his head. She asked of him and was told he had given his name as Barabal, a student from afar in search of stories to take back to his home across the southern waters. When his twists and leaps were done she spoke to him.

'I am told you are a student in search of stories.' From the way she spoke, with confident, imperious authority, he knew she was not from this place nor belonged to these people. He drew her aside.

'Madame,' he replied, still breathless, his dark eyes ablaze with curiosity, 'I am a student to please my father, but the truth is, as you can see, I am a dancing clown.'

She ignored his attempt to amuse her with those uninteresting deceits men think interesting. 'I have a sister who collects stories,' she told him, 'and if you come with me this night and tell me one, then I will take you to hear from her what she has collected from others.'

Barabal was an inch shorter than the princess Amy, which to her surprise gave her pleasure.

'I have such stories,' he said.

She took his hand and led him away.

On entering her dwelling, he whistled and slapped his thigh. 'Mabillon! You know of him here too?'

'We know of him, but I know of no one who has seen him.'

'Then I know just the story to tell you,' said the student, 'but in return for a kiss.'

She raised her hand to his face for his presumption. He guessed her movement, caught her hand, kissed the back of it and drew her to the fireside, where, between four huge cushions, he settled her gently but firmly. His firmness excited her, as did the promise of being told a story. Stories were her passion. She was possessed of an insatiable imagination needing constantly to be engaged. The mere promise of one filled her with excitement. And here, she could tell, was a master narrator.

The student was enchanted by the eagerness in her eyes. He brought her a dish of sweet marmatines soaked in the oil of their sour seeds. 'For a sweet and sour story,' he said. He poured wine for each, sat facing her, and began.

'As you know, the five heads of Mabillon are never needed together. A problem requires either intelligence, intuition, emotion, laughter or callousness for its resolution. Never all at once.'

The intelligent student's eyes were bright with challenge. The intelligent princess rose to his bright challenge.

'That cannot be true,' she said. 'There must be problems which require the application of at least two — intuition and intelligence, laughter and intuition, intelligence and laughter. And sometimes perhaps even three.'

She waited to be contradicted, alert for the slightest shift of his mind. No contradiction came. Instead he leaned forward to pour her more wine, brushed her lips with a light kiss which she resisted not, and continued.

'There was an old philosopher, adviser to the king and much beloved by every subject in the realm. He was nearing the end of his life, aged and demented from all the questions which he was asked but could not answer. Why do things fall? What lies between us and the stars? From whence comes melancholy? If men are born with unequal ability, how can harmony and peace be achieved? If God was always present and always will be, then what is beginning and what ending? Trying to imagine the nothingness in which matter began taxed him till his brain knotted itself from the tangle of possibilities. His last years were spent attempting to conceive a past and future embraced by infinity. It is terrible, this need in us to see whence grows what, to where and why.

'But he managed, for a while, to hide his knots of confusion from king and subjects, and continued to advise. The advice, however, led to disaster upon disaster, which, because he was so loved and trusted, no one thought could possibly be the fault of the old philosopher. Battles were lost; foreign emissaries quit, offended and displeased; merchants were guided to trade in goods no market demanded; laws were passed which confused justice and divided government from the realm; the crops failed. No one suspected the old, befuddled thinker except the old befuddled thinker himself.

'And so, because eminent men have access to oracles, the bewildered sage secretly called forth Mabillon to meet him by the Lake of Thronging, where he related how, deranged by problems to which he could find no resolution, he had lead his beloved countrymen into ruin and despair.

'The head of intuition asked him, 'And what do you want of us, to solve your problems or help revive your country?" 'Solve my problems," begged the sad old man, 'then I can help my king and country again.'The five heads, through the sternest of them, bade him lay his problems before them.'

The young student paused to consider the princess, who hugged her knees, leaned her chin upon them, gazed rapt with wide, attendant eyes, and held her breath for so long that her beating heart pulsated from wall to wooden wall. She thought: How could I ever have given myself to the freckled-faced dyer of cloth in whom neither thought nor story had shaped? The student bent to her again and placed a lingering kiss on her neck which forced from her the slightest moan, and continued.

'The philosopher asked his first question: 'Tell me how time began.' 'Time is a circle that repeats itself," said the head of intuition. 'That is poetry," said the philosopher sadly, 'not science."

The student again paused, drew the legs of the princess to him one by one, unlaced her sandals, raised a foot to his lips and gently kissed each toe. When he had done this to both feet, he continued.

'The philosopher asked his second question: 'How can ignorance ever know itself since ignorance is the state of unknowing?" 'Attend to the crops and the fruit of the earth," said the head full of feeling. 'That's husbandry," said the philosopher sadly, 'not wisdom."

Again the student paused. This time he pulled loose the bow that held together her embroidered blouse. It fell apart. He drew it over her shoulders and flashed his brilliant smile at her bold breasts and thrusting nipples set in dark haloes of raised flesh. He bent forward and took them one by one in his mouth. The princess cupped a breast in each hand, offering them. When her sighs grew, he ceased sucking and continued his tale.

'The philosopher asked his third question: 'Where will my soul go when I die?" 'It will hover," said the head serious with intelligence, 'until an offspring in your family is ready to receive it.' 'And if I have no children, no nieces, no nephews, if I am the last in my long sorry line?" asked the sorry philosopher. But, as you know, the heads are permitted only one reply.'

The princess nodded. She could not speak. Her eyes burned with expectation. She longed not only for what next he would tell of the story but for what next he would do to her. Oh, how could time have been wasted with a dumb dye-lad?

The student smiled at her eagerness, her tense body, the anticipation he could see in her eyes. He kissed her lips, eased her backwards into the cushions and slowly unbuttoned the long row of pearl buttons from the waist of her skirt to its hem. What a feast of flesh – a belly all aglow with the rich honey of youth. She closed her eyes, waiting for his touch. Into its tiny saucer he let ooze the cool waters of his mouth till they overflowed and slipped slowly down each side. She quivered, feeling the trickle of each rivulet, and heard the philosopher's next question.

'"How can I be remembered?" asked the bearded philosopher mournfully. At which the head full of laughter laughed and roared as though it would never stop. The philosopher wept.'

The young man from across the southern waters spread the princess's legs apart. He lay on his stomach before her and gazed into the moist lips of her cunnus. When she saw where his eyes were fixed, she prised apart the lips so that her story-teller could more easily see its succulent folds. His black eyes pierced deep the syrupy cavern. He breathed in its heady odour. His lips were upon her, drinking her flow. She writhed. But there was one more question.

'"Is there a final order to all things?" asked the philosopher. The four heads who had each given an answer to the other questions turned to the fifth head, whose countenance never changes. They waited. The philosopher waited. The stern, fixed face with no feeling, no intellect, no emotion and no laughter remained silent. Not a word did it offer. The philosopher returned to his king and people and began once more to proffer advice as he did in past times. The country returned to peace and the people to prosperity. Though not,' added the student, 'without vicissitudes, for no life and time is without those.'

At which the princess reclined, stretched wide her arms, arched her beautiful back, raised her belly, moaned a long contented cry and waited.

All this Jonas heard and saw about the princess Amy, and related to me, Coaxandria, who have here ordered and interpreted and summarized for the king, and for those who will read after.

ETHELDRA
~ THE FOURTH YOUNGEST

As would be expected of the keeper of King Melania's
gardens, the princess Etheldra's vast hut was festooned with
dried foliage bound and hung in sheaves from the walls.
Surfaces were flowery-kirtled and the air hot with smells
and ceaseless frondescence. The seasoned pillars of wood
writhed with vines and creepers thrusting multiformed
leaves and heavy-scented blossoms.

To inhabit the abode was to experience perpetual
thriving. At night there hummed through open window
and door the incessant flight of flies and minuscule
kaleidoscopic insects – cicada and cricket, midge, moth and
dragonfly. All seethed with the friendliest of motions while
this princess of earth, rain and sun radiated a powerful
confidence which comes from the knowledge that change
conforms to miraculous laws.

In such an explosion of foliage and smells, it was not any
man could be her companion for twelve nights. How many
could lie naked, risking the winged tickle of dazed and
flame-crazed moths? Which man could laugh her

mischievous laugh of wonderment at the slow, humping lurch of a centipede across the pimpled landscape of his pistoning rump? Who could idiosyncratically share her arousal by the smell of new-mown grass? But such a man did exist, Malmon, a man of science and system who came to her with flowers and dreams, ritually laid by her side, waited to be stripped and loved, stripped and loved her in return, then ate her tastily concocted topsides and tongues, trotters and brains, pasties and tarts, waffles and loaves, curds and whey, and drank her noggins and drams, her porter and mead – for the Princess of Gardens was also Queen Victualess. In return he fed her his own brand of pabulum: reports of his research, stories of discoveries from across the seas, hints of hidden worlds within a grain of dust.

'You should be the lover of my sister Beatrix,' she told him once. 'Your science is lost on me.'

On the third of the twelve nights Malmon arrived not with his usual bunch of flowers but with a bottle of wine 'made by my young assistant who shows promise in the field of astronomy. A star-gazer if ever I saw one.' He poured a glass for each of them, raised it to her health, 'Though God knows you could not be wished more health than you now possess', and together they rolled the taste around and around in their mouths.

'We do not have the earth for it in our parts,' he said, 'but damned if this young doctor has not found a patch somewhere that holds secrets unsuspected. What do you think?'

'I taste semion and novarine,' Etheldra replied, naming two rare herbs. 'You must ask him where he hides his grapevine. I would like some of that earth for myself in which to grow those difficult plants.'

'I will, I will!'

They drank in silence.

Malmon felt uncomfortable. The long mane of her hair was still furled behind her head. All was not as it should be. Nevertheless, when the bottle was finished, mostly by him, he stretched out on the bed, hesitantly commencing the routine of their pleasure, and waited.

Etheldra moved not. She squatted at this side, her back defiantly pressed to the wall, her eyes aglow with the wine of semion and novarine, her skin humming with restless frustration. When too much time had passed he asked, 'What is wrong?' She could not tell him. Her dilemma was acute.

She was a woman who tended what grew. Her vigilance had to be constant over that which was, by its nature, inconstant. If she wanted her father's gardens to be the most wondiferous in the world she could not prune only the shrub, merely the bedding plant, just the creeper. No, she must run to them all, check each month's bud, nurture the sapling, clip the sucker, cut back the wandering wisteria, manure the rose. All that lived had to be watered; what was dead had to be eliminated. Each protuberance looked and smelt different from the other. In her nose swam pungent perfumes, dizzying her, they leapt and changed about so much. And here was her dilemma: what commanded her singular loving care was, paradoxically, exquisitely various, whereas her nightly pleasure was in a man who changed neither in looks nor in scents.

Her loyal heart felt treacherous the moment she discovered this truth. But what could she do? Every instinct in her was attuned to variation, and the attraction of Malmon's mono-charm-and-smell had sunk like a slow summer sun. Yet he was a good man, of much erudition and some wit. He glowed still. Perhaps, like the celestial fire, desire for him would return again? She doubted it. Her natural gaiety was paralysed.

She said simply, 'I cannot tonight. Talk to me.'

He sat up, reached for the wine and asked, 'About what?'

'Oh, anything. Your assistant. Describe him to me. Tell me where he comes from. Explain his skills.'

The man of science stood up, ambled to the table laden with nourishment and declared, 'Well, if I cannot satisfy one appetite, I shall certainly satisfy another.'

Malmon possessed an equanimous nature. Experiment excited him but too many failures had tempered his expectations. He reached for a bowl of oats and raisins soaked in mead and covered with cinnamon and nutmeg, sat by an open window and slowly spooned himself into conversation.

'I found him by chance, you know. As with the best of my discoveries.'

When Etheldra saw that her withdrawn favours had not distressed her companion, her gaiety returned. She leapt to join him by her table of goodies, which she attacked with a mixture of high-spirited gluttony and relief. In between mouthfuls, she kissed him for his understanding, and even though she felt an ardour for him returning she dismissed it, knowing well the difference between gratitude and desire. She chewed, sucked, drank and listened with the same eagerness she proffered to her beds of plants and her passion. She was indeed a creature of the earth and changing winds.

'I was about to embark upon a long experiment,' continued her abandoned lover, 'involving the immersion of solids into chemical liquids to ascertain the effects upon them. A clumsy experiment as it turned out, but necessitating the building of innumerable dry-stone quads of wall in which could sit leaden vats. I approached a farmer I knew and had called upon before in times of physical difficulty, and asked him to build me the dozen walled edifices. He said he would have done so gladly but the crops were ripe and the weather uncertain, and now that the days were dry he must bring in all he could.'

'Oh, how I understand that,' said Etheldra, by now glowing and red-faced. 'I have watched my father's lands abused by careless husbandry and often thought I should turn my attention to horticulture rather than floriculture.' She was hot with food and drink. 'But go on, go on,' she urged, dipping into her bowl of honey cake and vanilla cream.

'The farmer was full of apologies and regrets, both because I pay handsomely and because he could see the quandary I was in. 'Ask my son,' he suggested, 'get him to help you and you will be doing me a great favour!' The son was an only boy among girls who was so tormented by his sisters that he spent his time out of theirs and everybody's way. Not that he was fit for farmwork, being, his father told me, fragile in build, and cursed with wandering concentration. 'I would not mind,' said the old farmer, 'if he had brains to replace muscle, but he is bereft of those too!' He was a very distressed and disappointed father. I took a chance and invited the poor man to send me his son.'

'What did he look like?' asked Etheldra, now completely captivated by the tale.

'Well, I could see why his father thought him fragile, but whereas I had imagined him to be small and wispy, he turned out to be tall and thin, and not fragile but curiously – elegant. Lumbering but – elegant. I have no other word to describe him. A mass of black, unkempt and curly hair, deep-brown, shy eyes, a long angular face and limbs which seemed to follow the wind rather than his wishes. And of course I knew within minutes of meeting him that here was no ordinary youth, and certainly no imbecile.'

'How did you know?' demanded a restless Etheldra. 'What did he do? What did he say? What did *you* do or say? Oh, I am so eager to know, so excited by your description of him.'

The scientist, who was arrested by all kinds of phenomena, was now startled by the interest he had awakened in his midnight princess. She was listening to his story but seemed animated by other envisionings. Observing her closely, he continued, 'Well, it happened this way. I took the lad – '

She interrupted him. 'How old is he?'

'Seventeen.' He watched her attention drift away from him. 'Seventeen,' he repeated. She remained dreamy. He began again. 'I took the lad – ' and on the word 'lad' she flashed back into his orbit. 'I took the lad to the stretch of land which I had purchased specially for the experiment, and explained the system of walled cradles I needed built for my vats. He paused for only a few seconds, during which I saw his face change from glum obedience to released intelligence, from dull vacuity to vivid imagination, from doubt to certainty. 'Why,' he asked, 'do you want to build high walls which must be climbed up and climbed down rather than digging wells in which your vats could sit and be walked between easily, and easily fed, and easily glanced at, and dipped into, and renewed, and tested?" He seemed not only instantly to have devised a better system than mine, he had also guessed at the various stages and processes the experiment involved. It was a metamorphosis heart-warming as anything I had ever experienced. To witness intellect falling into place, to watch features come into their own, to be the instrument by which natural talent flows into its proper channel, is profoundly gratifying.'

'Bring him to me,' ordered the enthralled Etheldra.

'Ah! The imperious tone!'

Malmon wondered much about his strange mistress who refused to reveal from where she came. Her nights were spent with him, but where her days? Which king was her father? Of which land? He had learned not to press. The arrangement had been attractive to him. Her easy, undemanding plumpness matched his taste, and pleasure-without-commitment matched his temper.

'For what reason should I bring him to you?' he asked.

'I cannot lie,' she replied with a mixture of sweet pity and sadness. 'Our understanding has always been that honesty must prevail. You knew our passion could not continue for ever, that one day I would be gone. Well, though the time has not come to leave, my passion, like young roots, gropes for fresh succour. I am overwhelmed by a desire to possess your young assistant.'

'But what pleasure can he be to you? He is shy, awkward, says little and, most relevant, he is a virgin!'

'I knew it! I knew it at once! He is a young shoot. And therefore am I inflamed. I long to tend and shape him.'

'But you are a flowerer not a deflowerer,' retorted her somewhat aggrieved partner, 'and his blossom is too tender to be so soon deblossomed.'

'I admit it, yes. Who would have guessed this to be my dark secret? To awaken, to initiate, excite first longings, to cradle fresh eagerness, bear new fruits, share first discoveries, ignite the first passion, receive the first thrust, witness the first pleasure, the first ecstasy – ah!' She was breathless from her list.

'You will never succeed,' said her diminished lover.

She regarded him with a mixture of coyness and mischievousness. 'I am shameful, am I not? But I will be lovely for him, and kind, and he will return to you wiser and more confident, and you will see, he will discover for you new stars and give them *such* names.'

'And what will I say you want of him?'

'To talk about the heavens.'

'All through the night?'

'When else does the moon shine?'

He smiled.

'We have never been your kings, have we?'

'But we have always been your queens.' She smiled back.

He embraced her and left.

The youth arrived the following evening as she was watering her plants. The air was cool, a little leftover warmth lingering from the summer's day. A fire was burning scented pine cones, and the room rocked with its offerings of foliaceous and culinary smells. The young boy, whose name was Tomaso, was blasted by conflicting odours as he entered.

Tall, thin with the promised shy, brown eyes and black curls, his every feature was alert with a slow but inexorable intelligence. She knew at once her brain would be no match for his. She possessed wit, instinct and the eternal if limited wisdom that comes from the nurturing of stems, stalks, root and branch. His, she sensed, was the quick mind that could carry abstractions and make connections. He understood her at a glance, after which glance he immediately averted his eyes. All advantages were hers, for she knew her goal and, surprising for one who hid behind no cunning corners of her mind, she had cunningly plotted each phase of the night which lay before them.

'You will not expect me to apologize for the heavy airs which greet you,' she began, 'for I wanted to feed you food you have never before tasted in return for keeping you awake and talking to me. Will you keep awake?' she asked.

'It is nights I am most awake,' he informed her, surprised at such a question of an astronomer. Then, fearing he had been too haughty, he lapsed into apologetic silence.

Etheldra thought she would not be able to see the night through, she was so weak with daring and desires. Feeling as anxious as he looked, she could bring herself to do no more than offer him food and wine. Both without exchanging a word.

The scheming princess was heavily clothed. No part other than her head and hands were visible. She wore a long, loose-fitting brown velvet dress which buttoned up at the side and covered her neck. Long sleeves wrapped her arms, stockings her legs and sandals her feet. Her famous long hair was wound round and round her head, covering the sides of her face. She seemed to be reassuring her young visitor by announcing celibacy. Though what need has the unthreatened of reassurance? She felt deliciously artful.

'Tell me about yourself,' she asked.

All his life he had haunted the countryside around his father's farm, a solitary soul inviting little conversation, asking only if anyone knew the whereabouts of books on science and astronomy. He had taught himself to read from the few he had stumbled upon and had read over and over again till he knew them word for word, gaining from them more than most gained from a hundred tomes.

He revealed little else. Of friendship and the heart he knew nothing. The meaning of eyes, the timbre of voice, the expectations of touch, all were alien. Her body spoke many languages to him but he understood only the language of her words. He was pure intellect. Etheldra perceived this. It quickened and challenged her.

'Tell me,' she asked next, 'what do you see when you gaze at the stars?' She took him by the hand and sat him at one end of the bed, while she clasped her hunched knees, modestly covering every part of them with her dress, and waited for his reply.

'When Camion, King of the Northern Straits and Hills, wrote the first *Book of Stars* six thousand years ago he began with this sentence: "I am so overwhelmed by the heavens at night that my mind pains with incomprehension." He ended his life never having comprehended what he saw, but what he saw he charted and named. That is a very special kind of bravery, I have always thought.'

Etheldra thrilled to him. Every aspect of the boy aroused her; his blushing youth, his shy brown eyes, his awkward elegance, his mellifluous voice and confident mind. But it was from his burning love of stars that she perceived the burned roots of other passions. How could a mere seventeen years possess such power?

That is the way with some, they need strive for nothing, all is endowed. Well, almost all. Gifts are endowed, innocence must be lived through alone.

Tomaso continued, 'King Camion was pained, but not me. When *I* look at the night sky I am exhilarated. Since King Camion there have been many to chart the sky and I know them all. The heavens cannot hurt me because I know my way round them better than the lanes of our small province. No, that is not true. There is a southern hemisphere. There must be many lands where astronomers have, unknown to me, composed maps.'

How careful, exact, precise, she thought. 'But do you comprehend them?' asked Etheldra.

'In time. The more constellations I can identify, the more I will comprehend.'

'Do you believe everything in this life is comprehensible?'

'It is not a question that matters to me. So much is, that I have no patience to consider what is not.'

'Tell me who came after King Camion and relate what they discovered.' she commanded, her eyes brilliant with pleasure. 'But first, I am hot. Be gallant and unlace my sandals.'

She stretched her legs towards him and pulled her dress above her knees. When he had unlaced one and proceeded to the other, she discreetly tucked her hands under her dress to roll down her stockings. He was offered only a momentary sight of flesh for, feigning accidental immodesty, she hastily covered her expanse of lambent thighs. The momentary feast momentarily confused the lank lad. He felt a new movement in his groin – the other 'lank lad' jumped. Now why? He had not made it do so, the action seemed to belong to a nerve with its own volition. Nor had it been merely a 'jump'. He identified it, scientist that he was, as a pulling back, a squeeze which rippled new sensations through his stomach to the back of his neck. Strange. Etheldra watched his mind attempting to wrap itself around the experience. What possible connection could there be between her stretched-out legs and the sudden pulse? He observed in himself one more thing to puzzle him – an urge to touch her flesh where it was whitest, high above the knee. It had all happened in an instant, the pulse, the urge, the bewilderment, the effort to understand. And in that same instant Etheldra had seen all, the leaping lad, the quickened lad, the puzzled lad, the absorbed lad. There is life in pure thought, she thought, which thought made her want to play all the more with this lovely, thoughtful boy.

She returned to hugging her knees and bade him continue. Who followed King Camion? King Camion's mistake, he told her, was to imagine that the earth was a small sphere revolving elliptically between two larger spheres, one light, one dark. For him, therefore, the sunlit day and the sunless night were constant and still. And because he thought the earth rotated in a spherical hollow between the two, all that was needed was to wait till his view of the stars came round again before continuing to chart them – for surely they began where he first sat to contemplate them? He could not conceive the need to plot the changing sky at night. A fixed map was all he could grasp.

'His map was used for centuries until along came the great Plunah of Greece. A giant of a man. They said of Plunah that it was difficult to remain with him for more than half an hour in the same space. Ideas came at him so swiftly that he staggered around like a man constantly bombarded with pellets of lead, the impact of which made him reel so violently that those nearby found it unbearable to witness. He talked non-stop, like a man possessed, as if failing to unburden himself at once he would drop with the weight of thought. It was Plunah who first suspected that we were one of many stars, all of which were in constant motion. With the help of his students, who later became the famous School of Plunah, he mapped out each night's pattern.'

Tomaso communicated his excitement to an over-excited princess. The effect they had upon one another was amazing to witness. She fuelled him into light. He blazed with words and information. There was a dark age, he told her, when powerful men insisted stars were holes in a sheet the gods drew over the earth to allow good citizens rest; those who tried to prove otherwise were cruelly put to death. He explained how newly discovered clusters were identified and by whom. He listed the names which different races and civilizations had given to what they had seen. He named the magical powers ascribed to different formations – Geophorim for fertility, Triangulata for courage, Dicynicon for longevity, Monkinius for beauty.

The more knowledge poured from him, the more he became animated. No one had ever asked so many questions nor drawn from him such lengthy expositions nor filled him with such energy. The air circled between them thick with urgency. The heat of his earnestness flowed back into her. Incandescent eyes returned his light. Light shone upon light. His senses were alert as never before. Her movements affected him strangely.

As though to calm the excitement of his stories, she moved her hands up and down her legs as if to smooth out, push away, to still the seething blood. The action, though intended to calm, agitated. Her moving hands shifted her long brown dress over her knee tops, so that the lower part fell into her lap. Now there was a feast of thighs, no longer momentary. And came that pulse again, not once, not twice, but again and again, sometimes singly, sometimes in stretches of three or four pulls. There too came the urge to touch. But touch he dared not. Instead she touched for him, her right hand moving up and down that taut, white skin with feigned casualness while her eyes said: Ignore what my hand does.

Ignore it he could not, such was the riot of his confused feelings. It seemed not only that *he* was touching her but that he was being touched! It had happened before. He had witnessed a minor operation and had felt the blade lacerate him. He had fainted. That branch of science, medicine it was called, could never be for him. He wanted to faint now. Why, why was there a connection between what he saw and what he experienced? It agitated him, so that he had to stand and pretend his story could not continue from a squatting position. Oh, horror and shame! He discovered the tensility of his young manhood. It stretched his garment, paralysed his tongue, crippled his step. He glared intently out of the window, his back to his hostess.

'I think you need a drink for a dry mouth,' she said.

He heard her rise and pour wine. She brought it to him. Her arm stretched round from behind. As the cause of his discomfort, she was content to wait for him to turn in his own time. When he did so, he was confronted with a vision which not only reawakened the pulse in his groin but touched off a heavy beat in his heart. Etheldra had taken off her brown dress and now stood in a long white chemise of thick silk. It was not merely in what she stood but where she stood. With her goblet in hand, her long hair undone and flowing down to her hips, she stood legs slightly apart before the fire. Through white diaphanous silk was silhouetted the ample body of earth's very own and flaxen temptress.

'Come,' she cooed. 'Sit by me and continue.'

Her eyes were still bright with interest, but now her voice had mellowed to maternal pitch. She stretched out her hand, mother to child, full of comfort and reassurance. He reached towards her unsteadily. She sat him on a bench facing her, the table between them. He was grateful for that.

'Or perhaps you would like to eat now? Yes, let us eat, and as you eat you can tell me what names *you* have given the stars.'

As though he wished to do anything but look at her, he eagerly swooped down upon her abundant provision. She had creamed a potage of roysters, seasoned with sweet marjoram. 'The herb of Mercury,' he told her. She had roasted the hind of the long handsteer coated with tamarisk blossom, 'governed by Saturn', and seasoned with Mother of Thyme, 'ruled by Venus', he told her. From fast rivers came platters of boiled whistings saturated with honey and hyssop, 'which herb is Jupiter's', and bowls of green speets and the root of snip and pate buttered with butter-bur, 'the herb of the sun', and chives, 'which belong to Mars'. To every flavour he gave its sign. Beside the savoury dishes were the sweets. The fruits of the muscard tree and the auvene-bush soaked in red wine and spiced with mace. The cake of angel-oat spiced with ginger. Egg creams and burnt sugar, boiled honey sticks, parteen pies spiced with cinnamon, and crust-covered casks of the jellied clotis root, flavoured with ground bitter almonds.

Abundance! *That* was the word to describe both the princess and her offerings. Abundance! It was there not only in all she baked and provided but in her plump limbs, her flood of hair, the intensity of her attention, the blazing radiance of her energy, the enormous embrace of her affection and the overpowering longing of her innocent stratagems – for innocent finally they were, despite that they had been calculated. Abundance! She seemed to him as vast as his heavens and suddenly as compelling.

As they ate, he told her, 'I name the stars by what they make me feel.' He pointed through the window. 'There is the 'Patient'' star, and beside it a cluster I call 'Grief''.' He pointed through another window. 'There spins a constellation I call 'Trapped'', it is so web-like. And there, much smaller, to its left, is one I call 'Joy'', it struggles so hard to sparkle.'

'Why do stars sparkle?' she asked.

'No one knows for certain,' he told her. 'I think they have their clouds, as we do, and if you look carefully, they have colour too. But the old astronomers say it is the way light travels.'

'Light travels?' she was amazed. 'How can light travel? It is not an object.'

He began to explain.

'Do not continue,' she begged. 'It is all too abstract for me.'

It was not, but she wished to take over the conversation for a while. After all, if he talked, he could not look at her.

'I would name stars from my plants,' she said, looking out of the window to allow him to gaze at her without fear of her intrusive eyes. 'Surely there would be an oak, a rose, a clematis, a writhing vine in your heavens?' She listed other favourites and described her joy in making things grow. She confessed her excitement at the scent of blossom, the aroma of old manure.

As she spoke, still gazing at the heavens, her hand, with feigned nonchalance, caressed first her neck, then slid to the bone above her breast, to the covered breast itself. A slow, casual massage that ended on her nipple, which if only he was facing her he would see was thickening beneath her gown. Round and round she stroked, knowing his pubescence was in turmoil. Suddenly she turned to him and caught him staring at her action. Again he blushed. How indescribable the pleasure his glow gave her. Why should a man's confusion be so delicious, so sublimely satisfying?

Still he made no movement, nor asked the question she wanted to hear. He must come to me, she told herself. I cannot bring myself to touch him. He must move first. He can. He will. I know it.

'Forgive me,' she said, 'the wine, the food, my chattering. I must close my eyes for a while. A moment merely. They say a day's energy can be recovered in ten minutes of sleep. Soon I will be with you again. Will you guard me?'

She stretched on a rug by the fire. Silk settled over the curves and hollows of her firm body. Her nipples and mound of hair would show through darkly, she knew. Let him gaze, let him feast, let his willow wand leap and protest. He need not be asked, he need only be stirred.

When she felt he had viewed this first vista like an appetizer, she turned with much artful sighing as if in sleep and lay on her stomach. Now her sleek garment fell around the high cheeks of her buttocks and slipped into their crevice. Here was a landscape to make a mad lad madder. Why, she was even becoming moist herself at the images of her own backside and the goings-on between her young visitor's thighs.

Ten minutes passed and she judged it time to turn again, an artful movement sliding down so that her silk stayed up and her dark pile slipped into tantalizing view. Yet her thighs remained clenched closed. All must be revealed, but slowly, slowly. Another ten minutes passed. One final movement – she stretched back her arms and bent her left leg out, exposing her dewy fronds. Silence. She waited.

A long, shy finger moved inside her leg, cautious, hesitant, but determined, up to her honeyed labia. Did she feel him scoop some honey to taste? Certainly it was oozing profusely from her. What would he make of it? Would he think her damaged? White blood? He came at her again for a second taste as though, scientist that he was, he needed to check first findings. She moaned in-voluntarily. The sound brought his explorations to a halt. She breathed loudly, as deep sleepers do, hoping to make

99

him feel safe. Within moments she felt his two hands take the hem of her dress and try to pull, gently, up. He wanted to gaze at her entire body.

Here was a problem. Her weight held back her slip. Unless she assisted him he would give up. As though a dream disturbed her she shifted back and forth till her chemise rose to her neck and the length of her was exposed. She shuddered. Oh! How would he interpret that? Would he think she was cold and must be covered? Please, no! Not yet. She held still. Something else was happening. The chill on her skin was hardening her nipples again. She could feel them rise. How would he interpret that? Would he understand she was really awake and responding to waking things? Please, no! She waited. He moved away. Her wiles and his innocence won. He understood neither her ruse nor the body's habits.

She lay exposed for a long time, so long that she feared he had moved from the room. She squinted her eyes to peer for his whereabouts. He was by the window, gazing at his stars. Embarrassment had overcome him. He had left her untouched. She knew he would return. What more could she do to help his resolve?

Etheldra was a princess born, but of nature's rough and wild spirit born too. She had gathered dung for her roses, buried dead birds, permitted worms to curl round her fingers. She loved all nature's smells and the mucky earth between her toes. Best of all she loved the touch of creatures. Large and tiny, swift of movement, slow of crawl. Near her were many such from the leaves of her plants. Silently she reached for two caterpillars and a small spider. On each breast she lay a caterpillar, in her navel the spider. She closed her eyes and waited.

They moved. Soft gentle treads across her skin, at home

on her, unafraid. Tomaso moved. She heard him. She felt him kneel at her side. He was gazing at the creatures on her body. One long green friend ambled down her left side, another aimed to be king of her right nipple, which he reached and sat triumphantly upon. The spider moved towards the forest. She knew Tomaso would soon bear it no more. She felt his finger gently remove them. He cover her with a rug and returned to the window.

She allowed enough time to pass so that it would appear she had woken at her own rhythm rather than his touch, and rose to join him. He looked at her enquiringly.

She asked him a strange question. 'Do you know what is happening?'

He shook his head.

'Tell me what you feel.'

His reply was careful but, oddly, breathless, as though he had been running. A heat, he said, had swept through him when he saw the moist, curled foliage between her legs. He described it.

She touched his face, then crept a hand inside his shirt to cup his smooth and hairless chest. 'What burning is coming from you. My poor one.' She wanted at once to embrace him but held back that he might continue describing his feelings.

'Every sensation is new. But more than new, it is doubled. When you touched yourself there and there – ' he pointed to her thighs and breast – 'I felt your fingers upon me, in the same place. And when I touched you here – ' he pointed between her legs – 'again I felt it upon myself.'

'Fortunate boy. Your pleasures in life will be twice that of normal mortals.' He went on to describe the pulling between his groin, the clenching of his stomach, the shiver in his neck, the weakness in his knees.

She leaned towards him, kissed his lips, caressed them with her own. 'What does that feel like?' she asked.

He thought for moment, weighing it, as all things, carefully. 'Like itself,' he said.

'And this?' She put her lips to his neck.

'Like itself,' he said again, but added, 'only more so.'

'And this?' She cupped her hand over what was the stoutest jack she had ever felt.

'Now,' he said, 'I have a tingling sense of incompleteness. I want to run, jump, bang walls with my fists. I can hardly breathe, I can hardly speak. Do not make me speak, just – just – I know not what. I want to say 'take me" but I have no comprehension of what that means. Take me, hold me, touch me, anything! But – ' then he found his words – 'complete my circle.'

Control burst free from her. She pulled him down to the rug, ripped off his shirt and fell upon him with kisses and bites, lavish as she was in all things. Here, before her, was a virgin boy to do with what she willed. She could hardly bear the thought, it made her blood race so.

'You are right,' she said, 'there is nothing to compare with this. It is like itself. Now, do you fear moths and creepy-crawly things? I surround myself with leafage, the window must remain open, all things will fly in. But our light is not what attracts them. They are attracted by fire and lamps. Have no fear of a flutter or two and I will give you a joy you will think comes from your most amazing stars.'

She kissed his face a dozen soft times, unhooked the cords of his pantaloons and knelt at his feet. Slowly teasing her own ecstasy, she pulled his leggings down and gasped at what sprang before her. An erectile so tall she almost swooned. She stood up, hoisted her clinging silk and played as she had always wanted to play but never dared. She spread astride her young protégé and slid her lushness over his ripened trunk.

'Here are soft clouds for your proud oak, my lovely boy.' She drew his hands under her chemise to her breasts. 'Teach your fingers the contours of this map,' she invited him, and clasping his slender arms for balance she gently rose and fell, rose and fell, as their throats hummed with cries, and his first seed found its first home.

All this Jonas heard and saw about the princess Etheldra, and related to me, Coaxandria, who have here ordered and interpreted and summarized for the king, and for those who will read after.

MABYLYE
~ THE FIFTH YOUNGEST

She lay beneath him. His hands pinioned her arms. Her eyes were open, his were closed. He heaved up and down. He sweated. The salt drops dripped over her. She felt him slip in and out of her tight, bored haven but was more absorbed by the fire's flames than his. Soon he shuddered, came with a mighty unmusical 'aieeeeeeee-hurmpf!' and collapsed on her breasts, between which he slithered in his own sweat, banging his nose upon her patient shoulder-bone. She held him tightly, and dutifully murmured 'Mmmmm'. That there was no enthusiasm in her voice his masculine vanity failed to register. Her eldest sister's words echoed in her memory. 'I am tired of the way I love.'

The fifth youngest princess, Mabylye, the lute player, large, carefree and loose-limbed, held her lover in her arms till he fell asleep, then rolled him away, wiped the sweat from his body, covered it to protect the heated skin from chill draughts – for though she found him tiresome, she did not wish him ill – and slipped on her bodice.

She nibbled at burnt pork. The sound of crunching in her

mouth pleased her. She sipped wine. Her fingers drummed the table. She shifted and sighed, nibbled and sipped again, loud, unregal slurping sounds defying the soundly sleeping Stephen to wake up. A melody came to her. She reached for her lute, sat on the bench by the fire, raised one leg to cradle her instrument and plucked a shape from the tune in her head. Music was a balm. No doubt of that.

Outside, her lover's dog whined as though competing with her inspiration. Truth was he cried to be allowed in, but she did not like the animal, there was something too knowing about him. She half suspected he was a magician from her father's court in disguise sent to find out where they went at nights. He was a mongrel besides. No breeding. You could not rely upon mongrels knowing their place. She tolerated him simply for her lover's sake. Stephen was a tanner and needed the dog to guard his stores. He insisted that between their amorous bouts the hound must be allowed in to eat and sit by the fire. She insisted that during them he must remain outside.

Mabylye fought to construct her melody until she could bear the competing howl no longer and opened the door to allow the delighted brute entry. Brute she may think him, but he was intelligent. Intelligent, cheerful and a forgiving creature who happily padded in, tail wagging, his joy obliterating memory of the princess's contempt. A ritual ensued. She swung her lute at him each time he entered, and each time he dodged her and forgave. The more often he forgave, the more exasperated she became; the more he revealed no sign of fear, the more irritated. It was as though the trusting hound understood her nature better than she herself and decided she was incapable of real cruelty. He behaved with her as a dear, forgiving and patient friend. She returned his friendship with swipes and snarls. The mongrel believed neither.

This night she was particularly restless. Her sister's words when they had all sat together, sharing their discontent with that withering derision few men can withstand, hung on her like a rough mantle scratching her smooth life. Her own unfinished sentence hovered like a tune she could not remember how to finish: 'My one bounces upon me and I think... I think...' What did she think? Her tanner's hide had lost its thrill? But how thrilling had it *ever* been? At its height, no more than three-quarters of an octave. She had never struck high C with him. Never! And as she strummed she wondered: Had her sisters ever done so with *their* first lovers?

The dog was simpering. She had let him in but had forgotten something. His bone. His stupid bone. She threw him one, stood up, paced, flopped, sighed and hurrumphed. She tried again to gather the notes in her head, to shape the melody she imagined she had heard. There she sat, her leg up on the bench, cuddling her melody-maker, humming and plucking. To no avail. The dog again competed, making other noises, grinding and licking his bone, knocking it about the wooden floor. She watched him. He sensed her eyes upon him and in turn watched her out of the corner of *his* eyes, gnawing still, both grappling and alert at the same time. 'Stupid hound,' she muttered. 'How can you be so happy when you are so hated?' He stopped, looked up, wagged his tail. She was talking to him! He waited for more words. All was wisdom to him. She flung her head in disgust. He returned to his crunching and snorts. Who could make music among such disgusting sounds? She sat leaning against the side of the fireplace, the lute flopped forlorn in her sprawling lap. She would wait till the dumb mongrel had finished, and looked forward to the pleasure of kicking it through the door, where it could scratch the earth and snap its futile life away at flies.

The hot room and steady rhythm of the hound's biting and scouring sent the princess off into a doze. At first she thought that if she closed her eyes it would be easier to concentrate and find the notes she had lost. Not so. Soon she was in a twilight sleep, dreaming. She dreamed a dream of song. It happened often – she would awake with new melodies in her. But now she dreamed of more than mere melody. She dreamed innovation. Her lover, who could pitch no true note in real life, was, in her dream, singing like an angel, a tenor angel. This was not all – she was accompanying him on her lute in a novel way, parallel but a third above his line, and while doing this the idea came to her in the dream to sing a third above her instrument. She had not heard such harmony before. It was a thrilling discovery. She leapt into her lover's arms to embrace him, and in the dream he held her with one arm and placed his other between her legs to lift her off the ground. They rose high into the clouds. It was exhilarating. New sounds filled the heavens in which her bovine body flew with her lover's hand between her legs. She loved and always hoped for dreams of flying, but to fly in clouds of music was undreamed of.

Slowly she filtered through into consciousness. The sensation between her legs lingered still, pleasantly. Suddenly she was very awake. That was not a lover's hand. That was the wet nose of a curious dog. Thwack! She struck the hound's hind so fiercely and – to him – unexpectedly that he was forced to prod his nose deeper into her before fleeing with a yelp to the other corner of the hut. She did not know whether to continue her rage and throw the room at him or attempt to recapture the sounds from her dream. She chose harmony rather than discord. But with her voice and guitar she could assemble only two lines. She needed a third. Amissia. The sister who sang. She must go to her at once.

Mabylye threw a shawl of scarlet and grey woollen weave over her, stepped into her sandals of antelope leather and ran into the night woods. Amissia's hut was the furthest from her own. She ran swiftly, her thoughts on nothing but the notes in her head. Thank God for dreams, she thought, and then stopped dead in her tracks and froze. Before her in the light of a full moon leered a she wolf frightened and poised. Mabylye must be near a pack of babes. She was terrified. She could move neither forward nor back. The thought came to her that she might play to it, but she dared move no limb; the anxious mother might think her movement was a movement towards her and leap at her throat. Stephen had told her stories of awful maiming by protective she-wolves. Her knees trembled, her legs turned to dust, her body was drifting beyond her control. She must swoon. And did. As she faded out of the moon's light, it seemed that two wolves leapt at her. She did not expect to see her sisters ever again.

When she came to, the sight before her made her want to swoon once more – the she-wolf lay stretched with blood oozing from her neck. How had this happened? From the shadows she heard another sound, the heavy breathing of another beast. Was the man-wolf about to revenge itself upon her? She peered deeper into the dark. It was the tanner's mongrel panting, waiting, guarding. He had followed her, knowing unusual events were taking place this night. He had sensed her restlessness, witnessed how she woke exhilarated from her dream; he knew the last beating was his fault for prying where he had never before pried nor been invited, and he had certainly known of the night's dangers. Everything drew him after her and now he waited, knowing this time no beating was forthcoming.

All this she knew that he knew. She knew more. She knew that she had always known it.

Princess Mabylye lay on her back on the damp earth, weak from her ordeal. A cool breeze steadied her. Refreshing. Her legs had returned but lute strings knotted in her stomach. She drew her shawl round her and stared up at the fast-moving clouds which covered, uncovered, covered and uncovered the full moon. The smells of the woods pleased her. Unexpectedly she thought of her childhood and the games she played with her sisters in other woods. A shudder caught her unawares – it was relief. She had been saved. She hummed to herself, as in thanksgiving. The patient mongrel slithered to her side, stretched and nuzzled into her armpit, where he now knew he was so safe that in his growling way he hummed with her. The friendship he had worked and waited for seemed to be taking hold of his mistress. As she hummed she stroked his ear. His tuneless growls melted helplessly into grateful sighs. She could not hide her smile. But what of the melody, the harmony? She must not lose it, she must continue to Amissia's hut. Resolve came and went. She was staring at the moon, mesmerized. Light and dark, light and dark. She could not turn her eyes from it and slipped into a trance like a somnambulist who had been called, drawn to answer – what? She knew not. From here on all she did seemed enacted by another self.

She stood up. Reached down for her lute and, with glazed eyes, turned round and round, searching for something. She found it. Some metres away were two very old trees growing closely together. So old that their roots rose above the ground, and so close that they formed a cove.

To this cove walked her new self as in a dream, the crack of dead twigs beneath her feet mixing with the hoot of an owl mixing with the low whisper of a wind mixing with the anxious whine of her furry saviour, who pattered backwards and forwards behind, wondering where she was going, to do what? She settled in the cove, raised a bent knee to cradle her lute and began to sing. As she sang she gazed at the moon, transfixed, as though singing to a stray soul who was marooned upon it and had called for comfort.

The mongrel moved restlessly around. Here was no one he recognized. She had been taken over and away from him. If he could understand nothing of her now, then how could he protect her? He seemed to want her to move from this spot. Rising on his hind legs, his forepaws cleaving to the bark, he placed his nose in her ear to whisper a message. She smiled but ignored him. He licked her face, nudged under her arm, urging her to move. She gazed on and played on. He fell back and regarded her. What had happened? Was she in shock? He looked around. Then back at her. He howled, then fell silent. He dropped his nose to the ground to sniff for danger. There was none. Could a dog in love be wrong? A dog in love could be wrong. He was confused and flopped on his belly, facing her, paws before him.

She was playing strangely. First sweetly and then frenziedly. He shuffled forward. Nosed the air. Shuffled forward again. She felt his breath on her stretched-out calf. He licked it, reassuringly. Be calm. I am close. Nothing to fear. He nosed the air again. Slid forward. His head was beneath her dress, as though here, if she was determined to settle for the night, he too would settle for the night. She closed her eyes, intense with song. She felt a long tongue lick the inside of her thigh. Her singing melted to a hum. The wet nose nosed further under her dress. She pushed it away. The mongrel paused, propped up his ears enquiringly. No resistance. He drooped his ears again and continued his cautious journey, tongue moving from calf to thigh to sweet moist harbours. Once more she pushed him away. Now he withdrew his head sharply to look at her frankly. What was she trying to tell him? She seemed not to know and hummed on.

'While from me, well – ' had said the loose-limbed Mabylye to her sisters, 'I will tell you this. I would be frightened to reveal what I feel. My one bounces upon me and I think, I think...' Her words returned. *What* did she think? What? What?

Suddenly, the hum transcended into one long clear high note. Her throat had found its C. She held it longer than any other before, thrilling to hear it pierce and echo through the spring forest, till she could hold it no more. At which instant she laid aside her lute, slid down into the cove, flung back her head, drew up her dress, opened her legs and with her fingers prised apart her moist lips.

'Come,' she whispered, as though she might be discovered and feared it. 'Oh, come, come.'

She heard the crackle of paws among the last dead winter leaves, felt the hot breath between her thighs. There it was! She arched herself up to a long rough tongue, lapping and rasping over the red bud which, moon-struck, she sought to expose. She howled the moon's fever as she heard her canine lover howl at the scent from her skin. He understood her pleas, and flicked his long rasp faster and faster, drawing in her sweet milk. The wise mongrel knew what the unfinished sentence longed to say, had always known, and came to her as she now came to him, overwhelmed, in a flood.

How happily the hound loped home, leaping up to her face, skipping round her, barely able to suppress his barks of joy. Not the royal princess, though. She moved slowly, deep in unease, dragging her lute along the rough earth, flinging off his advances, stooping now and then to throw at him a thick, dead length of branch. The imperturbable brute ignored it all, knowing she meant not one gesture of her anger. Friends and lovers were like that, gripped now and then by moods which had to be tolerated, lived with. It was the price you paid for love. So he pretended it was a game, dodged the missiles and retrieved them in his jaw to lay at her feet – thus we provide the wherewithal for our beatings.

When they reached the hut she tripped. Her sandal fell off. She bent to replace it and there he was again, nuzzling up her garment. She turned and swiped the dumb mutt with her lute so vehemently she snapped a string. Now the royal child's temper rose. She threw at him all she could find – stones, sticks, thick lumps of earth. He was impervious to it all and bounced out of harm's way as though in a game, which inflamed her temper even more that he refused to take her unease seriously.

Inside she sat at the table and worked angrily to replace the snapped gut, not caring that her noise might wake the tired tanner. Fortunately he was very tired – working day and night debilitates even the most ardent. He slept through her bangs and curses and the animated antics of his mongrel who paced the floor and talked to itself about his adorable but incomprehensible mistress.

'If you are not still this instant,' she hissed between her teeth at him, 'I will break the rest of these strings over your head.'

Her tone was effective. He collapsed with pained pride to his belly and lay with his head between stretched paws, a position from which with huge forgivng eyes he could gaze and adore. He became so quiet and she so absorbed that she forgot him. There she sat, heavy and sweating, splicing and tuning her strands, her concentration filling the room, until − again! There under the table! Breathing between her legs. She kicked him away. He returned. She kicked him away again. Again he returned. She kicked him again and again. Again and again he returned. Ah! He understood coy women. The fifth time she struck him with a wooden spoon, which sent him whimpering away in a state of confusion to his master, whom he licked awake and complained to. I thought I could humour a woman's unpredictability, he seemed to whine, but this one is beyond my charm. He flopped at his master's side and raised an indignant, disdainful nose into the air.

Stephen cuddled his quirky quadruped.

'And have you been protecting her?' The dog immediately forgot his chagrin and wagged his tail. 'And has she fed you?' The tail wagged faster. 'And has she stroked and fondled and lovingly cared for you while I slept?' The tail gyrated in a frenzy of delight. Stephen stood up and stretched. Not being as intelligent as his pet, he had understood none of his pet's tail's circumvolutions. 'I have such a hunger and thirst,' he said, oblivious to the unappetizing sight of himself clad only in a short vest reaching no further than his navel.

His uninhibited creature tried to make friends with *his* creature. Stephen swiped him away.

'I shall eat curd and honey first, then your deer's liver, then blackberries and nuts, then − but first, this.' He had filled a tankard with cider and drank, flicking his hand at his fond whelp's snout, which persisted in trying to nip his swinging authority.

'What's the matter with you, mutt?' he demanded. 'Frisky, are you? Well, so am I and I'll be at it soon and you'll have to be gone with your tail between your legs, because my mistress can't abide you.'

At which, to his amazement, the hound raced round and round the room in a surge of unaccountable joyous energy.

'Been drinking cider?' asked his startled master. 'Stop that! Stop! Sit or I'll thrash you!'

The animal obeyed, collapsing upon its stomach, its tongue lapping the air, panting from its pointless exploration of nowhere.

'Stephen,' called the princess Mabylye suddenly. 'I want your voice.'

'My voice?' He spoke with a mouthful of bread coated with deer's liver.

'You can sing, can you not?'

'For myself, yes, but not for anyone else. Especially not for you.'

'Not *for* me, but with me. I have a sound that has been going round in my head which I must hear. It is made at three levels. Do you know 'The Ballad of the Holy Tree"?' She was referring to a popular song of the day. He said he did.

'You sing the melody. My lute will play a third higher, and I'll sing a third higher still. Do you think you can hold?'

'I can but try,' he offered obligingly.

They began. The song went to pieces. They tried again. The sound they made hinted at possibility but could not be sustained. The third attempt gained strength, and by the fifth they were in full throat.

The tree grew tall
The strong men came
Their spirits lame
They have a task
Their axes fall
They make a wooden cross for him
They make a wooden cross for him.

The cross is spread
The sweet man nailed
The women paled
There is a thorn
Upon his head
They make a special place for him
They make a special place for him.

Oh bend your knee
Who e'er you are
Where e'er you are
Bow low before
The holy tree
And sing this holy song for him
And sing this holy song for him.

They sang it twice without stopping and were breathless
when finished. It had been a hard and speedy melody.
Stephen had thumped his fist on the table. Mabylye had
plucked her strings fiercely, banging one foot rhythmically
on the ground. The hut had throbbed. She was so thrilled
with her new sound that, driven by an excess of joy, she
flung down her lute and leapt into Stephen's arms with an
ardour both unfamiliar and, though he could not know it,
unrepeatable.

'Oh, glory!' she cried. 'I cannot wait to sing this new sound in the capital cities of the world. They will have heard nothing like it! Nothing!'

Here was a passion Stephen the tanner knew how to use. Had she not been such a heavy lady, he would have lifted her in his arms to throw her down upon cushions, but he knew his limitations limited though he was. Instead he pulled her down. This time Mabylye was ready to enjoy him, filled as she was with a sense of achievement. Now *there* was a truth: a woman requires more than any man can offer before she can offer herself to him. She did not care that she was tediously on her back again, that again he was tediously upon her, bouncing and kissing and sweating his leathery smells. He could labour as pedantically as he liked, and come. She was satisfied and at peace with herself.

His pedantic labouring was halted by a pathetic whining noise.

'The dumb hound! I have forgotten to put him outside,' he said. 'Look at him! Poking his nose into our affairs.' He half rose but she stayed him.

'Leave him,' she whispered in a low voice thick with unusual promise and anticipation. 'What harm can he do?'

Stephen was perplexed and looked from mistress to pet. Passion he could cope with; comprehension came, if at all, with difficulty. His mistress had her eyes closed, his pet stood eyeing him, waiting for his slow-witted master to comprehend. Cautiously Stephen bent forward to kiss her face. With his rump in the air he felt awkward, shy, exposed. He could not continue. Despite closed eyes, Mabylye seemed to understand his hiatus. She reached to pull him down to her lips. He sank upon her and thrilled to her tongue thrashing about inside his mouth, as though, fresh and eager, she had come upon him for the first time. He returned her eagerness.

But then she moaned. Why? It was only a kiss. She slithered about inside his mouth with greater urgency and moaned more. He was amazed that his simple action provoked such intense response. It was unnatural, his tongue had never before aroused such ecstasy. What was happening? Something brushed his rear. A furry skin. He heard another sound, another sucking. He pulled away and to his astonishment saw his happy hound licking the labia of his happy princess. He could not believe his eyes. There she was pulling herself apart to welcome a long rough canine tongue.

He watched on his knees as she wriggled and rose to his capable friend. A new excitement was overtaking him.

'Princess! Princess!' he cried. 'I shall come into the air if I watch any more.'

She pushed the surprised animal away and sat up. What could she do? Both were in wild states, their eyes frantic, their bodies on the brink of eruption. The interrupted dog squatted, his tongue hanging out, prepared to wait for their decision, knowing it would come. It did. The princess Mabylye sprang up, pulled her tanner man with her, sat him on the bench, turned her back to him, hoisted her garb, splayed her legs open and slowly eased herself on to his upright majesty.

Thus squatting, she looked at her new-found furry friend, whose intelligent eyes seemed to be sharing a secret smile with her. 'Come,' her eyes smiled back, and he strode in triumph to her pink crown, which with reverence and tenderness he lapped and lapped with the burning flame of his mouth.

The cry of three voices came that night from the hut of the bovine, regal lady whose delights were multiplied. A dream of songs had released them.

★

All this Jonas heard and saw about the princess Mabylye, and related to me, Coaxandria, who have here ordered and interpreted and summarized for the king, and for those who will read after.

AMISSIA
~ THE SIXTH YOUNGEST

Amissia knew, as she sat waiting and singing, that a singing woman was an erotic experience. But why? Cupping a hand over her ears, he could hear herself, audience to her own voice, producing the sounds she wanted, stretching, shaping them, modulating their texture. She could understand why a song held an audience, stirred, saddened, disturbed them, but wherein lay the eroticism? A woman walking, yes. A woman kneading dough, yes, suggestive – she smiled at the thought. She could perceive the eroticism of a woman in repose. But a woman singing? Was it, she wondered, to do with concentration? A woman absorbed is a magnet. When she sings softly, there is about her the intense air of sharing guilty secrets; she invites. When she sings out she exerts her entire body, surrenders to an irresistible abandon. Amissia sang conscious of a unique power, until –

– she heard his voice. It reverberated with overblown enthusiasms and expectations of pleasure, shattering the much sweeter music in her ear. He had a fine voice, but she had come to find him vain and tedious. The lifeless gaze of a disappointed princess greeted him as he bounced through the door with song.

Who was this frozen wench? Had she not demanded a bargain d'amour? And had he not honoured it? Eagerly of course; who would not for such a beautiful woman, all aflame, swarthy, almost black?

'My bugle was blowing and...'

'Do not, do not, DO NOT SAY IT!' Amissia exploded. 'I do not care if your bugle blows, or your horn, or your trumpet or whatever you call what flounders between your legs with which you want me to sing. I will not sing with it, to it, on it or about it, for I am bored with the melodies we play inspired by it!'

'Bored?' He could not believe she intended that word.

'Bored, battered, bitched, botched and bugled out of existence by them. I must...I wish...I need...' She spluttered in frustration. 'I do not know what!'

'That outburst has exhausted me before we have begun,' said her tolerant partner, who was not without humour, which is sometimes helpful when confronted with incomprehensible women.

'Good!' she threw back at him. 'Then we have no *need* to begin!'

'Woman!' he cried fiercely – it was time to abandon tolerance and assert manliness. 'Woman! Remember! *You* called upon *me*! I have not come this far to be rejected like a puppy suitor. Besides,' his voice softened, searching for understanding, 'what have I done?'

She softened with him, for she was not – as was none of the king's daughters – unkind. 'I am sorry, sweet puppy,' she sighed, and flopped into his arms, offering him apologetic kisses, though even those pale things soon ceased.

She was restless. He was confused.

'When confused – sing!' he said. He sang, slowly un-buttoning his kirtle, watching her as one would a pacified tigress, anxious its ferocity might return.

She let him sing on, wondering would he surprise her? A new melody perhaps? No such miracle. A boring man is a boring man. He can hide his tedium for a while, for a while it can be ignored, but in the end boredom will out like a boil through thick skin.

'Do not sing. *Please*!' she pleaded. 'Tell me a story instead.'

'You keep asking me to do this thing,' he complained, 'and I never can.'

'You never try!' How feeble men were. 'Now your dear little heart is still, your bugle and my passions sleep. Find us a story to rouse them.'

'I am not made to tell stories. I am made to sing!' he insisted, adding, 'Nor is my heart "little". It is a big heart. Vulnerable, passionate. You must not toy with it.'

'I do not ask for intricate plots – ' she ignored his sob – 'but lively anecdotes. Your experiences. Your other loves. They must have been strange, amusing, exciting.'

His vacuous eyes signalled the impossibility of this. She tried another track. 'Your friends' loves, then, they must have related what took place. Men always share their amorous escapades, if only to boast. I want to look into someone else's life. Are you not fascinated by other people's lives? Do you not look through windows, hoping to witness some strange, extraordinary act?'

A memory lit up his eyes. 'I went laying traps in the woods one night and passed a large abode lit with a dozen candles.'

'There! I knew you could find a story if you tried. A large

abode! A dozen candles! What a beginning. More! More! What more did you see?'The excitable princess pulled him down by her fire, poured him wine and urged him on.

'I peered through the window and saw two old people locked in fevered embrace. It was the sweetest yet strangest ceremony of love I have ever seen.'

Her round eyes widened. She was held at once. Tales of other people's lives gripped her with the amazement of a child.

'I have not told anyone this story before,' he procrastinated. 'To be honest, I am ashamed to have intruded upon their privacy. Private moments belong to their owners; to observe them is a kind of theft. I stole a precious hour from them.'

'To steal is to *deny*,' she corrected him. 'You did not steal, you shared. All stories are intrusions upon their characters' privacy. It is that very privacy which excites, and the presumption of poets is to share it with their public. Shameful, we know, to possess and be possessed by this demonic curiosity, but I have always been afflicted. From childhood. Cupboards, drawers, keyholes, windows. What protected itself from my knowing, inflamed my desire even more to know, and if I could barter my voice in return for the power of invisibility I would do it.'

'You would do that?' He was incredulous.

'Confession for confession!' she nodded. 'There is,' she continued, 'an old Druid legend that once every ten years the four winds blow from all corners of the earth upon the same spot where a living person stands, sits, sleeps or is at some task, and that person is filled with the power to become invisible. Man, woman, child, wise, foolish, rich or poor – the winds meet and where they meet the power is gifted. To be gifted thus – ah!'

There came to them the sound of a long, stifled moan.

'Did you hear that?' the princess asked, looking around.

'The four winds, perhaps?' His humour had returned.

'Tell me your story.' The mercurial woman spun back to him. 'Make me envious not to have witnessed it myself.'

'Is it so important for you to have been there?'

'How can you ask?'

'Then I will take you there. It is not far. I have little faith in my narrative powers...'

She was on her feet at once.

'But I am hungry,' he complained.

She grabbed two legs of roasted turkey, splashed them in sweet-pickled sauce, put one in his hand, reached for slices of cold venison, folded two into his mouth, plunged fruit into his pockets, wine into earthenware decanters, and hauled him through the door. Together they walked into the woods, eating, laughing, composing songs, inventing harmonies, pausing only to drink wine which excited their blood to hop, skip and dance them on their way.

When he guessed they were near, he calmed their high-spirited clamour and tiptoed as silently as can be done in woods full of dried and sapless twigs waiting to snap and warn of animals who preyed and pried.

It was found. A hut in a circular clearing. Not a modest hut as might belong to a poor woodsman, but one generously appointed, set within two circular enclosures, belonging perhaps to a retired bailiff who had once been attached to lord and manor. By the half-moon's light they could see that the inner circle was a garden brimming with the last of the summer's flowers. The outer circle was for vegetables. Half was cleared and newly dug over, the soil dark with rich peat. Four paths divided the circular habitation into four quarters. On the far perimeter was a small shed clustered around by fruit trees, heavy and scented.

'I think there is a dog about,' her singing companion warned.

The princess stuck a finger in her mouth to test which way the wind was blowing, and chose a path to take their scent away from the hound.

A light burned in a window. Like many of the houses scattered throughout the area, it was erected on stilts with a platform surrounding it. On to this they clambered.

Inside was an elderly couple of striking handsomeness dressed in nightshirt and nightdress, ready for bed. He carried in him a proud manager's life; she his proud partner. Both were tall and erect. The spirit with which each was born had brought them together and endowed their bodies with a majestic vigour. Work had not bowed them. Though bulky, he was a well-favoured old man with a mass of tangled grey curls for hair and a drooping brush for moustache. She, slightly shorter, had retained strands of black hair among the moonlight white. Her eyebrows were fierce, her dark-brown eyes passionate – God help those who threatened her patch. The princess Amissia loved them at sight. She longed to burst upon them with embraces, not to remain hidden and prying. Her guilt deepened but her curiosity increased. Conflict! She turned away.

'Will you leave now,' her not so riven companion asked, 'after we have come all this way?'

'Shame, shame. I feel shame,' she whispered.

'What will you do with your shame?' he jeered. 'Justify it? Suppress it? Buy dispensations for it?'

She would justify nothing to this little bugler.

'Live with it!' she replied defiantly.

'Like a dead weight?' he taunted.

'Like a dead weight!'

'Ah, but how much dead weight can you carry before collapsing?' he sneered.

'We never know until we have collapsed, do we?' she snapped, turning back and wishing he were anywhere but at her side.

The stately old lady was unbraiding her hair. When it was done, she turned to kiss her husband. Then she lowered the lamplight and both slid into their bed, set in a sculptured cavity in the wall, where they settled down to sleep.

Amissia was fascinated by the ritual with which they moved one with the other. He helped her withdraw pins from her hair and stacked them in a dark-blue bowl on a shelf over the fireplace, as no doubt he had done night after night since they were young and agile. She pulled back the sheets for him to crawl ahead of her into the bed to sleep nearest the wall, where no doubt he had always slept since they were young and agile. And since they were young and agile, no doubt she was the first awake to face the first of the day's duties.

Nothing more happened. The old ones fell asleep to sleep away the innocence of last days.

Amissia and her bored boring partner came a second night. Exactly the same cycle was enacted. On this occasion the dog barked and they had to retreat in haste. On the third night she brought some honeyed popernia given her by her sister, Beatrix, to quieten the animal. This time side by side with her tired and tiresome lover, hidden by the crazy foliage of a flourishing wistaria heavy with mauve blossom-like grapes, they witnessed a very different scene indeed. Another setting. Another couple.

A fire blazed in the grate, warming and cosy. A dozen vases of different shapes and colours lay scattered around the room, filled with freshly cut flowers, the summer's last. Aflame with reds, lilacs, purples and whites, the room had about it the atmosphere of a wedding celebration, further enhanced by the light of twenty candles. Shadows danced on the walls. On the table were wooden platters covered with fruit cut into small pieces. Dark-blue bowls brimmed with honey, jam, cream and sour milk. In a formation like skittles were a dark-blue jug of oil, four large terracotta pitchers of white wine, and – here was the strange addition – four large terracotta pitchers of mountain water, two of which were already empty and a third the old man was in the process of pouring. Both were in night-garments which, like all else, were different: flowing gowns brightly embroidered, fancifully fashioned, from Arabia perhaps, or China, enlivening the festive atmosphere with exotic promise. Each drank water in silence, ritualistically, saying nothing, waiting. For what? They drank steadily, glass after glass, till the third pitcher was empty, then they rose, moved out of the house and walked towards the shed where she raised her gown and passed water.

Even this was a ritual. As she squatted she bared her breasts, and her fond partner squeezed her nipples, gazing with fierce pleasure at her fierce waters. The beginnings of desire stirred in his features. When it was his turn to raise his flowery gown and piss, she stood behind him, leaned her face with affection on his back, reached in front with her right hand for his heavy spout, as if to direct its intentions, crept into his nightshirt with her left hand and caressed his nipple – the tender actions of an old nurse knowing how best to coax her child's bladder to play.

They were about to move away when the bailiff's wife caught sight of the dog stretched dozily by its kennel. She could tell at a glance it was not its usual self. She stiffened, looked around, listening. Amissia froze in fear. Sharing not stealing, she told herself. Sharing, sharing not stealing. But words can always be found to assuage guilt, and Amissia, princess and seventh youngest daughter of the king, was afraid. Not of being caught – what harm after all could come to her? She feared only confrontation with her shame. Stone blunts knife, knife cuts paper, paper covers stone, age commands royalty. The reprobation of those two veterans would mortify her.

Fortunately the hound, though unable to bark and bite, could rise on all fours and walk to lick his mistress's hand. Her suspicions were allayed. They returned indoors.

The ritual continued. Glass after glass of water before their fire, no word spoken, and two more excursions outside, playfully assisting one another to relieve their bladders. The last pitcher was coming to its end. Their animation was increasing. The old couple exchanged the smiles of those who had shared and agreed much since the days when their lives had been young and agile. For a last time – surely it was the last? – they visited their saturated terrain and released from one end of them what they had, for reasons unfathomable, poured into the other. Returning, they drank a glass of the wine and at once their faces lit up with the naughty energy of their agile youth. Well – almost! Their skin flushed red, their eyes radiated excited anticipation, the candle's shadows danced with the gaiety of heaven.

It was soon apparent that they had no intention of drinking the wine with the same speed and regularity as they had drunk the water. After the first glass they opened their arms to one another. They were ready. For what? She moved to receive her first kisses, which came like well-earned things. She matched wage for wage, ardour for ardour. Devotion and rewards. Each honoured each. Preludes. Beginnings. They clung to one another swaying, lipped tight in consolation, unhurried. Age knows its pace. With so little time, there is all the time in the world. Much more was to come. Their ritual had become many-faceted over the years.

From an ancient, simply-hewn oak chest he drew a rug of heavy silk, coloured dark red and purple, which he unfolded like the Sabbath's best, and ceremoniously spread before the fire. Then, standing before him she raised her arms as he lifted off her embroidered shift. Amissia marvelled. Before her was a woman of nearly three-score years and ten, whose breasts though hanging were full, whose hips were firm, whose buttocks had not fallen, whose shoulders were square and proud, whose back was straight and strong – tall, old, used and touchingly human. Of course folds of flesh hung down the middle, and skin on her hands and neck was wrinkled and cracked; of course the button in her belly was squeezed horizontal like a weeping eye, and brown spots freckled her, but to Amissia the older woman was luminescent.

It was the wife's turn to reveal the man. By what miracle did he stand both old and young before her? A leathery skin, it is true; a stomach without a waist, true; flabby muscles here and there, how could all that not be so? But robust, solid, a man who, like his wife, blazed. He took her by the hand and tenderly lowered her white length upon the red and purple silk – only the best for his dame.

From the table he brought the bowls, laid them by her side and began, delicately, to knead sour milk into her left breast, and cream into her right breast. Then he knelt behind her head, leaned forward, his belly hanging a little over her face, and with relish licked and sucked each breast clean, like a dog its rationed plate. Her nipples rose, dark brown corks from their dark brown discs, huge protuberances which the tip of his tongue laved, stroked, nipped and pulled. If he could have taken a whole breast into his mouth, he would have. Here was a hungry man.

While he was thus sweetly and sourly engaged, the good woman, her senses aroused, dipped a hand into the jam prickly with tiny pips of blackberries from which it was made, and rubbed some into her stomach. Next, to the honey, which she rubbed between her legs among the flaps of her old purse, deep into its ancient treasures, in the process of which was revealed a sight never before seen by our royal singer of songs and never to be forgotten.

From where the enthralled couple stood they viewed the old woman feet first. As she parted her legs to spread honey upon honey she exposed to them a pleasure-dome that rose one half-inch high, and which, when she pinioned it between her forefinger and thumb to stroke and pull, grew another inch. Amissia gazed jealous and astounded. Had age lengthened this knurl or was it a freak of nature? Did this mean the possibility of pleasure increased with time passing? She watched in wonderment as the old woman lapped up being lapped up, her eyes closed, writhing ecstatically from side to side, pleasuring herself. And to the young princess there flashed a truth about passion: ecstasy comes not merely from being touched but from the visible evidence that your partner aches to be touched as much. Look how the wife's eagerness delights and drives the husband, who thrills to her self-induced pleasure. She too had waited longingly, craving for this night to return with its intense, bizarre, sacredly private rituals. *That* was his great joy – his wife's dark desires. The princess would remember: whoever was to share her life let him know, let him see, hold nothing back. Let not the strangest need be hidden.

The old woman, roused, pulled her hungry husband forward by his hair to her belly where jam awaited him. Not too much! It was the honey between her legs she wanted him to taste. Sweetness would give him energy. As his lips reached there his trusty bone hung over her mouth. How their passions wrestled! He licking and biting that extraordinary spire, she pulling and sucking her long bronzed battler. Age may have its sad disappointments but there are compensations – revealed hidden needs, fantastic explorations, surrender, trust. The magnificent habits of a long life. Honours and rewards.

The princess turned to her pale-faced lover with his pale enthusiasms and observed, 'There was a Greek philosopher once who said old age is like being delivered from a multitude of furious masters. I do not see it.' *He* did not understand it!

The old woman took her time. Her old man's old man seemed reluctant to straighten his back. Her lips coaxed with tender cunning; her fingers pulled and caressed; her spirit and smiles reassured, encouraged. Rise! Rise! Trust me! I am your mistress who knows best. Rise to the pleasures she has planned for you, rise! Here are sweet things, soft cushionings. Find me, grasp me, rasp your faithful old parts upon me. Do not be sad that the young man has gone, that the old man wheezes like an old storm, that you need sticks to climb your hills, warm vests in summer. Forget the watering of your eyes, the cracking of your knees, the pained joints, the feeble grasp of your fingers, the ache in your heart. Rise! Be bold and brazen, these are not your last days. Rise! For are you not my beloved?

It was the young woman in her who spoke these things

to him as she offered her familiar mounds to his mouth, sighing with the urgency of time passing – the young woman who refused to go, to release her hold, who would not accept the old body which encased her. I am still here, this other woman pleaded, young still and beautiful. Find me, rescue me, do not abandon me.

Those sighs, thought Amissia. She had not heard their like before. In her own ecstasies she had screamed unbearable pleasure. Not this old woman. Her passion cried out to be remembered. Demanding, angry. Come! Remind me! No pain is too much! Do anything and all with me. So fierce did her sounds become as his lips rose up and down over her raw spike that Amissia swooned, and fell in a heap about her astonished lover's legs, clinging to him in her last second of consciousness. The poor man panicked and stood rooted to the spot, barely holding her. She revived slowly. They looked at one another. Perhaps they should leave? his eyes asked. Her response was emphatic. She returned attention to her old friends.

What confronted the voyeurs was another changed scene. The two old people, first ardours spent, were resting. No peak had been reached, both were still in a ferment of agitation. Were they deliberately holding back or were extremes required to reach their heights? He poured wine and knelt, offering it to her as to one wearied in battle. She drank, needily, and lay back. He too drained his cup. A new activity was to begin.

He turned her over on her belly and reached for another jar. Starting from the nape of her neck he poured its contents over her, down her spine into the cleft of her buttocks. Then he sat astride her and began a slow, firm massage, rubbing the scented oil into her skin, pausing to press certain spots as though to release energy, gripping her flesh in the vain hope that it could be wrung free of age. Her sounds were softer, sighs of contentment rather than regret, until his hands parted her buttocks and began to rub between her broad, taut cheeks. Then returned old moans of urgency. She raised her backside demanding more. And more he gave. Pouring oil upon his hands, he gently eased two fingers into the small crater which offers no helpful lubrication of its own.

Moans became cries of pain, pain felt, pain needed, pain called upon. She moved with him, back and forth, in and out, until it seemed she could take no more and slipped out of his reach. She turned to lie on her back, looked at him, a sign. He knew what must happen next. She was ready for it. She spread her heavy legs and with her fingers massaged her tower into view. He reached for another glass of wine and drank it in one gulp. Then he did something very strange. He scratched his finger between the cleft at the top of his buttocks and, as though the movement had touched a secret spring, out gushed his waters in a hard jet which he directed upon her swollen peak. She rose towards him to receive all, greedily, wildly, gazing intently with dark brown eyes from where it gushed forth.

The watching couple understood at last the reason for drinking so much water: the old lovers had known to clean the bladder of its sour odours. Only a faintly malodorous smell lingered, the pungency of which, when mixed with the wine, intoxicated the abandoned old woman as a forbidden juice. And how much there was. Warm and endlessly pouring.

Then it was her turn. Her eager partner lay on his back while she drank from a goblet, in one gulp, squatted astride him and gushed forth in a triumphant hiss over his face and into his mouth, which he opened like a young bird frantic to catch each drop. She was an endless fountain of wine! For the first time both old people laughed, like children in the rain splashing one another from gutters and streams. To see them in this state the princess could not recall the sedate and dignified old couple of the previous two nights who had carefully helped one another into bed to sleep away the innocence of last days. Here was no innocence, nor any sign of last days!

Amissia was exhausted and could barely watch more. The old lovers were exhausted too, and needed to rest. A sweet sight followed. Each fed the other sliced and diced fruits which they dipped into honey to revive strength, then washed down with wine in search of even greater abandon. And greater abandon came.

It was her turn to bite and travel over his body. She moved with the lasciviousness of a well-kept courtesan. Which this night she was. They had waited a month and now this night was the night of ravager and whore. Twelve times a year these wild and ravenous creatures emerged, called forth by gnarled old Eroxius, the too often misunderstood and misrepresented god of carnality.

She poured oil, rubbed him, slipped her body over him, bit his ears, his neck, the flesh of his sides, clung with her teeth upon his nipples till he screamed and had to push her away, then sat upon his tower and rode him while his right hand pulled at the teat between her legs, and his left at the teat of a breast, eyes closed, moving, gasping, laughing and shouting together, urging one another on and on. Yet though each new set of actions brought them to ever increasing heights of ecstasy, nothing had made them shriek that final sound, unlike any other in life, defying description for it is so utterly its own self.

The ritual was near its end. Both knew what must

happen. They drank the last of the wine. She looked at him as she always looked at him at this moment, for she needed to know it was still what he wanted – there might come a night when he did not and she would not wish to inflict upon her beloved what he could no longer bear. He nodded and knelt before her. She reached over to the table and drew off it a small knife. What followed next was swiftly done. She made two small cuts into each of his nipples, sliced a lemon in two, squeezed their burning acid over his cuts to mingle with the blood, ignored his howls, bent to his fallen pride which she revived with her mouth, and when it was risen turned to offer her back. He took oil. Rubbed it between her cheeks and into the small crevice, then eased into her his hungry horn, little by little, the old hugeness entering her like a friend, she clenching and unclenching, moving back and forth. He leaned over her, his hands reaching under her to part her lips, searching for that magic knurl. She felt sensations in two parts at once; he felt sensations in two parts at once: biting pain and soft suctions – for them both. Then! Then came the sounds which belonged to neither of them. Cries, lamentations, containing a confusion of ages. Each age in them howled together – childhood, adolescence, young man, young woman, middle age, all crying out their terrible unhappiness to be gone, gone, gone.

Their ecstasy was lost in tears.

Amissia, the singer of the nation's songs, thought she would faint again. Not only had such things never been done to her, the possibility of them ever happening had never dawned upon her. She and her bugler left their perch and returned home in silence. She could not make love that night. And when, some nights later, they did, it was not, she knew, this man with whom she wanted to sing.

★

All this Jonas heard and saw about the princess Amissia, and related to me, Coaxandria, who have here ordered and interpreted and summarized for the king, and for those who will read after.

MARGERIA
- THE SIXTH OLDEST

ℐt was true. She was not beautiful. A torso which hung with resignation close to the earth as though defeated by the knowledge of its inevitable return there. Lank hair, grey eyes, a face carved from flesh like dough, pitted skin, and a mournful gaze aware of its body's unloveliness.

But intelligence animates. When Margeria the lawmaker arrived at the simple thought which cut through Gordian knots of nonsense, when she formulated the logical equation for a right or a wrong, when she extracted justice from the murkiness of conflicting claims, she smiled, her features glowed, her grey eyes flashed with the pleasure of perspicacity.

Of all the royal sisters Margeria was the one for whom no man could be found. Her sisters had paraded before her an assortment of various males God had seemed driven to create: the rough, the refined, the imperious, the compliant, audacious leader, modest hero, wastrel fool, the unbelievably beautiful, the unbelievably innocent, the unbelievably damned, the sweetest of youths. She distressed them all with a mixture of fierce, uncompromising intelligence and her ungainliness. They would linger, eat her carelessly prepared but wholesome fare, converse some and flee. Her mind was unable to accommodate the slow, the simple, the frivolous, the unworldly. To her the modest hero was dull, the audacious leader pompous. But pity most the sweet-talker who roused her to fury. It was not her fault. She wished she were other. That was how she was made.

Nor did she fret. Her flesh had its season – spring. In summer her mind accelerated. In autumn she was spent. In winter all froze. But in spring there were stirrings.

It was spring.

Late spring. The being inhabiting her body was preparing to take its place in her summer head. There was little time left.

Jonas could understand none of all this. He watched uncomprehending the sisters smirk and frown as one by one the men were hopefully deposited in Margeria's room only to bid, some hours later, disappointed but relieved farewells.

'You will wither before your time,' warned Meliora, the second eldest, who herself *was* showing signs of withering, though not before her time.

'You *talk* too much, perhaps,' ventured Amabilia, the youngest.

'The pleasure is in sensation,' scolded Mabylye, 'not in thought.'

'Nonsense!' cried Amissia. 'The pleasure is in *remembering* the sensation and longing for it to be repeated. *That* requires thought.'

'Thought,' corrected the thoughtful Margeria, 'is not imagination, which is what I think you are talking about.'

'See!' cried Etheldra with consternation. 'If you correct every man you meet, of course his desires will deflate.'

'Perhaps,' suggested Enota, 'it is not a man she desires.'

The notion reduced the sisters to an embarrassed silence.

'Why is everyone reduced to an embarrassed silence?' asked Amy.

'*Can* you be 'reduced'' to an embarrassed silence?' asked Margeria, who seemed more interested to pursue questions of syntax than doubts about her desires.

'Have you *ever* experienced desire?' asked the still-fresh Amabilia.

'I think I have,' mused Margeria.

'Describe it!' demanded Beatrix.

'Ah, well...' Margeria became animated at the prospect of intellectual exploration. 'Desire is...desire is...it is...to want, no, to need, no, to want what you need.'

'Like a cup of water to quench your thirst?' Lenota was the acerbic one.

'Yes, that!'

'Ask the question you really want to ask,' Amy struck out. 'No one of you is anxious to hear Margeria describe desire in the abstract. You want her to relate the word to flesh. You want our sister of the legislature to define *amorous* desire.'

'Desiring the pleasures of the flesh,' insisted Margeria, 'is, I repeat, to *want* what you *need*. There is nothing evasively abstract about that.'

'You shape the king's laws,' Dionis reminded her. 'You must be more precise.'

Margeria could move forward only in small, careful steps.

'Very well. Amorous desire is to want what the *flesh* needs.'

'Then describe *what* the flesh needs,' Dionis pursued her.

'Ah, well, the flesh of each has different needs.'

'To *do* what? To *achieve* what?' Dionis would not relent.

'So,' parried Margeria, 'I am not being asked to describe *desire* but to explain what the body needs when it is in a *state* of desire.'

They all sighed and understood why men fled.

'Yes! Yes!' each cried in their different exasperated ways. 'Explain what you think the body needs when it is in a state of desire.'

'Gratification!' Margeria was confident of her response.

'Merciful heavens! Will we never be given a direct answer?' Liticia was the impatient one.

'My answers *are* direct,' insisted Margeria. 'Perhaps your questions are imprecise.'

'Then *you* formulate the question,' mocked Meliora, the second eldest.

'I think,' began the precisely minded Margeria, ignoring the ill-temper of her eldest sister, knowing that eldest sisters have herculean problems with which to wrestle, 'I think you want to know if I comprehend and delight in that extraordinary sensation known as 'coming" when the body and its secret parts have been stirred so ardently that something erupts and an energy departs, leaving you too spent and sensitized to accept further caresses.'

'Until some minutes later,' laughed Amabilia, the youngest, fresh from her glorious initiation.

'Or many minutes later,' smiled Enota, the second youngest.

'Or many many minutes, perhaps hours later,' cautioned Amy, the third youngest.

In this way Jonas heard each sister confess the time she needed for respite, up until the second eldest sister, Meliora, who said nothing.

The exchange had so engrossed and pleased the boy that

he sighed that sigh of contentment which those less intellectually endowed experience in the company of those who can assemble the loose ends of thought and weave them into thrilling tapestries of meaning.

This time only Margeria heard the sigh, and knew for certain there was a presence in her room. She of all the princesses enchanted Jonas most and so he was unaware she had detected him. Margeria continued.

'Yes, I do comprehend and have delighted in that extraordinary sensation.'

'But with whom?' demanded the exuberant Etheldra.

Margeria made no reply. Her secret was her secret and, as we shall discover, only Jonas was ever to be made privy to it.

Margeria turned the attention of her sisters to another thought. 'And now we come to the real question. The one *most* difficult to answer. The one I think you all wanted to ask. What *is* that 'extraordinary sensation"?'

'Ecstasy,' declared Amabilia with the certainty of youth.

'That is what you *feel*, not what is happening to you.' Margeria was in her element, enjoying herself.

'The blood is being brought to a boil,' said Beatrix, who should know about such things, caring as she did for the sick.

'It only *feels* like that. We know blood cannot actually boil!' persisted Margeria.

'The blood sings,' cried Amissia, the singer, 'and the body sings, and the heart and everything around you sings, sings, sings.' She was remembering her moments, dear girl.

'That is not what *happens*,' insisted Margeria. 'I know the moment is one of intoxication, but intoxicated language is of no help to the understanding of the nature of intoxication. Hearts, bodies, the blood do not sing, Amissia, pretty though that image is. It only *seems* to be singing.'

'Oh! It is impossible ever to know what is really *happening*,' exploded Dionis, the teller of stories. 'All we can do is describe what we *seem* to be feeling.'

'You are asking for a science that has not yet evolved,' Beatrix complained.

'What science?' asked the acerbic Lenota. 'One that can dissect ecstasy, innocence, melancholy, evil, joy, guilt, and codify their parts?'

'I am no match for the combined intellects of my sisters,' smiled Margeria, 'yet I humbly suggest, all human states, conditions, however intangible, have their anatomy.'

'For the discovering of which you need a poet,' declared Dionis.

'I do not accept that' said the lawmaker.

Silence followed. Each princess thought hard, searched her memory, mouthed different words to herself in an attempt to match them with that unique delirium known as orgasm.

Jonas held his breath. In that instant Margeria stared straight at him. He froze.

'What are you looking at?' Enota asked.

'There is a shape in the grain of the wood that pleases me,' she lied, and smiled her intelligent smile at the boy she could not see, which made her features glow with the understanding of things. How could one not love such a woman? Jonas wondered.

'*You* tell us,' Enota asked her at last. 'The anatomy of orgasm. Describe it.'

'That extraordinary sensation,' began Margeria, 'is surrender. The relinquishing of all restraint. We live tight lives. What is being stirred is a fire that melts bonds. It is the pleasure that comes from abdicating responsibility –

everything becomes possible, permissible, imaginable. It is the purest experience of freedom. The nature of physical ecstasy is release – release from the cautions of intellect, the inhibitions of the spirit, the impediments of the body; release from the world's demands, our neighbour's expectations: release from guilt, conscience, sensibilities, self-doubts, and the pain, pain, pain of each day's living. In that extended, intensely drawn-out moment, when our nerve ends rise raw, exposed, to their zenith, we are all equal. There is only one other moment in life when we are all as equal.'

Her sisters left her. Margeria was in control of, and at peace with, herself. Jonas, of course, dutifully remained. He felt relieved to have been mistaken – Margeria had not scented his presence, but what, he wondered, could now take place that would enable the king, her father, to understand this daughter's ways? She conducted herself as a woman utterly alone, humming, tidying up – concerned sisters leave behind disorder of many kinds – pausing to gaze with seeming absent-mindedness into the long distance ahead, or behind, it is never known, and talking to herself.

'Somewhere there *is* a man would bear with me, but what does it matter? A man can be such a strain, with few rewards. They expect, they are anxious, they agitate, complain. They have tempers with which I would have to comply, rhythms into which I would need to lock. Their whirl of life would swallow me up and disgorge me like a belch. In return for what? Alone, I make my own rhythms; move, think at my own pace. Or not move, not think at all if I wish.' This last thought amused her. 'Absurd woman. *You* not think at all? Your mind has a life of its own. What control do *you* have over it?' She hummed on to herself.

Her sisters had left because, rebellious though their

mood, it was the hour of pleasure. The night was cool and black. She closed the window shutters, bent to revive her fire with the pungent scented logs of the salomine tree, and prepared her two tables. On one she laid out the food she fancied for the evening – honey and raisin bread, maramunda cheese with poppyseed, olives, cold stuffed pheasant, boiled pears with crushed pistachio nuts and dates thrust into their centres, and a flask of red wine made from the chiappe grape.

On the second table she laid out parchments, inks and assorted quills, and from the floor picked up a fine copy of Plutarch's *Lives* copied by a monk of the Benedictine order – it was the life of Numa Pompilius, the Roman king and lawmaker, in whom she was especially interested. The laws of her father's kingdom were rooted in Roman law; she was forever noting its fine and precise language for her father's statutes.

'The reason why Numa impresses me,' she said aloud, as though someone in the room had posed her a question, 'is that his first act on accepting the kingship, which the Roman senators and common people begged him to take up, *begged* him, you know – was to dismiss three hundred men who had been the bodyguards of Romulus. 'I will not," he declared, 'distrust those that put confidence in me. Nor will I rule over a people that distrusts me!' A magnificent royal gesture! Would you not trust such a man to be your king?'

She looked directly at Jonas again. So naturally did she appear to question him, as though she could see him, that he was on the verge of answering.

Margeria smiled and continued, 'Oh, if only I had someone with me who could respond, share my conversation and the food at my table.' She turned instead to her book.

Was she settling down for a night of research into Roman law?

Jonas could not stop gazing at her. He found every movement she made enchanting, devoid of wiles. What was there about this heavy woman with pitted skin of white dough that touched him? Curiously, her skin was not so white now. Concentration, exertion, heat from the fire spread colour across her features. What *was* there about those features which, the more he gazed at them, the more they seemed to radiate? Was she *made* for a solitary existence? Did she blossom only when alone? How she glowed as she moved about her room between furious note-making, talking to herself, digesting precepts, arguing with the thoughts they prompted in her.

'We must remember, the law is not meant to discover and preserve truth. That much is obvious from the Romans. Truth? What is truth? asked a Roman general once. There are two kinds of human behaviour with which the law must deal: antisocial behaviour leading to crimes; and disputation with our neighbour. The law enables the criminal who has been antisocial to mitigate the crime; and it provides a framework of criteria within which the disputants can argue their differences. We must remember that law is not to do with truth, law is not to do with truth, law is not to do with truth.'

Jonas understood nothing of what this strange woman was muttering to herself.

Soon he could hardly hear, for now, on impulse, without warning, Margeria, still talking to herself, disappeared behind a screen to hide from whom he could not imagine, to do what he could not guess. Was her research at an end? Was she preparing to eat? To sleep? To walk out into the last of her spring? When she emerged he was stunned. It needed all his control not to cry out. This could not be the same woman. She glided from behind her screen in a long dress of plum-coloured fine velvet the cut of which seemed to follow itself rather than her body's outline. Her shape was hidden. Elegance replaced heaviness. For whom had she dressed? For whom was she humming with a new gaiety? For whom did her eyes sparkle?

Her pleasure appeared to be for herself. She cried aloud, 'Ah! To be alone and imagine the room is full only of those whom I would like to be with me. Or,' she added, as though addressing herself to a longed-for lover, 'to imagine a room of one.' She waited, expecting a response. There was none.

She sat to her meal. Alone. On a chair with a high back. Regal. Her thighs, thick though they were, gleamed healthily through the beaded cut in the sides of her plum-coloured dress. She ate slowly and, to the bewilderment of Jonas, chatted with friends on either side to whom she drank toast after toast.

'Here is to you with a head like a mushroom upon which the toad sits, may you live long. And here is to you with eyes like stars that scintillate only for me, may you shine for ever. And here is to you who have made me laugh ... and you who have kept me awake with your thoughts... and you who are so tall that you had to kneel on my floor to eat from my table... and you who, despite your fat belly, has travelled the world... and you whom I know but have never seen... friends! To you all!'

Jonas wondered who all these people could be. Especially the one she knew 'but had never seen'. Why single me out? he asked himself. She had seen none of the others. Or had she? Was the room inhabited by men invisible as he was? Or had the wine gone to her head? This was a strange woman. Jonas could understand nothing of her.

Her meal finished, she returned to her work table, prepared her parchment, sharpened her quills and sat poised, thinking. Jonas watched her thinking. He had never seen anyone sit so still, as though bound by a spell. Her eyes glazed over. Her spirit seemed to have transcended her body. Was she still part of this world? He was drawn to touch her, drawn as though what had taken possession of her was reaching out to him. He dared not. Fortunately. She stirred, like someone deep in thought whose limbs moved without conscious direction, as the onlooker pulls an earlobe, the puzzled man rubs his chin, the thinker strokes a brow. Similarly did this absorbed woman surreptitiously manoeuvre her sharp quill inside her bodice and move it gently up and down over what Jonas surmised was her nipple. It was. He could see it harden beneath her dress. Was this majestic lady contemplating the delights of law or lawless things?

Suddenly she stopped, catching herself in the act, surprised. 'What am I doing?' she asked. She looked inside her dress with mild curiosity as though something, not belonging to her, had accidentally strayed there. She laid down her quill and drew out her breast, regarding it all ways as though she had not known of its existence before. She ran her nail over the nipple and gasped with surprise as it thrust itself forward. 'Mmmm,' she muttered, curious like a scientist. She levered out the other breast for inspection, across whose dark bud she drew her nails again. Again the dark thing grew. She moved her nails round both at the same time. Round and round. Dipped her fingers in the red wine. Round and round. 'Mmmm! Mmmm!' she repeated, now no longer like a scientist. 'Would *he* know to do this? With wine-soaked fingers? Just this?'

She rose in search of something else. A copper flask. She

knelt by her fire and poured drops from its contents into the palm of her hand. The scent of it stirred young Jonas, it was his favourite – oil of seclucion, the exotic flower found only on the Phacean Islands. She rubbed it into her breasts, slowly, firmly, glistening her skin. Jonas had never seen a woman touch herself before.

She talked on. 'Could I do this before a man? Would it please me as much if I knew I was being watched?'

She moved in a way that made Jonas fear once again she was aware of his presence. She had knelt in profile, now she sat and swivelled her back to him, facing the fire, as though her next movement was one she did not want him to witness – the oiling of her legs. He could not position himself to face her – his back would be to the fire, he would burn! Besides, he would be too close to her, she would feel his breath. Could he sidle along the walls and catch her profile again? He moved. She swivelled her back to him again. Deliberately? He crept to the other side. Again she swivelled her back to him, rubbing, rubbing all the while, long oily movements up and down her calves, around her knees, her thighs and then – between. He knew but coud not see. He was tantalized, aroused.

This was not kind, not just. What was being enacted was being enacted for him. Jonas contemplated fleeing. But no! He had a duty and a future to settle. Margeria's next action ensured he could not leave. She rose to her knees again and drew down the dress to her waist. Indeed it *was* a monumental torso, and into it she rubbed seclucion oil, the aroma of which now pervaded her heated hideaway. Her caresses were firm and, like a rough man, her torso softened to her own touch. She was iridescent with strength and gentleness. A subdued Amazon herself subduing.

The Amazon closed her eyes and played fingers on the

stubs which stuck out from her breasts like eager spring boughs. Thus playing, she stepped from her dress, a marble of nakedness, and lay on her back.

'Could he ever match what my mind has the power to imagine? Would he move his fingers where I want them as I want them – the pressure just so, the rhythm just so?' She opened her legs. 'And would he know to touch here first?' She moved her nails in the hollow where thigh met mound, that mound which men cup lovingly and melt helpless upon. 'And would his finger know how sensitive was this thick skin stretching between my two holes? And would he dare to bite here on these wet lips, could he bear the strong odours, delight in the heavy old-cask taste?' With two fingers she scooped the viscid juices oozing from her cut and sucked them. 'And would his tongue find that centre of extraordinary pleasure and swim about in here, here, here? Would he dare? I dare him. Come. Out of the air, from nowhere, come. Touch me. Dare. I know hands and lips move in the space above me. I close my eyes. I see them. Face, body, limbs. Come. I dare who I cannot touch to touch me. Here is a body will bend to your wishes, answer your needs, transform itself for your pleasures. Come. You are there. I know it.' She flung back her arms and stretched, waiting. No movement answered her call. 'I will teach you,' she whispered, 'direct you.' Still nothing stirred. 'No one watches us. We can explore, you and I, do undreamt things. Come. Do not be afraid.'

Was she addressing herself? Did she believe she could force her material being to experience what it wanted, unaided, conjure sensations out of the incorporeal air? No imagination can be so powerful, Jonas reasoned. It must be *me* to whom she calls.

He gazed at the expectant flesh before him. It arched,

twisted, writhed and shimmered with oils in the fire glow. That body yearned, compelled. Dare he? He laid a hand on her belly. Margeria trembled. To feel what could not be seen, to make material her longings not in material presence but in touch, ah, that was a power to be envied. Presence would be no gain – eyes would inhibit, disturbing questions would be read in them. 'Will he? Should I? Can he? What is he feeling? What does he think? Am I pleasing? Will he please?' Margeria was distracted by no such eyes, no such questions, no such doubts. An unseen hand was upon her bare flesh. She could surrender to pure sensation.

What would the hand do next? She waited, holding her breath. It explored the roundness of her belly, defining her contours, then grabbed abruptly at her forest like a fearful thing.

'No!' she cried out. 'It is not an animal to be snared unawares. It will not run from you. Look, it stays, it waits. See how it rises to you, throbs for you.' The hand lifted. 'You were too eager, hand, too anxious.' She closed her eyes awaiting its return. She felt no touch. Coaxingly she said, 'Listen to me, hand, I will direct you. I know my body well, all its quick and tender parts. Now, tell me, hand, do you have a mouth?' Silence. 'I know you have a mouth. Make a hole with your lips. Imagine you are blowing cobwebs away.' She heard a whistling like the winds of night. 'Take my fingers, one by one, between those lips. Suck. Yes, so. Now with the nails of your other hand tear gently under the pit of my arms, yes – so. Down the sides to my hip, yes – so. And again. Yes. And again.' She opened her granite-grey eyes. Her fingers were moving through succulent air. She could not see, but certainly felt, what stroked her side. Ah, how tangible can be imagination!

'I have two sensations,' she continued. 'I need a third. I

can slide my fingers in your mouth without your help. Release your hand. Take this dark bud here, my nipple, squeeze. Yes. And pull. Yes.' She lay back enjoying the sensations, then asked, 'Do the hands and mouth belong to a body? If so, stride me.' She waited. The unseen mouth withdrew from her fingers. The caressing ceased. A weight moved over her, sank into her lap, heavy. Weight pleased her. She moved her hands over its flanks, up the sides, down to its belly, to – 'Ah! Now here's a stormy bolt from the clouds to set me on fire,' she said. 'And I will open my eyes again to look.' She did. 'I see nothing. I touch, but there is only air. I grip with my two hands a throbbing thing in space. Dare I believe in what I cannot see? Surely I would be deemed a mad woman to do that? I will let go. I will lay back. You have a tongue and three limbs. You could give me four sensations at once. I open my legs. Ease in your fiery lance. I offer you the palm of my hand. Circle it with your tongue. Spit on your finger and find my navel. Spit on another and find a nipple. Grasp my unlovely flesh. Bite where it hangs. Let your tongue explore every inch down to my toes. Take each toe in your mouth, one by one. To whom do I speak? Of whom do I ask? Am I a mad woman praying on the wind? Look, I will turn on my stomach. Find the nape of my neck, the lobes of my ears, the hollows of my shoulders. Trace the softness behind my knee. Tear down my spine, bite my sides, tongue every fold, every crease. I raise my hind to you. Pull their cheeks aside. See there a tiny crater? Pierce it with your tongue, fill it with spittle, bite and lick, finger it. Every part of me has a sense, a nerve end, a need. I turn on my back again. Here, my elbow, I shudder. Here, between fingers, I tingle. Here, beneath my eyes, I quiver. Here, and here, and here, I tremble. I am supple, see, I rise on my shoulders, my legs in the air. What do you see? White, wet juices pour from me. Drink them. They run down my cunt to the brown crater. One hole gapes, the other curls in upon itself. Moisten it with my cream, ease first with the little finger, ah! Yes! Now the middle one, ah! Yes! Yes! Now, quick, where is your prince of lightning, strike! Slowly first, slowly, slowly, now – plunge! Is that tight? Is your prince embraced? Captured? Chained? Move him, gently, oh gently. Yes. Move. Now, your hand, your hand. Your fingers in my – ah! It knows! The hand knows! But have you not two hands? Look at this. Regard, I prise it free for you. Yes. Now, prince and fingers, work! Fever! Delirium! Surrender! Everything becomes possible, imaginable, permissible...release... release...release...from the cautions of intellect...the impediments of the body...the world's demands... guilt...self-doubts...and the pain, the pain, the pain...fill me...ah, ahhh, ahhhhhhh!'

Margeria screamed, moaned and wept dry tears. Her body hung in the air, exposed to nothing, thrilled and spun about in space. Soon she heard another cry. A throat from the void. Hoarse at first, then jubilant. And into her back a long warm flow gushed and found its way to a deep and hidden home.

'All must be innocent till they are proven guilty,' she sighed as she sank back into her cushions. 'I must remember to tell the king, my father. All...must be innocent...till they are proven...guilty.'

A rug was laid over her.

'It must be the cornerstone of his law.' She was falling asleep. 'And soon, when I am recovered, I will pluck more justice from the air,' she whispered to whoever cared to listen. 'Soon. Soon...'

★

All this Jonas heard and saw about the princess Margeria, and related to me, Coaxandria, who have here ordered and interpreted and summarized for the king, and for those who will read after.

BEATRIX
- THE FIFTH OLDEST

The princess Beatrix, obsessed with time and the medicinal power of herbs, was indeed voluptuous – small, dark-eyed, high-hipped, raven-haired, deep-waisted, slender legs. A down of hair above her upper lip gave her an air of vulnerability.

Her hut was sparsely decorated – bed, table, benches and books, little else. Though when a fire burns, anywhere is cosy.

Which poems will he bring me this evening? she wondered. It was their fifth night together. She had listened to his versifications, his friends' versifications, the versifications of his friends' friends. All had followed the rules. All were dull. But she was polite. In between he read her the poetry of his favourite national poets. She could see why. Most were fine works. 'Besides,' he had said, 'the past is always easier to applaud.'

He was sophisticated, widely read, a much travelled man of the city-state's aristocracy. Around him he delighted in gathering artists and thinkers from among the city's cream.

His tastes, like his manners, were refined. He was that rare spirit who, though devoid of talent, was generous in praise of others. He had not written, nor, she guessed, would he ever write verse of lasting merit. Nevertheless she enjoyed his conversation, his enthusiasms, his gentle nature. She had a quick mind and opinions about every topic he introduced. More often than not she finished his sentences. He admired her work with medicines and hospitals, and often brought her news of fresh cures, or notes from passing Arab physicians on new methods of surgery. He was a delightful companion. Why then was she not full of pleasure at the prospect of his imminent arrival? Why did yet another evening of poetry, stimulating intellectual exchange and literary gossip fill her with impatience?

She heard the sound of a horse approaching. One horse? Or was that two? She opened her door. The two horses and riders galloped up. One alighted and embraced her, the other remained on his stallion and waited with an air trained to wait and obey.

'But what is this?' she asked anxiously. 'Are you not staying?'

'Forgive me, forgive me. I have been called by my father to a neighbouring town where he lies sick with a broken leg from a tumble. A man of panic – '

'Syrup of rockrose,' advised Beatrix.

' – coping with his days exhausts him at the best of times – '

'Juice of hornbeam,' advised Beatrix.

' – to say nothing of his state of shock – '

'Four drops from the Star of Bethlehem,' advised the princess, adding as he mounted his panting mare, 'Will I see you tomorrow night?'

He took time to answer, for his saddle had slipped and he was bending to notch and pull it up tight. He assured her he was indeed returning. And they were gone. She was alone with the unpleasant odour of horse-sweat in her nostrils, a table laden with food and drink, and no one to share it.

Well, she had her wish. She would not have to face more gossip and poetry. But what in its place? She hated changed plans. Time was precious. She had watched those terminal in her hospitals. In their pain they shared a common distress for time-lost-time-wasted which she recognized in the resignation of their dying eyes. Time was short. They all clutched at every last moment granted them.

She became restless and applied her mind to how the hours could be filled. Read? No, that was not her humour. Visit her sisters? That would be indiscreet. Go to the town where people meet, seek other companions? Tempting but – the prospect of finding no one to suit her mood filled her with dread.

What *was* her mood? She could not describe it. She was so used to her nights being occupied that to be companionless, without aim, was disorientating. Finding herself alone created a strange mixture of loneliness and excitement. The emptiness held promise. A void can be filled. With what? By whom? Idle thoughts. It was past midnight. Their huts were isolated. Nothing could happen, no one would come.

She looked at her array of foods. Each night's spread had been carefully planned. Over twelve nights no dish was repeated. She picked at the pickles, and rolled a slice of cured ox tongue, which she slowly nibbled. In one long swill, out of a bravado which came from she knew not where, she drank a glass of wine, hiccuped, and giggled.

What of the outside? She had never explored outside her hut for new or rare herbs. How thoughtless of her, she thought. Irresponsible. See how love is selfish? Whereupon she immediately reached for a lantern, covered her shoulders with a shawl, for this September night blew cool, and stepped naughtily into the night air.

How bizarre – dressed in her long, thin dress, holding high a lantern, looking for medicines in the night. Little could be discerned, each growth threw shadows upon the other, till – merciful heavens! There! White popernia! She gasped. Of the wild, purple variety known as the cornrose, she had stores plenty, but their uses were limited. The white popernia, difficult to grow in the soils around the palace, possessed a greater variety of application. Her last patch had been destroyed by blight from the elpha fly. How had these arrived here? What wind from where? Such a small cluster. Perhaps they had been planted secretly by someone for safekeeping? She carefully scraped away the surrounding earth and gathered them. Lunar herb, herb of the moon. Of the heads and seeds she would make a syrup to procure sleep for the sick.

Inside the hut she set some seeds to dry by the fire, crushed them, boiled the seed dust in water until one third of the water was left, which she then mixed with honey. The process took two hours and so excited her that despite the late o'clock she felt as awake as leaping salmon – just the right patient to sample the sweet sedative for sweet sleep.

Sweet sleep came not! Instead the oddest sensation: she felt a rein on the speed of her life, as though she had been hurtling through space but now her body floated. She watched her arm as it reached in a languorous arc for the water she craved to dilute the sweet taste in her mouth. She could feel her mouth, a cavern slowly opening to receive a liquid that slowly slowly coursed down her throat like an endless thick stream. Time, her oppressor, lifted and drifted away. She experienced the interior of her nocturnal retreat as a new place, divided very distinctly into colours and shapes. What she had contrived to be a sparse room was now alive with a myriad of shades and contours. She felt hungry. With a vague air of contemplation, she began to eat. Food had never tasted this way. Each taste was entirely itself. Each bitten victual splashed its own juice, slow explosions of glutinous texture, in her mouth. And aroma! She could slice the air into divisions of smell. Extraordinary! And when there returned the clop of a horse's hoofs again, the sound rose like thunder through her floors.

He was returning. Thank God! His father's accident could not have been that grave. The manservant had been left to help him safely home. This sound of life finally persuaded her that she had no taste for solitude. The prospect of poetry for a fifth evening caused her no consternation. She would view him as freshly as she now viewed the world around her, and in her present state his poetry would resonate with new meanings. She was surprised to discover how relieved she was.

Curled up by the fire, she awaited his breathless good nature through the door. Instead came a knock. She called, 'Enter.' The door opened. The huge figure of the man-servant loomed in the doorway. Outside she could see his stallion breathing furiously and steaming with sweat. He had been driven hard. The man handed her a note. It read:

I felt guilty leaving you unguarded. Here is my man. He will sit outside till dawn. Feed him. Do not engage him in conversation. His strength lies in muscle not intellect. Forgive his surly looks. He is utterly trustworthy.

Normally she would have acted at once – risen, been

civil, fed him, requested his needs as she had requested the needs of so many in her hospices. But her natural instincts were as slippered as her natural movements and, unnervingly, everything was magnified. She registered with alarm his huge moustached and bearded face. Stern eyes pierced into her with brute indifference, lifeless without purpose. What was her sensitive lover doing with such an uncouth manservant? She would ask him next night.

She floated up to a standing position and slowly reached to offer him a plate of savoury pancakes. He snatched them from her fiercely with a grunt she assumed implied thank you. She watched him eat, fascinated. Surprise made her mute. He was a figure some six feet tall and appeared – she could think of no other word – constructed. There was a torso, massive legs locked into it, two thick arms hung on shoulders, and two heavy hands plunged into arms. Before her was more a piece of machinery than a human being.

And as a piece of machinery he behaved with the hard indifference of iron. She did not exist for him, doubtless because he was reared knowing that he did not exist for such as her. To be so powerfully dismissed out of existence was both a new and, to her surprise, not uninteresting experience.

She drifted away from him to the door. Outside, the poor animal, a black Arab stud, was wildly pulling at its reins tied to the low bough of a tree, steam rising from its wet skin. She took off her shawl and slowly wiped dry the stud's back. Every so often she looked into the hut. The brute gorged on, ignoring her. It made her smile. She was not certain why.

Beatrix was not equinity-bent. Not that she was afraid of the beasts, she sensed merely that she would look absurd perched upon one. Founding hospitals was what she most enjoyed, tending to an animal in need.

At first the stallion's eyes had glared fearfully at her. He had jerked backwards, his curled nostrils flaring. But she had learned this of the horse: that if you blew into its nostrils it would become your friend for life. Gradually, under her firm strokes, her reassuring bedside voice, her gentle blowing, he becalmed. His breathing eased and he allowed his tight steaming skin to be rubbed dry that he might avoid catching chill. The animal's smell no longer displeased the princess. Instead there arose comfort from its heavy odour, an odour she linked to the power emanating from his impressive bulk. Odour, power, his trust in her all mingled and expanded into a portentousness she was, in her dreamy state, powerless to interpret. She hugged his head with sudden affection and kissed his long, black nose. The relieved animal nudged into her armpits, inhaling her own body's heavy odour, returning her embrace. The foam from his lips soaked through. The damp he left was not unpleasant.

Their trust and friendship struck, she continued rubbing him down. His sturdy chest, his forelegs, the curve under his belly. By now her shawl was saturated. There remained his posterior and hind legs. Without a second thought she reached under her dress and drew down a rough underslip. Though the night was cold, she had become immune to sensations of heat and chill. Besides, she would soon be inside. With this fresh cloth she stooped to dry the black beast's hind legs. And there she froze.

Had she not been hardened by awful sights of the sick and maimed she would have blushed. Hanging from a black pouch, uncertain whether to remain in or hang out, was the stallion's lance, limp now but waiting for the right cause to stir it into battle. Its meatiness riveted her. The upper part was dark, below was a broad band of pink flesh, then dark at the knob again. She felt an urge to grasp it in her hand and was at once ashamed. Nevertheless she could not tear her gaze away. Every detail of the massive bough intrigued her. Its bumps, its freckles, its treacly moisture, its hovering motion in and out of its pouch. It was impossible not to contemplate the sensation of such an eager engine inside her.

'Wanting that in you, are you?'

Princess Beatrix involuntarily screamed at the voice. The stallion bucked and neighed. She stood and faced the insolent hulk standing in the doorway. It was the first time she had seen any sign of recognizable life in him. Brief, however, for his mocking face returned inside to resume gluttonizing itself. He was as little interested in her answer as in the question he had asked. Thus there was nothing lewd in the tone of his voice. He had made a primitive connection between two objects before him, as food was there to be eaten, a command to be obeyed, a horse to be ridden.

She was angry, though. An emotion alien to her. Regal authority gathered its wit and rose to its proper height. She entered the hut, stood by the flames shivering from ire, chill, the aftermath of honeyed popernia and the heady sensations of her equinal encounter. She ordered, 'When you have finished, take a palliasse and covering to sleep outside. You will find a trough to the rear of the hut within which you can lie. It is a warm spot.'

Nothing in her voice touched him, however. His being existed beyond her reach. But whereas before neither of them had existed for the other, now something of her existed for him. What was he staring at? Not her face but her body, as though seeing through and beyond it. It was some seconds before she realized – her body's outline could be seen through her dress as she stood before the penetrating flames.

There, for some intense moments, they faced one another, each absorbing what of the other's senses they could. She perceived that he had no intimation of her as a being of authority, intelligence or feeling; and, because it was through people's eyes that she understood their intentions, she saw that none animated him. Pure appetite stood before her. His body had no concern for itself, as his gaze had no concern for her humanity, as his insolence had none for its consequence. She existed for him at a level hitherto unknown to her. The more he stared, the more she felt drained of all she was. It was extraordinary to be rendered so unfamiliar to herself. He was dismantling her, every thought, opinion, judgement, response, instinct, every nut and bolt of her identity. And, here was the unique sensation, with them went responsibility for all those things as she bathed in the luxury of helplessness. Before, she had floated filled with popernia but had been still *with* herself; now she felt light as a sucked-out egg, frail as its empty shell. It made her smile again. She was still not certain why, but remembered what an old patient had once said: 'I am happy to be ill. So many years of decisions. Now I am required to make none.'

Was the princess Beatrix ill? She knew only that she was in the presence of a man with whom none of the normal exchanges needed to be made, from whom no subtlety was forthcoming. There would be no explanation, no accounting, no bitterness, recrimination, disappointment. Nothing. That frail, empty eggshell could be filled, painted, split open, gorged upon or thrown away. Was this to be ill? Ill or no, decisions were not required of her. All was decided. Suddenly she was overwhelmed by his smell, an aroma heavy with indifference. It made her dizzy. She fell forward in a faint. He caught her.

She remembered these things: that he lifted her as though she were gossamer, that she was deeper into his body's smell, that he laid her on the bed, covered her, and that he had waited. For a long time. She must have slept a little. When she opened her eyes he was gone.

Again she was irritated, but for a different reason – his obedience to his master was complete. She rose from her covers. The air was filled with his odour. It reminded her of him. His image returned. Idly she dipped a finger into the honeyed popernia and sucked. At once the medicine mingled with what had been syruped before. She was afloat. Picking up the plate of preposterous properties, and covering herself against the night air, she glided out, driven by a singular intention. Nothing restrained her.

The servant had not taken her advice where to sleep but had bedded down beside his stallion, preferring his Arab animal's warmth to the earth's. The beast opened its eyes, alert at once. They immediately closed – it was his friend. She knelt and offered him some honeyed popernia. He licked her palm with slow affection. The rough tongue comforted her. She unlaced her bodice and on to her breast smeared more. The grateful beast licked again, this time his rough tongue rubbed her nipple. It gave her the pleasure she had anticipated. She did the same with her other breast.

With the syrup inside him, the stallion made strange whining sounds which awoke the servant, who sat up and understood within seconds what was happening. Was that a mocking grin he grinned? It could not be. Mockery revealed an ability to assess, evaluate. This man could only connect. And yet unmistakably a sort of cruel mockery enlivened his eyes. The royal princess answered his mockery, if that is what it was, with a steady gaze as she cupped her breast to the beast's mouth. At the same time she coated her fingers with more honey and offered them to the servant. He took her hand in his and roughly licked them dry. The horse, finding no more honey, bit her for attention. She jumped. It shied and tried to stand. It could not. His grey eyes clouded over surrendering to his state.

The servant rose. His movements had no elegance – how could they have? He was an awkward machine, abrupt with decision. Here was a situation he fully understood, here were connections he could make. But the honey slowed him down. She smiled at his momentary confusion. He moved to her as a man in a dream, she watching him all the while, her eyes fixed on his face looking for its intention. His features revealed nothing. He bent down, roughly pulled her dress from beneath her knees, parted her kneeling legs, took a handful of honey and rubbed it like ointment up into her swollen cut. She thrilled to his rough touch and when he understood her pleasure he unflapped his trouser to reveal a phallus as fearsomely hung as his prone beast's. She stared excited and awed as he rubbed honey on that too and with a laugh pulled her face towards it.

The stallion beside her, had he been in his normal state, would have risen. Instead he lay stupefied and content to watch her imitate him on all fours, her honeyed rump turned towards his languid head, her mouth locked on to the other stud's –

'I call it my 'nasty'', he said as a statement of fact. 'I have sweetened my nasty and sweetened your slash, now we can both be licked dry as ashes and dust and dust and ashes and cracked and crushed...' He made no sense, rather he seemed to enjoy the brutal sound the words made, stuttering on the crest of his brutal excitement.

The hot breath of a dazed animal filtered between her thighs where he dozily, rhythmically licked. She grasped the servant's honeyed 'nasty' to steady herself from the stallion's awesomely rousing rough tongue. It was of a thickness she could barely curl her hands around. The princess who loved poetry and intellectual conversation hugged the ground on all fours and prepared to do what she had not done before. Never had she seen so huge a weapon. She was not even certain her small mouth could enfold it. He gave her no time to wonder. He pulled her hair so that she opened in pain her mouth, into which he thrust his monstrous meal.

The two sensations were extreme. One soft and uncertain from the stupefied beast at her rear, exciting beyond anything she had before experienced; the other warm, hard and supremely pleasing. Her ecstasy was soon over. The servant wailed loud like a soul lost in this bewildering and unjust life while she screamed a muffled scream as into her mouth a hot bitter fountain jetted – for an eternity it seemed. She gulped and swallowed and sucked to draw more and more, every last drop he had, and even when she knew all was drawn she would not let go. He had to jerk her head away before he could withdraw and then, howling at the loss of his molten pride, he collapsed in a heap, whimpering, defeated. She watched him, not without some harsh satisfaction, as she turned her back and raised her haunches to allow the beast ample room for his tongue's gyrations. She wanted more of that too. But even he had tired. Both beast and master lay in a heap together, their pantings and moanings not dissimilar. The princess smiled, but now knew why.

All this Jonas heard and saw about the princess Beatrix. and related to me, Coaxandria, who have here ordered and interpreted and summarized for the king, and for those who will read after.

LITICIA
- THE FOURTH OLDEST

Liticia, who cared for the poor, had said to the king her father, 'The hours of light are for you, the dark hours are my own.'

It was no surprise, then, that her cottage was painted in dark colours, like shadows, and the carpets on her walls were woven of sombre hues. She moved in her space slowly, deliberately, as though each movement in life was to be savoured, each moment a lifetime to be lived. As the night approached, her mood and manner changed; her body tensed with expectation. On her face the flicker of a smile, in her heart the excitement of a plan, in her head the details.

The cottage was traditional. Three huge oak beams lay on the stone walls, horizontal with the fireplace. Narrower lengths of oak were mortised at right angles into them. The roof was thatched. Heavy dark-brown cloths covered the windows. Thick rugs, russet-dyed, softened the stone-flagged floors.

Into the middle beam had been hammered four iron

staples from which hung dark-grey lengths of rope. On each side wall at floor level, and in the centre of the floor, between the flagstones, were another four staples, to which were attached more lengths. Not one object of furniture decked the room. It seemed full yet was bare. Except for the rope. Liticia was happy with her nocturnal abode.

There was a knock on the door. Her two elder sisters, Dionis and Meliora, story-teller and diplomat, stood before her, dressed as she was in men's attire, all black. She urged them in swiftly.

'Do you have the herb from Beatrix?' she asked.

Meliora drew from a pocket two sachets and a small phial of water. 'Breathe,' she said, placing a sachet beneath Liticia's nose. 'But not too deeply.'

Her sister did so. The powerful sarcotic scent drove her eyes upwards.

'The effect is increased tenfold when saturated by water,' Dionis said. 'They will pass into another world for an hour at least.'

'And the wagon?' asked Liticia.

'Outside.' Dionis laughed. 'Oh, what a story I will make of this.'

'Does your spoilt aristocrat know?' asked Meliora.

'Nothing,' replied Liticia. 'I told him that tonight I wished to rest and that he must pass the evening drinking with his lumpen friend.'

'And is he the friend you want?' asked the oldest princess.

'Both,' whispered Liticia with a vague smile, 'here.' She pointed to the ropes. 'Helpless.'

'And she,' said Meliora, 'is the quietest of us all.'

'The one who works night and day tending the old.'

'How she ministers to them...'

'Bathes them, brings them food…'

'Ensures they have wood for fires…'

'Tolerates their smells, and complaints…'

'Like a saint,' said Meliora. 'I could not do that, confront the aged day after day and constantly be reminded of that time which must come to us all.'

'A time which is never far away,' added Liticia. 'So let us not waste *now* reflecting on *then*.'

One last article of clothing remained to be worn, a black hood with holes for eyes and mouth. They covered their heads. Three shadows glided into the shadows of the night, pulling with them a trundle on wheels.

The forest was known to the sisters. How could it not be? No crack or whine or flutter of wings disturbed them. That which is familiar is friendly. Soon they arrived near to the town via a path along which only the brave knowing no fear dared travel in order to reach an inn deep in the forest. Along it were expected the young man of Liticia's nights and his young friend. The princesses tied a length of rope to a tree on one side of the path. Liticia hauled it across and hid behind another, grasping its end in her hand. Dionis and Meliora stood hidden nearby, a sachet each in their hands. They had calculated the hour. The men would come soon.

'What if they trip and rise quickly before we can be upon them with our sarcotics?' asked Dionis.

'Then we will laugh loudly, step out and cry, 'Women of the night", and embrace them first with kisses then with sarcosia.'

There was no need to worry. Their nights were charmed. All went as planned. The two startled young men not only fell upon the rope but into each other's arms, which confused them further and made them easy for smothering to sleep. How the princesses laughed as they puffed and trundled the heavy gallants to their resting place: strung between dark-grey ropes, a pair to their wrists and another to their ankles. Dionis, being the story-teller, was the one best able to imitate the surprised faces of their captives.

'Poor things,' she said as they tied black lengths of wool to blindfold the lolling heads of the suspended pair.

'Poor?' queried Liticia, not without a hint of quiet lasciviousness. 'Why do you think them deserving of pity? They hang there for their pleasures.'

'But none *they* have requested,' Meliora pointed out.

'Therein lies *my* pleasure. To take from them what they may not wish to give but are powerless to deny.'

'Their helplessness is your pleasure?' asked Dionis.

'In part. And their anger. But I am curious too. I wish to discover if their helplessness is also *their* pleasure. If it is not, then I can turn their anger to – use.' Liticia was enigmatic.

'May it prove to be what you desire,' said the eldest.

'Be satisfied,' said Dionis.

They embraced Liticia and left.

Liticia changed her garments. From a corner of the room where lay a bundle of clothes she withdrew a long kimono of blue and wrapped herself in it. The dying fire needed more wood. Three goblets had been prepared into which she poured dark-red wine. She checked the dishes of foods lined up on the floor, turned the wicks higher in their lamps, and sat, her back to the wall, her knees drawn up to her chin, sipping wine, contemplating the two young men, a gentle, unfathomable smile on her face. Muddy leaves hung from them as they hung from ropes. She awaited patiently their return from sarcotic sleep.

Out from which they slowly rose like mists from the sea to break upon a sort of daylight with starts and cries, pullings and peeks, and demands to know where they were and who was there. They heard only each other's voice.

'You?'

'You?'

'Untie me.'

'I cannot. They have tied me, too.'

'Where are we?

'I do not know, and yet – ' it was the lover – 'I smell familiar smells. As though I had spent my childhood here.'

'Is there someone else in the room or are we alone?' asked the friend, whose name was Martin.

'Ssh! Let us listen,' replied the lover, whose name was Kindred.

Liticia held her breath. They heard nothing.

'How did it happen?' asked Martin.

'They fell upon us. A half-dozen or so.'

'For what motive?'

'I fear we shall soon know.'

It was time, thought Liticia. She rose.

'They are coming,' cried Martin. 'Who is there? Kindred! They are coming to me. I am to be slain. Kindred!' he screamed.

Liticia's hand gently touched his face. She traced a finger down the left side of his cheek, round his ear into the nape of his neck, where she circled some, and stopped. Martin uttered his friend's name again, a thousand times softer, and now as a question.

'Kindred?'

'Martin?' whispered Kindred. 'Are you still with me? Are you in pain? What cruel thing is it they do to you? Martin? Speak to me.'

But Martin made no sound, for soft lips were kissing him.

'Martin? Martin? Oh, my God, Martin!'

Kindred imagined his friend was dead. Or if not dead, then dying. Or soon dead. He heard a ripping sound, signalling to him that his friend's shirt had been torn apart at the breast in preparation for the knife.

Martin felt his shirt torn apart and pulled down over his shoulders to his waist signalling he was being prepared for the knife. First the kiss of death and now the knife of death. He felt cool breath upon his skin. He shuddered. Ah! This is cruelty, he thought. He dared not breathe. His teeth clenched in anticipation of the painful thrust. His heart was breaking with the pointlessness of it all. His head reeled, thought tripped over thought in an effort to understand. But no knife plunged. What happened instead was hardly to be believed. The finger that had traced his cheek now traced the curve of his right breast, slowly; a smooth cold finger, each circle diminishing in size and moving in towards a nipple which stiffened even before it was touched. When it was touched he moaned.

Kindred, thinking it was his friend's dying gasp, said, 'There has been no greater pain in my life than now, now that I am unable to reach out my arms to comfort you.'

But his friend's moan became a sigh of pleasure and his friend's reply amazed him.

'I do not think it is your comfort I am in need of. Your explanations perhaps.' And he moaned again, for now another finger, this time slippery and wet, was circling his other breast. Soon two slithery fingers circled both breasts and teased two nipples at their tips. His moan broke into gasps.

'They do not murder you,' cried Kindred, 'they torture you!'

'Yes,' replied Martin with that edge of complaint to his

voice which could arise from either pain or ecstasy. 'It is a
kind of…' He was stopped by two tender fingers pressed
against his lips, a silencing touch which at last reassured
him. Fear vanished. Perplexed curiosity took its place.

'Martin,' cried a terrified Kindred. 'Are you gone? Am I
to be next?'

The answer came at once. Two hands ripped apart his
shirt. His time had come. 'Our father which art in
heaven…' He began to recite the Lord's Prayer.

Here was a body she knew well, one that needed to be
touched first at the back. A knife cut everything away. The
knife's tip was drawn down his spine.

'Cruel! Cruel!' he cried. 'Plunge if you must, plunge!
Why taunt me with steel?'

Her fingers probed the soft centres of his spine and sides.
Silence. Neither man knew what to say. Liticia had
difficulty in suppressing laughter. Two naked torsos before
her. Suspended. Hers to play upon. She moved over both at
the same time, closing her eyes the better to feel their
different textures, to smell their different odours. Now she
was behind them, caressing their backs, their necks, their
ears; now she was in front of them, pulling at nipples,
cupping breasts, squeezing, tearing at skin. Weals rose on
their bodies. She had to restrain herself. Gently, gently. How
easy it was to abuse power.

Liticia drank more wine and stepped back the better to
look at them. What fine torsos they were. One light-
skinned and hairless. That one she had sucked and bitten
many times. The other, Martin's, was darker and – it was
this that gave her unexpected pleasure – covered with a
mass of black curls forming patterns as though a
woodcarver had indulged his delight. She was breathing
heavily, like a runner. The men said nothing. From suspense

or embarrassment? She could not decide. I will give them cause to be embarrassed, she thought, and ripped down their codpieces, leaving two surprised phalluses to fall and droop in shame, as though, once hopefully hidden, they now had been found out.

Here was a sight to be relished. There the lads hung, well-hung. She gazed and gazed. And wondered – if she stared at them, would they rise? If she concentrated, would she induce, by osmosis, their recrudescence? Or would exposure to air, mere nakedness, be sufficient to rouse their shy, sly heads? Can the body's sensual proclivities overcome the soul's little shames? Nothing happened. What could she do? She sat to contain her beating heart. What could she *not* do! Images came to her. She breathed deeply. Excitement affected her like asthma, and she parted her knees as though needing to breathe between them. Oh, if they were not blindfolded what would they see now. She closed her eyes, instinctively clasping her hands between her legs. How wet she was! Her fingers wriggled between creamed labia. She wondered – what was the cream's taste? She tried to identify it. She licked her fingers. Slightly bitter, not unpleasant, like the body's healing herb made into balm. But there are tastes, smells, conditions which metaphor fails to illuminate. They are simply themselves. So much so that they *become* metaphors, unable to serve any other function, occupying a pure, lofty position in the linguistic order.

She pondered an idea. Creaming both hands, she rose to her manacled men and rubbed her balm into their breasts, massaging her juices deep into their skin, reaching down again and again to replenish her fingers with the pungent lubricant. She offered her odour to their nostrils. They stiffened, writhed a little, groaned. Then stopped abruptly on hearing the other's sound. Why has my friend groaned the same groan I have groaned? They were perplexed. In darkness little can be assembled. And whose was the third groan? A greedy groan. It was greedy Liticia, who, like a child in a fit of generosity that had given away more of its honeycomb than it had intended and had regretted its hasty gesture, was licking her own effusion, fearful its springs would dry up. Satiated, she withdrew to wash one nectar down with another, and waited by the wall for her excitement to subside.

In the silence that followed, Kindred's slow memory slowly shaped itself. The smells of the room, the odour in his nostrils, the meandering touch on his skin, all took shape in his consciousness.

'Liticia?' his voice croaked.

'Liticia?' echoed his friend. 'Who is Liticia, for God's sake?'

'Do you feel you are being caressed by a woman?' asked Kindred.

'*Feel*?' replied his see-sawed friend. 'I *know*!'

'Liticia?' called a cautious Kindred once more.

There was no response. Instead he felt two oily hands clasp and pull at his prince of parts.

'No! he cried. 'Stop!' he cried. 'Who are you?' he cried.

To no avail. He wriggled, he swayed, he quivered. He thrust forward, attempting to bite what he thought might be before him but was not. He snapped at air. The pulling persisted.

'Have you no shame?' his voice trembled. 'No pity for *my* shame?' his voice quaked.

No being responded, except the bent being between his legs, which unbent like offended youth happy to defend the slightest slight, slighted or not. The sensation was one he had never experienced: his royal member had leapt to act but *he* was shackled! His legs were apart and bound, his arms raised and roped, while his thing, his thong, his far-flung fancy threateningly thrust at nothing and no one in mid-air. Here was power and powerlessness! A warrior armed with a mighty sword impotent before enemies! The oil of pithicon rose to his nostrils. The pulling ceased. He slumped in his spun, jute chains. Not for long, oh not for long, for lips now lapped at the exposed warrior and a tongue searched, found and stung with kisses his pissing niche wherein is hid a powder keg of explosive pleasure.

Kindred exploded. In sound. In sound so loud with strange agonies that his abandoned, dangling friend, Martin, became alarmed.

'Is this it?' he called fearfully. 'Has it all been a sweet misleading preparation for death?'

'Death?' His friend's voice emerged as a yodel. 'Death? Oh, yes. This *is* a kind of dying. Lord save us, we are in the hands of a plundering – aaaaah! – mad oooooh! – witch – aayeeeee! I can promise you nothing but turbulence and delirium.'

Nails scratched the length of his chest, up and down. He moved, despite himself, in and out between lips formed as a velvet orifice for his battering-ram. Deeper and deeper it battered until he felt a throat. Unexplored territory! Too much to bear. Too bare to control. Ahhhhh! and oooooh! and ayeeeee! and mmmmm! and mmmmmmmm! and mmmmmmmmmmmmmmmm!

Liticia received what she had sucked hard to win – the warm and acrid taste of a spent man. The flow of it against the roof of her mouth seemed endless. She had never milked so much from her lover. It splashed her lips, her face, her eyes. Each time that she sucked more, more came. She could not swallow fast enough. And like the discoverer of hidden treasure, she screamed her delight. Mmmmm, mmmmmmmm, mmmmmmmm, mmmm mmmmmmmm mmmmmmmm, until the spending was spent and the mmming had mmmed away to silence.

Kindred whimpered. He felt like a virgin who had been forced to surrender what she most cherished to someone she cherished not. A soothing hand was upon his cheek, a cup raised to his lips. He drank. Wine. Warm, comforting, burning, revivifying. Lips kissed him. He recognized them. He wanted to exclaim 'Liticia'. Lips kissed him again to secrecy. A voice whispered in his ear, 'I will release you soon.'

Liticia needed to rest. She sat once more on her haunches by the fire. She perspired. Unconsciously, she wiped a hand beneath her armpit, brought it to her snub nose. It was not unpleasant. She tried to identify the quality of the odour. Here was another of those experiences which could be compared to nothing else. Sweat was itself, not comparable *with* but compared *to*. And because it was itself, it was lifelong, to be lived with daily, reassuring because it was familiar, because it resulted from effort. The body's breath, evidence of endeavour. She was happy to sweat.

But this other fine fellow, what was to be done with him? With Kindred after his 'dismal flounderings' she had tossed and turned at his side, stirred by 'such other things I would do and have done'. Was she not doing them now? Not all. There had been a hidden part she had wanted to explore with him. He had not permitted. Regal though she was, there had been wishes she respected. But now? Who was in control now? She closed her eyes. A certain image took shape, intoxicating, irresistible.

To pursue her dark longing, this swarthy lad needed to be denuded. Ignoring his protests, she firmly ripped apart hosen and shoon. Now, here was a well-thighed man. Naked! Captive! Hers! She marvelled as her hand moved proprietorially around thick-muscled legs. Was that slumbering land-lubber throbbing in its sleep? She caressed and squeezed, she kissed and bit. It leapt a little here, then there. She smiled. Later! Later! She would soon attend to this ripening spike. There was elsewhere she wished to wander and wonder.

Martin was a simple soul. Very little on this earth signified great meanings to him. He was here to work, be a companionable and available companion to his friends, an obliging neighbour to those in need of him, a dutiful son. There were only these three things in life: duty, work, pleasure. And pleasure was not to be defined. It defined itself, was at this very moment defining itself for all it was worth.

'Kindred!' he cried out. 'I must speak. You must speak. Someone must say something, for what is happening cannot continue in silence. Aaaaah! Nothing like this has happened before. Aaaaah!' and, 'Oooooh! I stand helpless. Strung helpless. I do not know if a woman touches me or a boy or a spirit. Aaaaah! Aaaaah!' and, 'Oooooh! Are we to die, Kindred? Is this the way we are to end our days? In blindness? Understanding nothing? Oooooh!' and, 'Ayeeeee!' and, 'Ahahahahah! Do you understand any of what is happening, what is going to happen? Oh, noooooeee! My merciful heavens, oooooh, ooooooooh, ooooooooooooh!' His 'oooooohs' sounded unnaturally feminine to himself

No wonder. Hands had prodded a path down his back and now, the unimaginable! His firm flanks were being prised apart and he could feel hot breath going into that whorl from whence hot breath normally comes out! And following the breath — a tongue. His friend spoke at last, strangely tired and resigned.

'Martin,' he sighed. 'Martin, fear not. Surrender. All things are explained in time, and in time can be avenged.'

Martin surrendered. Here was a touching of a spot untouched before and — caution flew out with the fire's smoke — it was not that unimaginable. It was even acceptable. He found himself pushing out those fine flanks, the better to be approached, entered. Fine flanks, thought Liticia as she circled the tip of her tongue on the faintly farted-upon font. She did not mind. The taste was soon lost in her saliva. Inebriating, dizzying. To be so close to such private functions increased her abandon. She drove her tongue into the tight, resisting cavity with greater vigour. The more it resisted the more urgent her thrusts. The orifice clenched. She must be gentler. She reached between her legs for lubricant and fingered him softly. He relaxed. The learning lad unclenched as he felt a finger find his hidden hole. In it went, and out, and in again, and out, and further in, and further in. Liticia remained inside for many minutes thinking — how comfortable it feels, warm and tight and cosy. Another palm crept beneath his bundle of twins. The palm moved. The palm moved up. The palm fondled. The palm stroked. The palm found oooooh and aaaaah and ayeeeee and mmmmmmmmmmmm.

But the roped male, billowing in and out like a sail battered by a frenzied wind, protested. Put to a severe test, even simple souls will reach at least one moment of perception more complex than the sum of their parts. As Liticia played and plagued the now willing boy's body, the willing boy called out.

'This boy is a willing boy, but is he to be sucked upon like dead meat? Is he to be made ecstatic strung up in air?

Are his affections to be boiled out? Vaporized? Will you play music upon him and not permit him to sing his own song? Where is the loveliness of love? Where are your lips? At least your lips. Without lips all is barbaric!'

The not-so-young princess who tended the poor and the old understood at once. Passion was an arid experience without that one contact which made humans human – the kiss. The kiss, which began life as a nose smelling skin two thousand years before the birth of our Lord in the land they called Indie; the kiss, the key to paradise, said the Greeks; the kiss, the kiss, the young man wanted her kisses to tell him all was not bleak. She loved him in that instant, and forgave him everything. Hoisting her robe she moved round to face him.

Martin felt these things: lips and lips heaping kisses; the soft flesh of female parts pressing, gyrating; his Lord of Hosts rising; his heart beating; another heart beating; two arms around his neck; a body raising itself; two legs around his hips, and then, ah then ,a long luscious cavity sliding like a sly guest to his host, back and forth, back and forth, a tight rocking of his ample generosity, accepted, taken in, fussed over, devoured. How he moaned, gratefully kissed, and offered up his gifts like any good host.

Liticia was a delirious child again, swinging on her royal swings, pulling on the ropes to rise higher and higher. Now she could cry out, 'Come to me, fettered hawk. No honey boy or mother's pride now. Here is your true home. In you go. In, in, in you go. Your talon, in. Take wing. Imagine that you have a princess riding you this night. A royal cunt has clasped your thighs. The years fly faster than the wind. Soon we will be God's dust at his feet. I have a fire burning me. Quell it! Where are your rains. Give me your storm. Storm hawk caught in a high wind. Here! Here! In here!'

He came like a long scream. She felt his beak swoop into her, piercing her skin. Oh, how he came, with a vengeance for his helplessness. Bleeding his seed. Spilled seed. Lost seed. Lost. Lost.

Liticia returned to her squatting place by the fire, exhausted and dissatisfied.

That was him. That was them both. Now what for herself?

She drank wine and quietly regarded the forlorn young strung men before her. Limp they were. Defeated things. Ravished, drained, depleted things. Should she lower them? Feed and succour them? Nurse their raped prides? Offer them the chance to retaliate? Render herself helpless to their mercy? Suddenly she asked, 'Are you afflicted with obsession?'

'For God's sake, Liticia,' said Kindred, 'unbind us. You have had your pleasure and – '

'Not you, yours?'

'We feel foolish.'

'And hungry.' Poor Martin.

'And stripped of your power?'

'And stripped. It is not fair. Not sense. What was there for you? What purpose was satisfied?'

'Did you not enjoy helplessness?'

'Who in his right mind would enjoy that?' asked an amazed Martin.

She realized she could not discourse with them. Here were unsubtle minds, possessing no true strengths, incapable of perceiving the joy of surrender. *They* must hold on at all costs. Maintain control. Direct their fortunes and the fortunes of their neighbours. Helplessness was anathema in the vocabulary of their narrow lives.

'I will unbind your eyes,' she decided.

They regarded the exhilarated woman before them, wondering what devil had taken possession of her. They looked at one another and each blushed for their ripped, naked condition.

Liticia smiled. 'I cannot unbind you completely yet. I fear you may be too angry with me. I want to soften your tempers. Hungry, you say? I will feed you.'

And there, as they hung between beams, she broke off legs of duck roasted in honey and offered it to their wrenching teeth; she fed them sliced chicken stuffed with pork and veal, boiled in white wine and brandy, seasoned with garlic and parsley, coated in jelly. The jelly she smeared on their lips with her fingers. There were cabbage sweet and sour; artichokes stewed in oil; carrots in hot cream; dumplings of yeast, flour and sugar; quince marmalade on Turkish bread; syllabub based in Rhenish hock and spiced with mace and rosemary; chestnuts boiled in claret and mashed with cream, and all washed down with wines they had never before tasted. As she fed them she talked.

'The only obsession from which I suffer is ageing. Some people find themselves able to imagine life within the skins of animals. Not me. They know, with fine imagination, what it feels like to have four legs and be mute; to have no legs or arms and be earthed ineluctably to surfaces; to be in flight suspended on the wind, surveyors of vast landscapes which are theirs to swoop down upon for prey. They are obsessed with what barks, purrs, slithers, flies, crawls, gallops, swims or roars, and they make of them passionate pets. Not me. Age obsesses me. I had no inclination to lose myself as a cat but from childhood I could creep into and know what it would be like to live within decrepit skins. As I grew tall and strong, I could sense the ache of joints; as I delighted in my body's powers, I felt intimations of failing sight; as I marvelled at my suppleness, dexterity, mobility, as I ran races with my sisters, as I thrilled to energetic games of bat and ball, swam, skipped, leapt, danced – in all *that* I could feel the oncoming stoop, the hobble, the pitiful dependency of diminished powers. In the years of my blossoming I was ageing; at the height of my fervent, youthful energies I could feel the pain and humiliation of decline. It was like a curse upon me. There!' She had fed them their last tart, quenched their last thirst, wiped away their last crumb. 'All has been done for you. It will never happen again. Be grateful. Am I forgiven?'

'Liticia,' Kindred said, 'none of this was necessary.'

'You mean you would have brought your friend at my request? Allowed me to bind you at my request? Relinquished your command at my command? Submitted to my will? Two men? Together? Side by side?' She ridiculed them.

'And now what?' asked Martin. 'My arms ache. These ropes bite into me. What more do you want of us?'

They had understood nothing of what she had confided in them.

She made no reply, simply stoked up the fire, returned to her place by the side of it and sat with delicious omnipotence watching their eyes widen with incredulity as she raised her knees and opened her legs, exposing to them what she seemed unaware of possessing. Her grey-blue eyes roamed lazily around the bare room as though her thoughts were lightly stuck to walls from where she plucked them.

'And so,' continued the calm and quiet daughter of the king, ignoring Martin's question, 'I have passed my young womanhood in guilt for the suffering poor and aged and suffered the dread of myself ageing. Has anyone else revealed such fears to you before? Are they the same fears you fear?' She could not decide if their silence denoted stupefaction or stupidity. She continued with gay in-difference. 'Do you not find it strange that not one mortal on this earth resembles the other in any aspect? We do not look alike, feel or perceive alike. For each of us the same landscape falls differently before our eyes, as painters know. No two people on this many-peopled planet experience the same emotion in the same manner. Joy lights up our hearts in different ways. Is that not an extraordinary fact about life, its variety, its delicious multifariousness?'

The only fact about life they found extraordinary was their stranded situation and the grey-eyed temptress before them.

'Release us,' begged Kindred.

She seemed not to have heard him. Instead she closed her eyes and, humming to herself, fondled her soft, fleshy parts. They begged no more. When she paused and looked up, there both stood – raised roused revived and rearing.

'I can release you now,' she said. And did so.

The young men acted at once. As though by pre-arrangement, their manhood fused in unison, their singular manly determination as one. With none of the delicacy she had shown them, they roughly grabbed her arms and legs and in an instant she was trussed and hung where they had been trussed and hung, her robe torn off her.

'Ah, how helpless I am now,' she tearfully cried. 'I see vengeance in your eyes. I have not softened your tempers. My guilt is proclaimed. You will punish me, I see that. But one request. I was cruel to your pride, not your bodies, and so I plead – allow me to name my punishment.'

The furious clod-headed youths agreed. What did it matter how their poor hurts were healed?

'Imagine me,' she sobbed, 'as a misdemeaning child. How

must I learn my lesson?' She gave their slow minds time to think. They needed help. She closed her eyes, hung limp on her ropes and whispered, 'Chastise me.'

At first they did not comprehend. 'I think,' said Kindred, as a dawn, if not of mankind then of some small hesitant intelligence, crept into his eyes, 'that she wants to be smacked.'

'Smacked?' His friend was flabbergasted.

'Slapped.' Kindred felt the need to explain further.

'Spanked.' Martin was anxious to show he understood at last.

'Beaten.' Kindred was beginning to enjoy the prospect.

'Trounced!'

'Flogged!'

'Whipped!'

'Scourged!'

Liticia feared they would work themselves up into such a lather of onomatopoeia that they would exhaust their appetite for action.

'Do it! Do it!' she urged, her eyes still closed.

She heard the shuffle of uncertain movements, the hesitancy of awkward limbs. A hand struck her left flank. A shy slap. The crack echoed. A heavier hand struck her right flank. There was weight in it but no sting. A second hand struck from the left. More force there – a learning hand. From the right a second slap. More confident, that. Left, a slap, more sting. Right, a slap, more anger. Left, right, left, right, left, right. The rhythm of chastisement accelerated. The slapping hardened. The stinging on her skin spread like a hot spring pool. Their enthusiasm turned to frenzy and boiled over.

She cried out. 'Wait! Wait!'

They were grateful to be called to a halt. It had been tiring.

'You do not wish me *all* ill, do you?' she whimpered. 'One man's hand will suffice now, surely.' Her flesh was red where the blood had risen. 'I am so tender there. The pain must be increased, I accept that, but will not one of you ease it a little with a caress, here.' She thrust forward her pelvic mound. 'While one beats, let the other console. Upon my drenched lips below one of you compensate for the pain. Strike but caress. Beat but soothe. Pleasure and pain. Do it!'

They did as she ordered. It seemed to them they had no alternative. Something in her voice commanded obedience. As of right. Vague intimations of metamorphosis drifted through their befuddled minds. Who the chastised child, then — commander or executant?

On her raw, worn buttocks came harsh blows again. Into her saturated cleft roamed rough fingers. The hand found its sting, the fingers her crux. From behind and before, Liticia was attacked and fondled, punished and rewarded, inflamed, reduced, rendered helpless. Ah, pain! Ah, ecstasy! She protested. She writhed. She begged them to pause. She wrenched and pulled to break loose. She screamed for mercy. To no avail. The beatings and rubbings built to a crescendo of exquisite agony. She shuddered, and from her bosom came a wail the pitch of which brought the crazed men to halt. She called out to her father for forgiveness. She wept.

'I think tears are meant to be ignored,' said the spoilt Lord Kindred. 'You take her from the front and I will whip her with these same ropes she bound us with.'

Incapable of distinguishing between right and wrong, good and bad, ravishing and revenge, they prepared to replace the pleasures of chastisement with the vengeful spites of their manly cruelty. They were to be denied.

The door burst open. Two ferocious women hurled themselves in, flourishing long scimitars. Meliora and Dionis towered over the startled, naked men, their steel poised high above their heads.

What a silence was in that room, as though all had been turned to stone for future generations to gaze, reflect upon, perhaps concoct wild stories round, deciphering their mute significance.

Meliora threw them some shreds of clothes. They understood. They dressed. They fled.

'Are you satisfied?' asked Dionis.

'I am satisfied,' Liticia replied.

They took her down and tenderly laid her to sleep.

All this Jonas heard and saw about the princess Liticia, and related to me, Coaxandria, who have here ordered and interpreted and summarized for the king, and for those who will read after.

DIONIS
~ THE THIRD OLDEST

𝔗here he was, above her once more, pressing himself up and down breathing heavily, sweating happily, occasionally opening his eyes to smile benevolently upon her, checking she was aware of her good fortune, grateful for the gift of his horn of plenty.

When he closed his eyes to press on, the story-teller's mind drifted. Here was a burly sergeant-at-arms who could ram for eternity without the need to scatter his seed to the applauding crowds. That had been amusing, once, as most things are, once.

Then he had confessed, neither she nor his wife were his real passion in life, but a small squadron of men he drilled for a local lord who had little need of protection, the drilling was for ceremony. Oh, his pride that they did shine in their metals and leather, salute like clocks and march like machines. They could run with the deer, hit bulls with their bows, hold endlessly still like owls, and fast for days on water, snakeweed, heartsease and purslane. As with an iron rod he disciplined his men, so did he discipline his iron rod.

Dionis had been satisfied with such sustained control, once. Now he moved with the tedium of a windmill.

And once she had enjoyed the affection he displayed for his men, though it dismayed her that of their histories he knew nothing nor cared. The teller of stories badgered him many nights for the stories of their lives.

'Surely,' she had asked, 'your men have tales they share, exchange, hear from visiting strangers? They may not tell you of themselves but they must talk of others.'

He told her only of their colourful splendour and what praises had been heaped upon him and them for their military skills. They had never fought battles, but should that day come they would, her sergeant-at-arms assured her, be crowned with glory. 'A man is what he is, not where he comes from,' he had declared, pompously pulling at his ginger moustache. She had enjoyed his ginger moustache, once. Finally she gave up asking.

He was a young sergeant-at-arms, though how his rank had come about he could not explain, for there were neither corporals nor officers for miles around. No ranks to rise from nor any to aspire to. How did he begin? Who appointed him? Perhaps there *was* no squad of men. Did that account for why he could not relate their histories?

Something, however, had to account for his staying powers. His mother's milk? His father's will? His wife's routine of demands? Nor would he speak of his wife, except to say that she came from far over the sea and was unfathomable, which intrigued Dionis still more. How did she arrive? How did they meet? Why had he loved her? She pressed for those details which can bring the dullest life to life. He did not love her, he said, it had been an arrangement. His mother had bought her, or rather paid her. She was healthy and unlike anyone in the district. Offspring would be enriched by a new strand. His mother viewed her family as she did her herd of cattle. And that was all he ever said. Our agreement, he reminded her, was for nights without questions. But, she protested, those who love telling stories love asking questions. Her stories were becoming stale. The inclination to recount at all had dimmed. She was not of that school which could invent, fantasise. Her tales were rooted in events, in what actually happened, what had been lived through by someone. Nothing was more extraordinary than other people's lives, she avowed. He was not forthcoming, however, merely coming.

Oh, ye gods whose task it is to protect us, will he never cease his pumping? Why did she continue with these arrangements? Why does he not go home to his wife? Why did she not *send* him home to his wife? Was she not after all a princess? She would be glad when this trial period ended and they could all return to the normal routine of court life. It had been a good idea, once, to escape at nights from their father's shelter to pursue unchaperoned pursuits, give rein to their free spirits, explore desires. But, the sisters now agreed, they had moved from sheltered days to sheltered nights, from fetters to fetters, from unworldliness to dull-worldliness.

It is curious, she thought as she lay there, taking her punishment and remembering the ecstatic state of the quiet Liticia, my sisters who are not story-tellers have imagined happenings and made them happen, while I, no other teller of tales better than I, I must *wait* for life to happen. She paused, as all tellers of tales pause in the midst of their complaints about life when they come upon a phrase, a line, an observation that pleases them despite their suffering. Now *there* is a good beginning for a story, she thought:

There are those who *make* life happen and those who *wait* for life to happen. This is a story about...

At which moment the door burst open unceremoniously upon their ancient ceremony and a strange woman loomed in the portal. She was a mass of black everything – clothes, hair, eyes, intentions! Here was a gypsy come to murder us, thought Dionis unperturbed, her legs in the air, her allocated lover nigh upon his goal, too absorbed to notice. Being a military man, he possessed little imagination and, concomitant with that, no fear. The door has flown open with the wind, he thought. Nothing was going to deny him the rewards of his long labours.

'I am coming,' he cried, as though he were the first man ever so to do. 'I-am-come-ing.'

The princess thought it wise to warn him they had a visitor.

'I think *she* is coming to murder us,' she said.

'I am coming,' said the intruder with resignation, 'to take him home!'

He howled. Dionis could not recall if this was the howl normally accompanying his triumphant arrival or one of despair for being discovered. Military actions must be seen through to their end, however. He emptied his horn before turning at last.

'My wife!' he cried, with the amazed alarm of a general whose rear had been unexpectedly attacked by the enemy.

'But no one knows where we are or even that we exist,' said the princess Dionis, pulling her dress down to its modest level. 'How can your wife know? Did you tell her?'

'He told me nothing.'

'She knows everything,' he said morosely. 'The names of stars, the virtues of wild plants, the language of animals, the

189

best recipe for rabbit pie and how the world began.'

There is no sadder sight than an exposed husband. Double exposure – to be caught *and* naked – is purgatory, shame upon shame. The sergeant-at-arms was a sergeant lost, defeated, desolate. His spirits, his honour, his authority, his proud sword, all were down. In such a moment is wondrously revealed the Elysian bond between women. Their disguise falls away, they assume their true shape – God's chosen guardians of men.

Where till then it had seemed they were men's companions, partners, help-mates, love-mates, soul-mates, mother-sister-next-door-neighbour-mates, now, in such moments of male deflation, women rise to their natural authority as emissaries sent forth on earth to guide, to garland, to approve, adore; to convince, cajole, persuade, reproach; to wean, suggest, encourage, cheer; to blackmail, stricture, praise, support; to flatter, threaten, censor, urge; to damn, to plague, to woo, wham, bang or exercise whatever other means prove efficacious at that moment in order that men be controlled – for the greater glory of God, that is. There exists only mankind and heaven. The function of womankind is to steer men through heaven's gates. They mostly fail. And it is then, when women confront their failures, that the disguise falls away, their bond is revealed and they are seen for what they really are – not of this life. Men are earthbound. Women are ethereal. Men are merely God's creatures, women, free of earth's natural demands and its conventional expectations, are God's appointed castellans to whom he has licensed the universe.

This it was that Dionis and the gypsy woman – for that is what we will call her – recognized in one another.

'Take him home,' sighed Dionis. 'Feed him, he has not yet been served his food.' She pointed to the sumptuous spread which, like all her sisters, she had prepared for her borrowed lover. 'He needs revitalizing.'

'Body *and* soul, it seems,' said the gypsy, her intelligent eyes flashing conspiratorially at the princess.

'And will you diminish me still more,' asked the sergeant-at-arms, drawing together what dignity they had left him, 'by talking of me as though I were not here?'

'Dress yourself, husband,' said his wife with firm tenderness. 'I am no stranger to the impossibilities of this life. We will return hand in hand to what we know best, and mend the cracks of your fallen state. There are many years left for soldiering and other of life's small pleasures. Pack up your parts. I have no fury. Come, it is about time we had children before my body loses its strength.'

'Do not forget,' said Dionis, 'these victuals, prepared for him with effort and some affection, enough for a family of ten. Let it not rot for sourness' sake.'

The gypsy accepted with grace and took him and his fodder home.

With charity, forgiveness and a fine meal for his stomach, they had asserted their control of the poor sergeant-at-arms, whose sad glory shrank even more. Thus diminished is the way through heaven's gate!

Dionis was alone. Must she be so until these probing days were done and all the sisters satisfied? Two angels had passed one another in the astral night. It was time to contemplate earthly matters once more.

Here was a muddle. The sisters had escaped to find pleasures of the flesh and she was pleasureless. Pleasure-of-the-fleshless. Each had devised nocturnal escapades, but while *they* were embracing partners, *she* was partnerless. Embraceless. Engulfed in a bored and aching yawningness. She yawned, plucked at a pickled herring, bit into her buttock of brawn – too much nutmeg, she thought – played with her Dutch pudding, sipped her sack posset and wriggled her toes. Sipped and sipped, reclined against cushions to the side of her fire, thinking she had no need of sergeants-at-arms, no need of sergeants' arms, no need of sergeants' legs, nor their chests nor any old part of their old parts. Here was undemanding solitude and a good drink. What more was there to life? Sack posset! The sergeant's favourite: eggs, red wine, cinnamon, mace, nutmeg, cream and sugar. Warm and comforting. Sip, sip! Down to her belly, sip! Out along her legs, sip! High into her head, sip, sip! The recipe for sack posset came from a story told her by an Englishman.

'Stories!' she exclaimed aloud to herself. 'What *is* a story? Not the truth, that is for sure. And yet, when told, recognition lights up in men's eyes. What can it be? Fascination with men's fortunes? Incredulity at men's ways? Awe before God's playfulness? The *sound* of words? The *teller* not the tale?' Sip, sip! 'Thank you, Englishman, for your story and your sack posset.' Sip, sip! 'If I drone on like this, drink on like this, where will it end?'

At which moment, for the second time that night, the door burst open. It was the gypsy.

'Welcome,' said Dionis, though she was not sure why. 'I have been waiting for you!' That too surprised her. She was not certain it had been a wise greeting.

The gypsy woman said nothing. She entered, closed the door, took a seat opposite Dionis and accepted a goblet of sack posset. Here is a handsome woman, thought Dionis. But why has she come?

There is a regal woman, thought the gypsy. I know why I have come.

I am telling a story, Dionis rolled thoughts around in her

head and sack posset on her tongue. I must look and describe her. How? Should I *compare* her to this and that or simply *identify* the parts? Should I liken how she sits to the heavy solidity of a cuddly bear? Or should I list her square jaw, her wide face, her high forehead? Should I compare her loftily combed hair to a dark tower, her firm shoulders to safe rocks, her ample bosom to the comfort of strangers? Or should I merely name her fleshy arms, her broad hips, her lean legs, her slim ankles, her delicate feet, her long straight toes and the black flashing of her smiling eyes?

'Why are you smiling?' asked Dionis.

The gypsy replied. 'Now it is my turn to look at you.'

'What do you see?'

'Someone tall and slender. Someone soft and anxious. Someone vulnerable and concerned. Your head moves from side to side in pity, even though there is nothing to be pitied.'

'You use words which do not belong to your station in life,' said Dionis.

The dark gypsy woman laughed loudly. 'Oh, we have stations in life, do we?'

Dionis wondered how this woman would behave in court if she knew she was a princess?

'Where are you from?'

'I am from a country beyond Switzerland, Belgium, Normandy and England. It is called Ireland. Words come with our blood from birth. The milk we drink from our mothers' breasts flows with words. There is language on the Irish winds and in the earth. Language feeds what we feed from.'

The gypsy, whose high-built black hair wound in and out of itself stacked with copper pins, withdrew the pins. A coral avalanche cascaded round her pale face. The fire sent out a great heat. She unbuttoned her blouse that her skin might breathe. She gazed intently at Dionis. Suddenly she opened her arms and said, 'Come.' The princess was surprised. Perhaps she ought not to have been but she was. A woman's arms? What comfort in a woman? To exchange gossip and heartache with, yes. To offer, seek advice, yes. Console each other, warn one another, mock men together, yes. But touch? Be touched?

'I think not,' she said.

The gypsy asked, 'Would you like me to go, then?'

'No,' Dionis confessed. 'I am in need of company.'

They sat in silence for a long while, softly sweating in the fire's heat. The gypsy began to hum. Her voice was deep and seemed to come from her stomach, almost as though it did not belong to her. The humming drifted into a song.

> To my bedside there came a lass
> The trees grow tall the tide moves out
> Who told me that two galleon ships
> Are out to sea and poised to fight.
> The tide moves out the trees grow tall.
>
> Why have you come to my bedside
> The tide moves out the trees grow tall
> Because your brother minds the guns
> And when the battle starts will fall
> The trees grow tall the tide moves out.
>
> So rise and come prepare his grave
> The trees grow tall the tide moves out
> Here's one we love for heaven's gate
> We must be gone or we'll be late
> The tide moves out the trees grow tall.

Dionis wept. Tears from nowhere. The gypsy's song? Her silly sergeant? Her sack posset? The weight of the sad old world's sad stories? All these things.

The gypsy opened her arms and again called, 'Come.'

Again Dionis shook her head. 'I am not made that way.'

'Am I?' the voluptuous gypsy from Ireland asked.

'I do not know you,' Dionis said, trying to stem her sobbing.

'You know me well.' The gypsy paused. 'You did not send me away.'

Dionis at last controlled her tears.

'How strange. Of we sisters it is I who console and am their confidante. I who listen, sympathize with their complaints, mend their problems, attend to their fears. Why am I like this now?'

The gypsy slid from her chair and crept to lean between the legs of the princess, her strong back against regal breasts. She said nothing, she did nothing. The princess could feel herself tensing at the gypsy's closeness. From anxiety or expectation?

'Are you tensing from anxiety or expectation?' asked the gypsy.

'You read my thoughts?'

'They say,' said the gypsy, 'that if two women who have never known one another live together for long, their menstrual cycles begin to coincide.'

She lifted the feet of the princess into her lap and slowly massaged them. Her fingers knew the whereabouts of every nerve and their function. Dionis felt like a bottle full of flat wine and stale juices which, with each small pressure, lowered a little more until she seemed drained of twenty-eight years of accumulated poison that somehow had dropped into her feet and was now spilling out through her toes. Had not the gypsy hung on to her, a foot in each hand, she felt she would have risen, floated off. She felt so light.

In this way did the black-haired lady claim her. What had begun as an easing of tension became sanction to move over her body where she pleased. And she pleased. Fingers strayed to calves and trickled down to feet. They strayed to thighs and ran to knees. She had wanted to be touched and was being touched, by whom did not matter. The military man had understood nothing of such movements. His landscape was ditches and oaks and the commanding heights of tiny hillocks. Nothing like this, the soft mound of a belly, the curve between rib and hip, the dip in the buttock's side, the pelvic lanes covered in gorse, smelling of smoke converging upon lips of sweet slime. Dionis was helpless as she lay, the princess of story-time, astonished, on her back with no robe and a mountain of woman with black hair leaning over her. How did she know, this dark mountain, where to run her fingers, stroke with her palm, lick with her tongue? Her tongue! A woman's tongue lapping her salty skin! A wet, flicking interloper into crevices where no one had been but her; where nothing had touched but her own hands.

The gypsy rolled her on to her stomach. She felt those heavy breasts on her back, warm breath on her neck, a mouth biting, kissing, circling, sucking. Dionis writhed and quivered, gasped and sighed. How, how did this woman know? Did she give what she herself longed for? Is that how we love? Then what she longed for, Dionis would give!

The princess moved quickly from under the huge gypsy and, grasping her shoulders firm as rocks, eased her back. She knelt by her. Looked at her. The gypsy heaved, her body signalling, calling. But Dionis could not bring herself to touch the other woman's flesh, merely to caress it with her eyes, every part familiar and yet utterly new. The gypsy's eyes were closed, her body trembling, a shudder of small shiftings.

Dionis lifted a thick strand of the woman's black hair and stroked her breast with it, back and forth, across her nipple. The nipple grew. Dionis watched it, fascinated. She touched it with her finger. It grew still further. She bent forward and took the small stub between her teeth and gently bit. The gypsy moved and moaned. Holding on with her teeth, she flicked her tongue to and fro. The gypsy writhed and plunged her hands between her legs. Dionis looked there. The lips were parted and from between them seeped such honey as Dionis had not imagined possible. She dipped her finger there and tasted. Once more, deeper, with two fingers this time. And tasted. The gypsy gripped the hair of her head and pulled her down. 'Drink, drink, drink,' she pressed. Dionis drank. She drank and sucked at this well of well-being where she had not been ever before. Shrill cries struggled from the gypsy – as though to escape an unbearable pain. 'Stop!' she screamed. 'Stop! Stop!'

Dionis raised her head. The gypsy rose to her knees and gripped her shoulders, gasping for breath. Here before her was a wild woman – black eyes now burning beacons of fierce light, holding on to her as though fearful the world was ending. Hands crossed their no man's land. They stroked each other to a calm. They were still. The fire flickered. Restless shadows surrounded them.

'You have never touched nor been touched by a woman before?' asked the sergeant's wife. Dionis shook her head. 'And was he the first man to enter you?' Dionis nodded. 'Then you know nothing.'

'I know what I know. When I know more I will know what I know not.'

The gypsy leaned towards her lips. She is going to kiss

me! Instinctively Dionis averted her face. The gypsy gently pulled it back. Her tongue brushed the lips of the princess whose lips stayed closed. Why? Had not those lips just drunk from the most private of wells? The gypsy's fingers caressed instead. Dionis shuddered. The fingers coaxingly prised her lips apart. Before she understood what she was doing, she took the fingers into her mouth and sucked. Again the gypsy offered her lips. This time Dionis stayed to receive them. More. She leapt at them. Grabbed at them. Drew them into her mouth. Tongue entwined tongue. Breast upon breast. They grasped, they squeezed, they pinched and dug their nails into one another's back. They drew blood.

Again, breathless, they held each other away, but held. And laughed.

Uncontrollable laughter. Till their eyes watered.

'I lie with him,' Dionis struggled to say, 'always me beneath and him above.'

'And he pistons up and down,' spluttered the gypsy, 'up and down, up and down, up and down.'

'With such pride for his stamina.'

'No medals for *ours*!'

'And when he is done he imagines that is all.'

'And you feed him?'

'And I feed him.'

'And he says nothing.'

'Oh yes, he talks − of his platoon and their spit and polish and precision and marksmanship. He loves his men. No doubt of that. Better than a king's platoon is his platoon!'

'What platoon?' asked the wife of the sergeant-at-arms.

Dionis was shocked, surprised, a little saddened. Her brave military man had commanded nothing! Silence. Then both laughed again, huge and incredulously, with no thought of cruelty for, being God's guardians, they could not ever be cruel, could they?

Now the gypsy positioned herself most curiously. First she raised Dionis to her knees. Then she parted them, rolled on to her back, and slid between them till her face was directly beneath a quim dripping like over-ripe slices of peach. Her hands gripped the hips above her. She pulled them down. Dionis felt a long tongue push up and in. No horn of plenty, this, but oh more welcome than his piston of tedious regularity. Here was a long erratic tickler; a tantalizer of wit. It moved. It stopped. It flurried. It stroked. It was brazen, it was coy. And then – what mischief now? It had tiptoed along the roof of her cunt and stumbled over a pebble. A pebble? What had this wicked tongue found? Where was it that she was so driven to squirm and twist and scream aloud. She must find the same spot in the gypsy. Would she too scream and tremble with such ecstasy?

She found it. There in that dark show of promise, in all that translucent cream, a pink twist of tiny flesh. She bent down to it. Pulled with her lips at it. Teased it with her tongue. Gently tried to bite it away. And then – sucked, as *she* was being sucked, growling from her throat as she heard growling beneath her, trying to escape the mouth round her lips as the lips in her mouth were trying to escape, turbulence mounting. They hung on. Passionately. Each to the other. That turbulence must erupt. It must. Each would make it erupt. No – no – no – no – oh, please, no-ooohh.

It was indeed like the world ending.

Oh, sweet woman, sweet, sweet woman.

Here was a passion of parity. A symmetry of sensuality. No convulsions of defeat. No crumbling into submission. No ugly struggle to dominate. But the flow of give and take. Here was the relieved embrace of equals.

All this Jonas heard and saw about the princess Dionis, and related to me, Coaxandria, who have here ordered and interpreted and summarized for the king, and for those who will read after.

MELIORA
- THE SECOND OLDEST

$\mathcal{R}$ estless! Restless! She was restless. She stared at Aldus in dismay, an old man on his back, jaw open in a gasp, a dribble of saliva betraying him, snoring his way through dreams which,when he awoke, he would forget, and if not forget, be bewildered by. She had worn him out. Amorous endeavour had exhausted him, decanted his bitter wine.

Why had she chosen the eldest? She, the diplomat. Assessor of character! Estimator of worthiness! Evaluator of virtues! What virtues? What worthiness? What character? How weary she was of conventional assessments, weathered rituals, stale cautions, the tried ways of good breeding, good sense, goodness; how impatient she was with tender, honeyed and tediously well-meant male solicitude. She had loved her way through the years and now her nerves were numbed by the boredom of predictable decisions. She was surfeited with the old man's ridiculous cries and her own commonplace moans. Their strenuous inventions, finally, were not worth the effort. She craved release from the prison of self-censure, the strictures of upbringing. She wanted to cast anchor from herself, permit strange currents and rude winds to take her where they would. Restless, restless, oh she certainly was that.

In such a mood she wandered from the hut through the forest. To do what? To go where? Here among lofty trees in the gossamer light of a half-moon could be found only the untroubled breeze of a summer night made for delicate young lovers. Here was no promise of turbulence, no threat of the unimaginable. The anxiety of a lost hedgehog was the most that could disturb such a night. She walked chastising herself with memories of lost nocturnal hours which had filtered away, taking not only her youthful blushes but her youthful expectations, leaving her heart cankered with doubt. Very little could penetrate such powerful discontent. Not even that which had been stalking her for nearly half an hour. Or rather 'those' who had been stalking her for nearly half an hour.

Following her, parallel to her route between the tall trees, keeping to the moon's shadows, gauging their prey, reading her features, whispering between themselves, trying to explain the meaning of her concentration, the reason for her solitary stroll, were two small strange predators who choked between argument and hesitation and finally, roaring with haste, rushed upon her.

Meliora, a princess of ancient lineage nurtured by centuries of iron rule and defiant breeding, normally confronted the world imperiously enough to wither all manner of human predators. But coarse natures are controlled only by strength. Regal bearing diminisheth them not, nor imperious flame frighten them. A long whip curled its sneer round her, binding her arms to her body and bringing down her pride. Though often handled by men, never had she been manhandled. What was hers and hers alone was now invaded, enveloped by rope and rudeness. She screamed, writhed and made futile efforts to hurt with her free limbs. From their laughter, she knew she was adding to their pleasure rather than disturbing it. Steely with impotence and royal resignation, she quelled her wrath, clenched her teeth and awaited their intentions.

They said nothing, though intentions they had. What kind of being were they? Dwarfs, certainly, but from where? A circus? A village of dwarfs? Servants of a robber baron? They drew more rope from their mud-coated satchels and strung her up between two trees far enough apart to contain the span of her outstretched arms and parted legs. Was she thus to be ravaged? Must she hang there bound and defenceless while they exercised dull appetites upon her? They stepped back to gaze at her. She searched their eyes for an answer. No extraordinary lusts struggled there, only the weak fevers of habitual serfdom flickered with brief freedom. They stood weaving wordless hands in argument until, to her chagrin, one each side, they raised her dress. Unauthorized eyes inspected her like a beast of burden for sale. How did they dare, these erks, skivvies, villeins?

'Villeins! Skivvies! Erks!' she cried.

Neither sense nor sound penetrated them. As she hung like indecision, exposed against her will, she mocked herself with recriminatory questions. You craved release from the strictures of upbringing? Your nerves were numbed by the boredom of predictable decisions? You wanted to cast anchor from yourself, permit strange currents and rude winds to take you where they would? What of these *rude* winds, then? Will they cure you of your restlessness or rather make you crave for the return of those weathered rituals, stale cautions, tried ways?

She answered herself: but it was to be *my* choice to cast anchor, *my* decision, made freely, not imposed. She reflected contemptuously: Oh, so it was to be *your* decision to be deprived of decision? What strange antilogy was that? Suddenly she was alone. They had left her. No finger had been laid upon her. What was to happen?

She hung between the tall talifers for many minutes before becoming intensely aware of her exposed position – a stretched-out invitation to the forest's denizens! Her plight focused her attention upon each part of her vulnerable body. And vulnerable it felt – available to whatever cared to alight upon it. Bracken had slipped between her toes making her conscious of her feet; the careful midnight wind billowed her skirt and crept up the long length of her legs, chilling unimpeded expanses of flesh; the sleeves of her dress had fallen, exposing armpits to the tickle of air; palm, knuckle, arm – all bare.

Made sensate thus in such tiny, intimate areas, so all other exposed parts cried out their nakedness. Feel here! called the thin crease behind her knee; and here! whispered the soft hollow where her elbow bent; and here and here and here! Suddenly she was neck and nape, shoulders and shivering spine, clenched buttocks, and finally, there! My God, there! With all the earth's seasons breathing up into her damp, unguarded entrance, free for any idling insect, reptile, dumb beast to forage for food, drink or habitation. The commanding princess commanded nothing. Not even her voice. No one was near enough to hear it.

Something moved. She would have screamed had not the terror of what she saw paralysed her. A snake, green and busy, curved its way towards her. She uttered a soft cry, not too loud for fear it would behave erratically. It paused, reared its head and swayed like a confused, long tongue challenging the alien airs. What new, immobile object lay before it? And what were these foreign scents? Meliora could not discern what species it was – harmless or envenomed. Moonlight subdued its colour. The wavering shape moved closer, trying to understand what it saw. Closer still to test safety. Then in one swift, daring dart it rushed and stretched up in lofty curiosity three feet before her. The princess was a breath away from hysteria. She managed to strangle a whimper. The reptile froze, momentarily warned. Then she saw – it was coloured green. A mere grass snake. Harmless, fangless, venomless, like a bewildered old man desirous only of friendship, puzzled that most living creatures fled from him as though his proximity to death was the world's only threat. She sighed, and in sighing realized that she had not breathed for so long her heart could be heard in her head, and no doubt throughout the forest.

Meliora, utterly relieved, found comfort in his company and spoke aloud to him. 'Would that I knew the language of wild places, I would give you messages for your swift comings and goings. Oh, would I give you urgent motions to make.' The timbre of her voice attracted the tame ophidian. It slithered to her feet, paused and curved back, as though seeking permission to approach and speak with her. Or was he searching out the shortest way to her lips to hear more clearly what she said? Deaf old man! She could help him not. Whereupon he took decisions for himself and, to her confused thrill and dread, proceeded to wind its way up her leg to her thigh, where, reaching the crossroads below her belly, she felt the creeper hesitate, peer this way and that, halt to check scent and bearings, and then – no! She could not believe it, it would not be possible – imagination unscaled – the fond serpent foolishly, rashly, erroneously surmised her dewy door to be his route to her attention. What else in the past had, with her blessing, found its way into her moist house of delight compared not one bit with what now nosed and played its lost way up and around inside her, thrusting here, thrusting there, perplexed, chagrined a little, impatient to get somewhere, anywhere, banging its head against cushions of quite another slime, wriggling for egress, wriggling for light, wriggling, wriggling, wriggling till she cried out, 'Stop! stop!'

The thing was half-way in and half-way out, learning nothing for a long time but for a long time probing into her more deeply than any man's length had ever been able; probing, and rubbing her hothouse walls, while, helpless to remove or improve for pleasure, she hung on till this unattached member of an outcast species came to its senses and, understanding finally that it had taken the wrong road, left her limp and tingling in her bonds. Like a grumpy old toothless man hissing complaints at the stupid problems with which life confronted him, it slid up her belly, under her arms, across and around her breasts, at last flinging itself into the hollow of her neck, where, exhausted, it coiled and settled for rest. Had it been blessed with the power of speech it would have said, 'I have arrived, I am here, say what it is you want, and, when I have caught my breath, I will be gone in a trice on your errand.'

She felt like Eve with evil about to whisper in her ear. Here, though, was not evil, just a poor tired thing come to comfort a poor tired thing. And with a familiar smell about it too! Cat-like, the snake rose a little to brush its head against her cheek for reassurance, and waited.

'I have eleven sisters,' she began, more to keep company with herself than imagining her words conveyed meaning to her mute companion, 'and each one with her partner would cease at once whatever sweet amorous invention they were exploring, whatever ecstatic height they were approaching, to rescue me if they but knew.' She raised her head and looked in the direction from which she thought she had wandered. The sleepy coil at her ear raised its head as well, following her gaze. 'Could it be *so* far away?' she sighed. The serpent sighed with her, recoiled, dozed a little to recover from his escapade, then suddenly leapt from her and was gone. She cried out at the loss, feeling, as never before, the unbearable pain of loneliness, a loneliness exacerbated by her aching suspension; alone, powerless, exposed, and held high to what fate the rude winds had stored in its box of vindictive spites.

Though it seemed to her like an aeon, all this had passed in a mere score of minutes. Was she feeling fear? Fatigue? Curiosity? Boredom? Outrage? Resignation? She was left no time to decide. There were sounds. Persons approaching. Help, perhaps? Had Aldus come in search of her? Had her sisters been alerted by the deft grass-dweller? None of these. She urgently needed to flush and, shame upon shame, as feet approached, her bladder pressed.

A flowing torch floated before her. The moonlight quivered pink. On either side of the flame stood the two rough churls, grinning, pointing and looking pleased with themselves. The torch was planted into the ground. Before her stood a most extraordinary figure scrutinizing her strung-up form. A man, fine-boned, whose strangely exquisite looks were flawed by over-excited eyes and over-calculated attire – black trousers, black boots and a white shirt with a collar made to lie flat but which, perhaps because he thought it lent him an interestingly demonic air, he had propped to stand up around his neck. A cascade of black hair matched striking black eyes set in a face unnaturally pale, almost white, as though powdered, or bloodless. At his side sat a huge wolf-dog as grey as its master was black, and seeming to have been acquired for the powerful harmony of tones man and animal made alongside one another. He bore himself like a lord whose life was lived solitarily, exuding an air of eccentricity that allowed no partnership, declaring itself singular and beyond the reach of questions. Was he less than thirty-five years of age? Certainly he looked as though he had forgotten that nineteen had come and gone.

For a long time he stared at her. She returned his gaze with royal fire, reading in his eyes the same regal language her own had learned to speak, informing him silently, steadily, that she was not to be trifled with. He turned to her, signalled to the two men a gesture they understood, for they at once set about making a fire. The lord drew up a stone on which he could sit, ponder and view. His beast settled at his side. Why had he turned from her? Had he read something other than warning in her eyes? Had she involuntarily signalled that restlessness which she had imagined had been successfully hidden? It was obvious now that her imperial glances had failed to impress him. Her strength drained, her heart humbled, and a voice came from quite another, unknown, part of her.

'Please. Release me. I must return to my kinsmen.'

He turned to her with slow contempt. A minute like an hour passed. His rude silence angered her. She found again her royal demeanour and answered piercing gaze with contemptuous piercing gaze. Nothing moved him. His spirit was as denuded of emotion as his face of blood. Denuded, that is, of all but that over-intense excitement in his eyes so constant that she thought it the natural, fixed countenance with which he had been born.

Could he speak? His servants were obviously mutes, their arguments over the digging, gathering and laying of the fire were snarled grunts. But the master – what *was* it that emanated from him? Was his demeanour evil or merely cruel? She had not been instantly released, therefore she was being held for a reason. What reason? And why did she feel no real fear? It was illogical but something in the way they all moved and behaved with one another spoke of strange but not mortiferous intent. And inexplicably, elusively, she sensed – what? Familiarity, that which was recognizable, but what?

The three sat staring at her. Clothed though she was, she felt naked. Why did they stare so? If they will have her, then let them take her now, at once, and be done. Again she became acutely aware of every part of her body and what could be played upon it. She shivered. Excitement like distant thunder rumbled through her discomfort. Threat or promise, the storm was imminent. And to add to her discomfort her bladder threatened its own tempest. Now she was plaintive.

'Please, please release me. There are private attentions to be paid.'

He spoke at last, remarkably, and in a voice which seemed to come from the back of the throat rather than the chest. He asked, 'By which you mean?'

'Come, come! You can tie me up again, but allow me personal dignity.'

'Placed as you now are,' he gaily chided her, 'that is an absurd thing to say.'

What metamorphosis! Excited eyes became, moment-arily, merry eyes, sufficient to reveal here was no monster. A curious fanatic of sorts, but one indulging his fevers within bounds.

'I promise not to run away.'

'A sensible promise, since impossible.' He paused. 'It is to piss you want, yes?'

Princess Meliora lowered her eyes.

'Then why not here?' asked her tormentor. 'Why is it more shameful to be seen passing water than imbibing it? Have you ever reflected how odd an action it is to eat, to drink? Watch.' He made another gesture to his men, one of whom drew a fruit from his bag and began to eat. 'He opens his mouth, he bites, he chews. And he chews and he chews and he waits and we watch him, and we regard the foolish expression of pleasure in his eyes as taste assails him, texture tickles him and satisfaction is swallowed to fill a gap. And then what does he do? Why he bites again, and chews again, and repeats again the entire ungainly process. What could be more clumsy, unsightly? Even when someone not rude as this fellow here eats, a woman of high birth, yourself for example – oh yes! I know you to be high-born – do you imagine that because your mouthfuls are daintier, your chewing not so pronounced, your look dreamier, that your appearance is any less ridiculous?'

He signalled another of his strange but perfectly comprehensible signs to one of his men, who, to her mortification, went behind her and raised her dress.

'Relieve yourself,' he invited her.

She clenched her teeth, hurled contempt at him and tightened the sac holding her watery shame.

The lord sighed, rose, stepped behind her and executed a movement most odd but one which, had Meliora accompanied her sister Amissia to the old lovers' hut in the woods, she would have instantly recognized. With his forefinger he scratched the top of her buttock's crease and, as though he had turned the wheel to raise a dyke, her floods could be held back no longer. The evening's wines gushed from her, warm and hissing. How could this happen? Was *nothing* left in her control? Had she not been so amazed, she would have been furious. Relief followed amazement, and incredulity followed relief – for the other rough mute leapt up and thrust his face beneath her fountain, laughing and drinking for all the world as though life's elixir had been granted him. She watched him thrashing about in her waters. Her flow and his glee seemed endless, and she was surprised to discover herself enjoying a sense of small power.

The scratching stopped, the pouring ceased, the two little men returned with their grunts and groans beside the fire. Not the lord. He was busy about something else. Instead of allowing her dress to fall back he tucked it into the leather belt around her waist and returned to his stone. All three were again squinnying. She was half bare and could feel their eyes like fingers shifting and ruffling about her pubic hair. The waiting, the waiting! It was the quality of the waiting. No one had ever dared tantalize her with time, and yet the waiting filled her with not unpleasant expectations. She became curious, wondering what next was to follow.

Minutes passed in silence. She felt the warmth from the fire upon her flesh. It was comforting until – he mouthed another clicking sound and the being whose existence she had forgotten, for it had lain so still, rose high on its four legs, stretched, and nonchalantly ambled towards her. Her eyes opened wide with anxiety as she watched the huge dog sniff at the ground before her, perplexed by what had rained there. It raised its head to her bush, sniffed again, long and deep, its hot breath clammy on her. She froze at the thought that he might bite, and closed her eyes in terror. No animal had ever before been privy to her sanctuary. Hers had been a chapel reserved only for those who knew how to kneel and pay homage. The boring may have found their way to her, never the dumb.

The hot breath removed itself. She heard a slow, lazy shuffling around her. The beast was now behind. Again the sniffing. Again the hot breath on her flesh. He was still uncertain. What could he want? She felt a cold nose nozzle between her flanks. She tautened her buttocks. The hound growled, her tight hold relaxed at once! Let his nose probe where it wished! She even found herself helping the dumb thing by sinking a little towards a squat. Anything to appease its curiosity and not tempt its teeth to pierce her skin. This foraging could not last long. What interest could such an animal have in her?

She soon discovered. Eyes still closed, she experienced an entirely new sensation. A rough tongue flapped between her crease and found the smallest of her holes. She heard a cry. The dog? No. Her own voice. A nerve had been touched. But then? Tongue and hot breath receded. She heard him move away. As she guessed, he was not interested in her. She sighed relief and kept her eyes closed ostrich-like, imagining that if she could not see the animal she would cease to exist for him. But in closing her eyes two things happened. Concentrating on the prying quadruped made her forget she was not alone. All her attention was upon what it would do next. Again the waiting. Why? Had the animal learned from its master to take time over decisions? Apparently so, for suddenly it was there again. That hot breath before her. And now its long tongue! Licking her! Searching the soft lips hanging between her legs, savouring her taste. Oh, heavens! Licking and thrusting and drinking as though she oozed milk. She surrendered to the sensation, writhed with the beast's eagerness, thrust her groin forward to its lapping, and heard herself moaning until – click! A mouth made a sound. The mutt returned to its master's side. She remembered where she was, opened her eyes and found all three, still there, intent upon her. *He* was amused. *They* were wide-eyed.

She spoke: 'Well. Now you know. I am held and helpless. You can do what you wish. I cannot control what my body will feel. You have a compliant victim.'

'I know what I have,' he replied. How confident this throaty voice sounded, as from a man wandering through his estate where every stone, lush blossom and wild herb was known to him.

She seemed to be his domain, understanding her feelings, anticipating her thoughts. But the waiting, the waiting! What next? What, what next? As she stood, strung and defenceless, her imagination feverishly at work trying to guess what could be in store for her, she recalled a little puppy she had as a child. Her greatest pleasure had been to feed, teach it obedience, make it wait. She would hold morsels in her hand for ages watching the young thing sit, pant, gaze at her, plaintively waiting for her offering. It could hardly sit still and would shift from paw to paw, uttering soft whines, urging her to hurry and feed him again, becoming so excited it would pee. His excitement had given her a sense of pleasure and power. She had made it wait. Now she was the puppy, being made to wait, excited. Theirs was the power and the pleasure.

He spoke: 'You must be aching,' he said, not unkindly.

'Oh yes! Yes, yes, yes!' Did he intend to release her?

He did not. Instead he signalled new instructions to his factotums, who with alacrity and delight sprang up to fulfil his orders, though how they understood them was beyond her. They knelt before her, rough-skinned but firm-fingered, and began to knead her flesh from ankle to neck. Four strong hands upon her, about her, pulling and squeezing with a pleasing, unhurried skill on her legs, her flanks, her belly, buttocks, back, her arms, her neck. Her bones relaxed, her skin became warm. The warmth grew and spread, making her blood race, relieving strain and releasing energy. What had been a body of aches became a body alert as they rolled, pummelled, manipulated her muscles and flesh. The aching eased. The princess had been frictioned awake. She looked at her captors with new feelings of fondness. Nothing about them was any longer menacing. More, a bond had grown between them. Resistance had been replaced by acquiescence, acquiescence by desire. She could conceive of nothing they might do that would not please her. Her body yearned to experience everything.

But for what were they preparing her? The most curious part of this invigorating massage was that their fingers touched not one private part. The omission made her wonder. Why had they avoided those sensitive places? The more they had touched, the more aware she became of what was untouched. When *she* was all movement, *they* ceased. She could not know this was to be the pattern of the next hours – conflicting sensations. They withdrew from her, returned to their peering, like sculptors stepping back to reflect on what they had achieved.

Again the waiting. Would she accept that too, as she had come to accept her captivity? And he? If she was to be held for pleasure, wherein lay his gratification? It confused her. The waiting made her salivate; they were feeding *her* appetite rather than their own; she was being subjected to contrasting impressions; she was being roused to abandon and then neglected. Her captor showed no inclination to participate at all, merely to watch. Yet bondaged she could offer him nothing. And how perfectly he judged time, stretched it, stretching with it her nerves. So on edge were her senses that his slightest movement made her heart beat faster, her vulva throb.

What now? Why had a smile appeared in his eyes? Why did he look at her as though his only pleasure was his effect upon her? He reached for something which turned her trust to terror. An object she had noticed before was drawn out from his boot. A whip, elegant and brown-leathered, carved with mythological heads at the top, tapering finely to a whiskered end. Had she misjudged her misjudgement of him? Was there to be cruelty now? Had her skin been prepared for the pain of whipping? Contrasts?

He said nothing, merely circled her. She felt the slender tip stroke the back of her legs, the inside of her thighs, her armpits. Each area touched by the leather was more sensitive than the last. He twisted the stick playfully into her belly's dip, stroked her belly's side, pulled it back and forth under that moist palace of pleasure, horizontally, searching. All his movements had been of that nature: seeking a response. She stifled sounds in her throat. She shuddered. Was that all he wanted, her responses? He seemed satisfied and returned to his place.

The next pause was taken up with preparations which revived her fears. As the master sat the servants rose. They moved very slowly. One to build up the fire, the other to withdraw from his sack the long lash which had first bound her. He flicked it in the air. She heard its crack. Again and again. The cracks echoed. She watched him aim for a leaf on a tree and bring it down. His companion set up fine twigs on distant stones for him to flick into space. He could make the tip of his lash encounter any tiny object or area he wished. She watched him with fascination and dread. Was that tip to be flicked and flayed over her? And with what accompanying pain?

She was, the next instant, to discover. The little man moved a distance behind her. Crack! A tiny area of her buttock was stung. Not lashed but nipped, so that she was uncertain whether to laugh or cry out. It was pain, but short-lived. What began as pain faded to a sting. How odd! The sting lasted an instant, while the warm urtication spread and remained. Another fierce flick followed. Again the momentary sting followed by ripples of heat. And with each flick the heat grew, accumulated. Tiny areas were stung again and again, until all parts of her buttocks were on fire.

This was pain and not pain. Her body writhed, uncertain how to react. Her cries of 'oh, OH, oh, OH!' and 'ohoh!' were bewildered cries, each 'oh' striking a different note, her scales all awry. When she knew that she could bear no more, that she was on the verge of real pain, the cracking ceased, and she felt a hand cup her swollen, salivating vulva, its lips parted, the pebble exposed, and a tongue slowly lap, soothingly. Here was a contrast exquisite beyond any she had ever known. Behind her the burning, before her the gentle sucking. The burning tingled, the tonguing thrilled. Two extremes. She moaned with such gratitude that the faun-like man was spurred to greater plunderings.

Now was to be heaped sensation upon sensation. She felt another presence behind her. She turned to look. The whipper had abandoned the leathery slash for his fleshy lash and was rubbing that most enormous weapon with oil. Why? To do with it what? She soon discovered. Her flanks were parted, a large finger probed her small hole. She was to be entered from behind! God help her! Here was a mad mouth sucking her front, and now a fantastic tool eased into her rear. Her instinct was to tauten her muscles. No pleasure in that! She concentrated and relaxed. A round head entered. Then withdrew. A practised, oft-used tool this, one that had obviously mortised many tenons. It knew well how to cajole, tease and persuade small places to be generous hostesses. When the head was comfortably embraced, the remainder of the long limb begged way to be made for it. And make way she did, squatting as she had done to accommodate the dog. The warm length slid in and out with ease, enabling her to concentrate on rhythms. Lips pulled and bit at her cunt's teat; a powerful thrusting moved in and out of her behind; her flesh continued to smart; and now a fourth sensation assaulted her. The top part of her dress was ripped open by the one who was sucking before her, his fingers twisted her nipples and pulled at her breasts. Could she bear more? Here was an ecstasy of which she had never imagined herself capable.

But where was the perpetrator and controller of all this? She opened her eyes. He sat, as before, eager only for her responses. Something in the fever of his gazing touched her. What was it? Then it struck her – the boy had entered the man's eyes. A child was confronting a spectacle. She was now driven by a strong desire to please both herself and the 'child'. Her moaning mingled with wild laughter. She writhed with greater violence. From behind came a shrill cry. She felt a warm fluid well within her. Another sensation! To be poured into! More! More! She wanted to be filled. She felt herself to be a receptacle and ached to be used, brimmed full. But he withdrew, the little man, spent and staggering.

What of the licking lackey at her front? Did he not have

troubled waters needing to flow into a gentle harbour? She had not long to wait. He replaced his little companion at the back. Oh, how she welcomed him. Long as his predecessor but more vigorous because fresher. Suddenly, absurdly, it became unthinkable that her rear chamber should ever be unoccupied! She thrust herself back, arching her spine, lifting her end, hostess to the world! But who was to replace him to the fore exposed there and abandoned? Would they exchange places? No, not that. Something more thrilling still. The great beast, on command, lumbered to its feet and lurched obediently forward. Now *there* was a tongue. Rougher, longer, able to fulfil the duel role of entering and caress. What triumphant chords would she not reach now that all the orchestra played upon her! Tromboned from behind; nipples plucked; an obliging dog's tongue bowing the cello between her legs; the taut, drummed skin of her bum still stinging; and now nipping teeth on her back in frenzied rhythm. Contrasts! Contrasts! She was flooded with contrasts. *And* she was watched!

Why *should* being watched increase pleasure? She was not by nature an exhibitionist, which anyway seemed facile as explanation, nor, absorbed by pleasure, had she concentration to spare for answers. Inspiration, however, moves in mysterious ways. Sharpened nerve ends sharpened her mind. The explanation came as a revelation. The pleasure lay in the knowledge that one's own excitement excited others. Which knowledge sped her to climax. She convulsed, rocked, erupted, wept. Into her cavern creamed forth a second coming and, oh, she wished the gushing never to cease. Warm with liquids, stings and polished parts, she soared and glowed.

The dog, knowing its duty was fulfilled, left her; the

second little man, littler now, slunk off to join his shrunken brother by the fire. She slumped in her ropes, overcome by gratification and weariness. The tall, pale man approached, a flagon in his hand. He offered drink to her lips. She accepted gratefully, greedily. The drink was strange. She had not drunk any such before. At first it tasted bitter, then warmth spread through her, rising from the pit of her stomach back again round her breasts, into her eyes, through to her outstretched arms, and spreading down, burning her belly, weakening her knees.

He untied her. She buckled to the ground. He left her there and returned to his viewing post, knowing what would happen. And what would happen? What had he given her to drink? From the leather that flicked her skin, from the hands that pummelled and caressed, from the long voyagers who had navigated her back ways, from the flapping, rough, drunk tongue that lapped lovingly her effluent font, all made her body intensely aware of itself from top to toe. She was aflame with memory.

But what was that burning nectar doing to her? Her senses were in anarchy. Each tiny sound magnified into a shriek; the forest quarrelled, its bracken proliferated; moonlight exploded and scorched the night's sly colours with sorcerous hues; the fire flashed demonic messages of hell. Yet nothing frightened her. She was queen, possessor, victrix of it all. And with conqueror's confidence returned appetite – gluttonous, ravishing, voracious. She rose from her knees and started towards Him. He jumped back. The dog growled. She was not to be allowed near. Her attention roved, wildly. The two serfs lay stretched beside one another. She pounced on them, ripped down their buttoned flaps. There they were, her two marauders, limp now, drained, doped things. She would soon pump passion back into place, tongue new turmoil into these lazy heroes of bygone days.

She peeled back the skin of one. Yes, it was there, red fruit for plucking when the bough grows. And how the hoeing of her tongue, the spading of her teeth, the spittle of her mouth, nourished up the sap. The bough grew, thickened. Her mouth could barely encompass it, her throat gagged as she coaxed the fruit to ripen, turning her eyes up every so often to make sure she was being watched. He must not miss what she was about to suck forth. It was coming, coming, she knew, for the heaving and groaning grew, till at last, into her mouth spat the white acrid history of generations. She drank, she swallowed, and with the insatiability of Bacchus turned to coax the second bough awaiting her nourishing mouth. A second ripening, a second succulent surge. She was in the grip of brazen abandon. She pulled her bodice apart, declared her ample breasts to Him, and from her mouth spat seed into her palms which she rubbed there, watching Him all the time, her eyes commanding Him 'Look! Be roused! Open for me! I can draw fruit that will make you giddy and raw.'

Indeed he was shaken. Had he released in her inexorable powers beyond his control? Whom had he imagined was his captive? He had only ever toyed with and roused skin-deep girls, never a princess. She gave him no time to reflect or escape, for she was upon him with hands and lips eager to thicken his bough, rouse his sap, ripen his fruit. She craved more seed. But, lo! Fruit, sap, bough was there none. Here was no seedling to plant. Here instead were the fertile grounds in *which* to plant! Holy mother of Mary, He was a She! The princess held in her hand the grapes of her own sex! She froze, her thrashing spirits wavered, confused. The contact was entirely alien, disorientating. He/She froze as well. For Her/Him too the contact was unfamiliar.

The two servants came to their feet, a little unsteady but steady enough to draw their whips and be at their master's/mistress's command. The hound opened one threatening eye and stiffened itself in readiness to leap on a word. Thus all waited, again the waiting, poised for decision, ready for action.

The mistress raised a reassuring arm and uttered a calming sound. The dog returned to sleep, the servants settled to observe. The startled princess withdrew her hand. It had been plunged in viscidity. She looked at her fingers, creamed and sticking to each other. She pulled them apart. Like a babe who comes to know the world through taste, she put two fingers in her mouth and slowly slid them in and out. Smell and taste were familiar and not familiar. The odour was strong, mixed of fermented cheese and sweat; the taste was gum from an opiate plant, intoxicating for its strangeness, yet strangely comforting. But perhaps the most intoxicating taste came from the commingling of gnomes' nectar and the nectar she had just tasted from her fingers. A tempest was brewing in her blood.

The princess looked at the mistress who had been her master. Roles had reversed. The mistress had taken control. The old mistress knew she was controlled. The slave had usurped power. She who once had power flinched, shuddered and waited. Fingers plunged again between her moist thighs. The intoxicant was gathered. The princess thrilled to its texture, then bent to inhale. She felt dizzy and eager. Clothes were an impediment. She stripped her captive captor of her boots, leggings, shirt, all. And disrobed herself. Here now was sight by the forest firelight. One lean, small-breasted, coy, uncertain woman grasping the earth with her back, and over her her amanuensis, voluptuously fleshed, luminous.

The unleashed princess lowered herself over her ex-mistress, her skin feeling the temperature of the waters she was about to enter. Skin touched skin, nipple to nipple, breast upon breast. Pleasure was there. Ah! moaned the mistress. Good, whispered the princess, and dived to those viscerous lips and drank.

Here was a strange thing. Playing with her mouth, her lips, her tongue as she had been played upon made her aware of her own untenanted inns. She ordered the two amazed guards to come behind her. Her upturned rump spread open as she moved her mouth in and out of the delirious figure beneath her. How she yearned to possess a man's torch between her legs. How incredible it must be to protrude, to proclaim such a limb, enter between moist, warm, odorous cushions, and be clamped. Her tongue was not long enough to dip deeply. Her fingers then, then her small hand, up to her wrist, she could turn inside, caress the inner walls and at the same time tongue and circle the tiny pink protrusion, that third nipple.

But where were the little men with their grand inquisitors? Why had they not accepted the invitations of her gyrating, restless rear? She turned. Poor nothings could beget only poor nothings. Their yeast was spent. They must wander in the wilderness of the night with unleavened loaves between their legs.

Between biting and chewing the wanton woman beneath her, she cried out, 'I am bereft!' The wanton woman beneath her looked up. At once she understood and with her mouth made a clicking sound. The regal princess, fulfilling a man's task, had resigned herself to receive no more that night. The most unheard of was yet to come.

Something was being held over her. She felt a furry belly

on her back and lump in her buttock. The hound was upon her. She was being offered the grey beast. As she moved in and out of the mistress, the mistress's pet moved in and out of her. A length like a spear pricked her. Here was no skin-covered limb serving her, but raw flesh on a long bone. She was being taken by an animal, possessed by a canine thing, while in her mouth she possessed a thing female.

The bitter drink revived itself within her. The tempest stirred wildly in her blood, she breathed deeply before turmoil. Great gasps were upon them all. Three ululations shattered the moonstruck forest and warm waters flooded her at both ends from 'master' and mastiff. The crazing potion struck her hard. She could take no more. The night was at an end. She swooned out of this world.

When she surfaced through layers of dreams and opened her eyes, a circle of familiar faces were peering anxiously over her. She was upon her bed in her hut. A green coil lay on her belly, messenger once, guardian now.

All this Jonas heard and saw about the princess Meliora, and related to me, Coaxandria, who have here ordered and interpreted and summarized for the king, and for those who will read after.

LENOTA
~ THE OLDEST

Let us consider Lenota carefully, she who continually warned, 'We are not alone, sisters, I tell you we are not alone.'

It is curious how certain qualities or features of a person impinge upon us before others. Of one we may observe how fair her features are, of another how tall, what pellucid skin, how fat, thin, voluptuous, what a loud voice, what succulent lips, look at that bulbous nose! Of another it is their quality we first observe — sunny with laughter, disturbingly restless, ebullient, foreboding, or dark, dark, dark. Ask a friend about a friend. Responses are revealing, often telling as much about they who respond.

With Lenota most would agree she possessed a feature which also revealed a quality — her eyes. Orphan's eyes.

She entered a gathering with eyes declaring two things at once — pity me, help me. Whence came such eyes? What experience informed them? She was no orphan. Of all the daughters here was a best-beloved, the eldest. Could it have been that as her sisters were born she saw, with each new arrival, an encroachment upon her territory? Her father's love, if seen as a cake, was all hers in her first years. With each entry of a new sister another tranche was removed. In the end eleven parts of his affection had been dislodged, eleven parts of her father vanished, and her mother to a nunnery! Is this not a kind of orphaning?

What next do we notice of Lenota? After her striking eyes, other features impinge in quick succession: she is small, well proportioned, dark-complexioned; then other qualities – a quiet air, an ability to glide up to us unaware, to hover, measure and wait to be stroked, told how well she looks today, allowed into the company, permitted to speak, and *then*, then is manifested her second startling quality: an incisive intelligence. The sad, pathetic sister becomes the sharpest, wisest, often most acerbic of them all. She utters her perceptive observation, her penetrating comment, her potent advice, all with a confidence completely at odds with her manner. It is disconcerting for strangers, who begin with pity but must soon pull back as though stung by a snake they had mistaken for a doe, for she uttered that which demolished their argument, uncovered their falsehood, revealed their shallow intelligence, exposed their motives, shook with penetrating questions the foundations of their cherished and comfortable beliefs. Of all the sisters, Lenota did not fulfil what appeared to be her promise.

For her sweetness her sisters loved her. For her intelligence they admired her. For intimations of things beyond intelligence they were driven to distraction and scolding her. None of which stopped them providing for her. Before returning each morning to the castle they saw she was becoming paler and thinner, but this they attributed to the intense effects of passion. Every night they filled her hut with food and fruits for her lover, and since the food had been eaten they concluded all must be well. She continued to warn they were not alone and they listened with respect, for she might be right. But what was to be done? If there was another presence, it seemed not a malign one, their nights were not disturbed by it. Whoever it was, *if* it was, seemed indifferent, helpless, at worst a harmless voyeur. Or perhaps they were haunted by a blind, afflicted spirit doomed to wander eyeless in death a world it never understood in life. The afflicted spirit notwithstanding, all must be well.

All was not well. On the first night her lover had taken her but she had been unmoved. From then on, night after night, he came but loved not again nor was loved. Instead Lenota read to him from books which lay scattered around the floor of her unkempt room, furnished with odds and ends which she had idly taken from the rooms of her sisters. Plants from Etheldra, statues from Enota, tapestries from Amy, an embroidered cushion from this one, a carved shelf from that one, woven rugs for walls and floors, plates and pots of no special shape, strange paintings. There was no consistency, no apparent pattern. And herein was manifested another of her qualities – artful disorder. For though each scattered piece belonged to a sister, yet *she* had selected it, she had scattered it. Casual though her plundering had seemed, yet calculated it transpired. Her chaos vibrated with the distinct tone of her taste. Selection was all.

For this reason her allocated lover had returned again and again despite the absence of earthy passion from this first of the king's daughters. Here was a room and a being of endless fascination. She confessed to him that her plague of doubts about this life and the life hereafter so preoccupied her that she was left without appetite for pleasures of the flesh. Where he lived there was no such life of the mind and spirit. His father tended the herd and he, named Lenaeus, was apprenticed by his father to learn the skill of butchery. Because his pleasure in flesh was not unmixed, his response to her mind and spirit was more certain.

Lenota had smiled: 'My sisters have found for me a man with blood on his hands,' she had said. 'I wonder why?'

'It would make me unhappy,' Lenaeus had responded, 'if you thought of me in that way only. I suffer with each slaughtering. I am able and proficient but I find no satisfaction in the labour. It must be done, for men eat meat, but I have devised ways of execution with the least possible pain, and more – please do not laugh at me – there is a maid with a loud and rich voice who sings so that they may be distracted and pass from this life with music in their ears.'

'It were more honest to let them know their fate,' said Lenota, not at her most alert, for her vivid imagination conjured the terror and the pain and, as with us all, her body and soul were enthralled between fascination and disgust.

'More honest perhaps,' he had replied, 'but not as kind. I have heard much talk of the virtues of honesty but in my limited experience I have found neither man nor beast who lived comfortably with honesty all the time.'

Lenota found some truth in this and, for its unadorned perceptiveness, she had warmed to the young brute. 'Brute' because he was a thick-set youth, short, heavy and muscular, not much taller than Lenota. And, like his mistress, his appearance deceived. From his squat massiveness one expected a corpulent mind, an obese sensitivity, but 'brute' though his stature, his mind was slim, agile, his sensitivity delicate, not made to carve animal flesh.

So they passed their nights talking of the soul and questioning whether such an intangible quality could be identified and, if not, then how could one verify its presence in the human personality. It cannot be heard, seen, touched, Lenota reasoned. Surgeons cannot remove it. Poets sang of it but, she asked, could poets be trusted? She had intimations beyond intelligence but they were not located in the legerdemainian fields of poetry. There, words were employed. She, on the other hand, drifted towards realms devoid of word, thought or action, towards an existence of insubstantiality. Lenaeus noted this. He ate, she did not. He drank wine, she water. As the nights went by she became more – incorporeal.

Once she had asked him, 'Do you wish you were someone else, or somewhere else, or that you pursued another skill? Would you like to be a lion, a woman, live in China, be an emperor, a physician, a cloud, a star among stars?'

'None of those things,' he had replied, 'but something else. Look.'

Round his waist hung a magnificent leather belt grooved with the sinuous shapes of root and branch. Attached to it a pouch of crimson velvet. He unhooked the pouch, placed it upon the table and unfolded its four corners. Lenota gazed, enraptured. Twelve pieces of jewellery were within. He laid them out alongside one another. All were of gold and precious stones. Two pairs of earrings: one, pendants of rich blue lapis lazuli; another of hanging vines with black coral for grapes. Four pins in the shapes of leaves – oak, ash, elm and sycamore. Two brooches as snakes with purple amethysts for eyes, and two more as the sphinxes of Egypt with eyes of green emeralds. What had impressed Lenota most was the thinness of his gold pins. She could not understand how this had been achieved. Nor whence came such precious metal and stones.

He explained. To assuage his guilt for slaughtering animals he had tanned hides and wrought works in leather – satchels, pouches, belts, all intricately engraved. These he traded for the gold and gems with travellers passing through. He had worked hard and late into the night, needing many leather artefacts to exchange for only few pieces of rough stone. Lapidary and leather craftsman both. Lenota was impressed and moved. But how did he contrive such fine pins? A thin groove cut in stone, he explained, the gold melted and poured in. What could be simpler? No one had thought to make such thread-like stems for jewels till now. Indeed!

Lenota looked at them night after night. She would read to him, feed him and ask to look at his handmade treasures. She would stare with great concentration as though each piece implied a significance she struggled to comprehend. What did she seek? What lay there for her? What was hidden in the gem, the gold, the leaf, the vine, the sphinx, the snake? Night after night she contemplated his delicate handiwork. Night after night she refrained from eating, became thinner, more fevered. Her eyes grew wider and receded into her head. Her cheeks sank, her cheekbones became more pronounced. Each night she read to him with mounting fervour. He begged her to eat, a little bread, some fruit, a few nuts. She refused. Her skin became translucent. Her blood glowed. She gazed longer and longer at the serpent, the leaves, the vines, the sphinx. Her eyes shone black, shone blue, shone purple, shone green. A haunted, wild look spread across her face.

One night Lenaeus asked if he could pin the jewels upon her. She cried out with a sound he had heard from no beast or human before: 'No, no, no-o-o-o-o-o-o-o!' She wept and screamed from deep within her, as though his words had been a sword piercing her and she was shrieking for mercy. Her sounds made the hair on the back of his neck rise. A shattering sound, incomprehensible. It frightened him. He could not know her shrill declination mirrored ecstatic affirmation.

Lenota could see she had distressed him. For the first time since that solitary night of love she held him in her arms, stroked his face, comforted him. 'There is within us all,' she explained, 'two people. I have heard that in some there are more. My sister Dionis told us once the story of a man who was known to six different groups as six different persons. To his parents as one, to his wife and family as another, to his friends as a third, to those with whom he laboured as a fourth, in other villages as a fifth, to his priest as a sixth. I am not always myself. Though you may well ask – who is "myself"? Forgive me.'

'You must believe me,' he said, as he lay like a young protected foal, 'that I am happy just to be with you. My pact was to serve you, not, it seems, with my manhood, but I am content nevertheless. To share your presence, listen to you read, hear your thoughts, to take pleasure in the pleasure you take from my jewels. I would do anything that pleased you.'

'And what would please you most?' she asked.

'Were you to accept a gift of whichever piece you choose. That!' he replied.

He did not look at her as he spoke these words but gazed instead into the fire as though all such dreams were burnt in flames to become ashes. She made no reply but cradled him. She stroked no other part but his face. He did not touch her. They sat in silence.

She said, and her voice came as a fearful whisper, 'I have no holes in my ears for your rings.'

'That is not a problem.'

He leapt joyously to face her. His joy froze. He saw a changed woman. She seemed not to see him. Her eyes were wide, but looked inwards. Something possessed her. She wants to please me, he thought. She would like to wear my earrings but is sensitive and fears pain. Yet she is prepared to suffer pain to give me pleasure. Oh, I think I love this woman.

'I have pierced the ears of women and girls before,' he said. 'I know the secret. Will you trust me?'

She said nothing, simply nodded her head vaguely, as one resigned to a fate. He had misread her state utterly.

Into a saucer he poured a little of the acid from a soused tomato. From a flap of his crimson pouch he extracted a long thin needle of gold, which he laid in the acid. His jerkin of leather had been decorated with strips and squares, a square of which he ripped off and laid aside. He drew a burning candle towards him, knelt behind her, wound her hair in a pile which he knotted above her head so that the nape of her neck and her ears were exposed, and reassured her: 'This will not hurt, or only a little, and not for long.' She made no response but shuddered, as one does from a passing terror. He felt her stiffen.

He withdrew the needle from the acid, took the blunt end in a clean cloth, held the sharp end briefly over the candle flame, wiped it on the cloth and held it poised, ready, in his right hand. The first two fingers and thumb of his left hand he dipped in the acid, then firmly rubbed and squeezed the lobe of her right ear until he judged it numb. Quickly he reached for the leather square, which he placed behind her lobe and thrust the needle through flesh into leather, turning it round and round. He felt her body tense

231

even more. A natural reaction, he thought. He repeated the procedure with the other ear and into both he placed the earrings of gold vines and black coral grapes. He faced her.

And gasped, amazed. Could a person change so many times? Where was the world to which she was transported, for she was not of this world. Her beauty was ethereal. Two tiny spots of blood rested on her ears, rendering her pale skin paler, the blackness of her hair blacker. The coral flashed. The earrings became part of her. Had some mysterious force driven him to fashion them for whom they were destined? Are lives impelled in straight lines to meet and cross inevitably at preordained points?

Now ensued events which Lenaeus would remember until his last days. She expressed wishes but he could not match them with the woman with whom he had spent these nights, who had read to him from the books of philosophers and ancient mystics. She spoke to him, but it was not her voice. It came from the pit of her stomach, or somewhere outside her. An echo of her voice, low, deep, commanding. Its quality of unearthliness transformed him into a state of narcosis. He obeyed a woman who was and was not she. The dark is light. The light is dark. The lion lies down with the lamb. And it is written 'for ye are like unto whitened sepulchres, which outwardly appear beautiful, but inwardly are full of dead men's bones'.

She asked, '"I would do anything to please you", were those your words?'

'They were,' he confirmed warmly.

'And are they true?'

'Oh, they are true, so true,' he answered with emotion.

'Do you understand them?'

'What is there to understand? Seven simple words which can mean only what they mean.'

'Seven simple words with shadows,' she insisted darkly in a dark voice, 'for what may please me may offend you.'

'Nothing you could ask of me would offend,' the gallant lad insisted.

'Offend, frighten, cause anguish. You are too young and cannot know of what this life is made.'

It was true what the princess spoke. But confidence rode him. His ardour grasped him in its stride. He knew that what he was about to do was right, was what had to be done, the moment called for it. He took her in his arms and kissed her lips. He encountered no resistance. Rather a passion whose eerie, moist calm betokened an unprecedented storm. Suddenly her whole body was in a state of turmoil, as in a fever. She eased him away. His arms lingered on her, more to steady her, for she swayed and trembled and seemed in the grip of a monstrous spirit that tried to suck her into itself and out of this world. She took control of her state, looked once more into the eyes of Lenaeus, and requested those rituals the memory of which he would take to his grave.

'Take up the second earrings, those pendants of blue stone, and place them here.' In one movement she peeled the top part of her dress down to her waist, took her two breasts in her hands, and pinched with forefingers and thumbs her nipples. 'Through here. Those thin, fine needles, here.'

The young man was stunned. 'Through that thick flesh?'

'Do not ask.'

'It will cause pain.'

'You vowed. Anything to please me. The pain will please me. Now do as I request. At once. It is essential that you act immediately. Immediately!' Her fingers squeezed the brown protuberances until it seemed she could bestow all the pain she desired without his assistance.

He acted with speed. The whole jewel into the acid to cleanse it of impurities; the square of leather beneath the flesh as hard background on which to apply pressure. And then – in! With all his skill and power. A swift action. It took longer to pierce this flesh than the ear's lobe, but his firmness met only slight resistance.

Lenota gripped his head of hair with both hands and choked back her cries. The first pendant was hung. The second followed. A slow, continuous easing of the gold pin into the nipple. Again her cries. 'Oh, that is a joy! A great and wondrous joy. There is no pain in it for me. Yes, there is pain but no pain. Suffering but no suffering.'

The peasant boy gazed at this princess whom he knew not as a princess but felt to be a queen, his queen. What spirit burned in her burned in him too. He waited for her to speak again.

'Those brooches. The green-eyed sphinxes. Here!'

She pointed to the top of her breasts. Must he pierce her soft skin there? He would obey, he was now her slave, her adoring, unquestioning slave. Once more he applied his swift skill and the pins were eased through the white flesh. She screamed in ecstasy. This time blood was drawn. It surprised her. She put her fingers to it.

'Now there is blood on both our hands.' She smiled. She tasted her blood and found it sweet. 'Drink,' she commanded him.

He placed his lips on her flesh. He drank her blood.

She pulled at her belt. Her dress fell to her ankles. She stepped out of it and stood, with her legs astride, defiantly.

'Those brooches, the snakes with purple eyes. Here!' She pointed to the soft flesh inside her thighs. 'Let serpents creep into me.'

He acted quickly, pinching her skin and pressing the pins through. Blood gushed, ran down her legs. This time her screams went on and on. Pain was pain and suffering was suffering was suffering was suffering.

She held out her arms to him. He took her hands, his eyes searching for her wishes. She wanted to lie down. She needed his help. She feared collapsing into a heap. He helped her on to her back. She was now in a trance.

'One last request.' She opened her legs. 'These folds of wet skin, look how they slip about in my fingers. See how like autumn's leaves they curl. You once passed through. And here – ' she pulled the folds apart and revealed the tender push of flesh – 'here wherein lies the secret, the secret, ah, the secret. Do these things for me. Take this in your lips, suck and discover the secret, then when I cry out 'Now!' take the oak, the ash, the elm, the sycamore and pin together these wet folds of skin. Do not hesitate and do it swiftly.'

Lenaeus placed the pins in acid by her side. He laid on his stomach between her open legs, from the centre of which came forth a heat he found comforting. Before lowering his lips to that secret place, he glanced at his lady. Her eyes were wide open. Her pupils had risen high in their sockets, leaving behind the whites. She was in a state of rapture. Her fingers were upon the coral pendants piercing her nipples. She moved them back and forth. He bent forward. He found the bud. He gently sucked. She writhed. The sound which had first made the hair of his neck rise now grew again from within her. It began low and rose to a shriek. The hair on the back of his neck prickled once more. She released hold of the gold vines in her breasts and grasped his hair. The shrieks became tears, the tears a torrential sobbing, the sobbing wrapped around a word.

'No, no, no, no, no-oh-Oh-Oh-OOOOOOH. Now!

Now! Now!'

Within the count of eight, four pins of oak, ash, elm and sycamore were pierced through her labia folds. She spread out her arms and shrieked to the dark heavens, 'O Lord, Lord, Lord, I am coming. Your sinner comes. Open your gates. Your sinner cuuuuuuuuuuuuuuuuuuuums!'

Lenota swooned.

Her lover of this last night knew what had to be done, for now he was in rhythm with her. He withdrew from her flesh each piece of jewellery except those in her ears. He heated water over the fire and bathed her body. Then he lifted her in his arms, laid her gently on her bed and covered her with a dark-blue, soft woollen covering. From an earthenware jar he poured Samaritanian oils into his palms and rubbed her feet in them. With what remained in his hands he soothed the skin on her face. Then he kissed her eyes, her hands, her lips and left her in a deep sleep.

He did not know who she was or where she came from. She had created a womb into which he had fitted. He would fit with no one else like this ever in his life. He parted from her. He would never see her again.

When she awoke, the youngest sister, Amabilia, was at her side.

'Wake up,' she said. 'The nights are over. We must return to our palace, our father, the busy days of the court. Recover! We have made our journeys. There is work to be done, and many wait for us. Come through, sister. We must be back with our world in time to catch the dawn.'

All this Jonas heard and saw about the princess Lenota, and related to me, Coaxandria, who have here ordered and interpreted and summarized for the king, and for those who will read after.

THE OLD KING
HAD SAT LONG HOURS

ᴛhe old king had sat long hours listening to
Coaxandria. When the narratives were finished, he bowed
to be excused, and retired alone to his chamber.

There he lay upon his bed plunged in contemplation.
The more he thought, the deeper sank his eyes with
sadness into his head, as though seeking to retreat from
sight. He struggled to interpret the histories which had
been related to him. All night he lay wrestling with
indecision. Then he rose with the sun, washed, changed
from his royal clothes to the simple garb of a peasant,
rolled some breads and onions and a handful of coins into
a scarf, and, without saying farewell to anyone, walked
away from his life.

He had lived his years. There was nothing more to offer,
nothing more to receive, nothing more he wanted to
know. All but his last tears had dried up. He wished quietly
to recede, like a dream of time, live out his last handful of
moonlit skies, and not awake in another's dawn.

He was never seen again by any living soul. He left

behind him no note, no message, only the vast space that his magnificent regal presence had once occupied and which, now, twelve fine and worthy daughters filled.